BOOKS BY C.K. SORENS

TRIMARKED SERIES

Trimarked
Afflicted
Tattered
Tempered

❖ ❖ ❖

THE DJINN OF LAS VEGAS

Eighteen Wishes

This novel contains content that may be triggering.
For a list of possible triggers, please visit
https://www.cksorens.com/trimarked-trigger-warnings

This is a work of fiction. All of the characters, organizations, and events portrayed in this novel are products of the author's imagination.

TEMPERED

Copyright © 2026 by Carrie Sorensen

All rights reserved.

Edited by Hannah at Dark Muse Studio

Cover design by NMT Design Studio

www.cksorens.com

ISBN 978-1-954054-16-5 (hardcover)
ISBN 978-1-954054-15-8 (paperback)
ISBN 978-1-954054-17-2 (ebook)

First Edition: March 2026

*For those who were forged by the fire
and learned that choosing themselves
was never weakness.*

C.K. Sorens

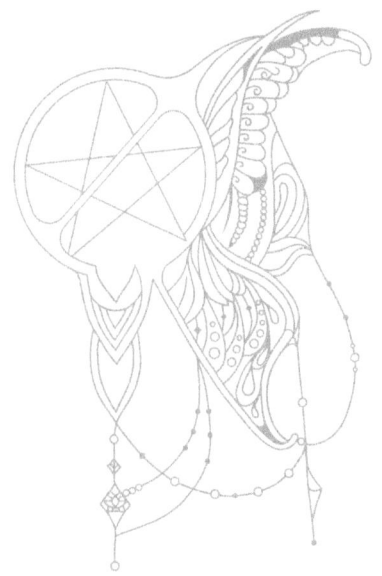

Tempered

Trimarked Series
Book Four

1

NICU

Fractured silence echoed in Nicu's ears. Altaya stood at his left and three other Fae on their flank. Devi hovered on his right, lips thin, skin pale with disbelief.

The windless space of No Man's Land stretched before them, unchanged for two decades, its ground covered in decayed forest. Behind them loomed the Helduan sequoia, scarred from its battle against the dome that held Trifecta captive. Blackened branches curved against an invisible resistance while others sprung free through the new cracks and fissures in the magic.

Yet all eyes fixed on the smallest change, low against the ground. A fragile plant only inches tall despite being minutes old, growing where nothing else did. The lone sign Ember had been there, her absence pressing harder than the silence.

Beside the sequoia, Tristan Glynn stepped forward, fists knotted at his sides as if the force before him posed no threat.

"Aim at the Wizard!" Nicu barked. The order should have been instinct. Yet the four hunters held their bows fixed on the space Ember had occupied only moments ago. The longer they hesitated, the tighter frustration coiled in Nicu's gut. Then the bows dipped, pulled off target, their arrows slack and harmless.

"We need the Council," Altaya countered, voice clipped.

"It's really best for all of us if you don't." Tristan's voice returned to civility, though it held the gravel-deep tones of his disappointment.

The hunters turned as one, long strides carrying them back toward center. A day alongside the Trimarked Guardian had not convinced them to use caution when contacting the Council in Center. Nicu's jaw tightened. Devi's mint-green, gem-like eyes shifted to the Wizard.

Tristan's smile broke at the edges as he met Nicu's gaze. "It seems neither of us can control everything."

Devi stayed rooted in human territory where she could still cast, an advantage Tristan lacked in No Man's. A few steps into Witch land would have given her more strength, but the tree would have blocked her view of the Wizard. Keeping Tristan in the dead zone also benefited Nicu who relied on other skills: physical strength, agility, and the kind of mental acuity honed from years of watching for betrayal.

Yet none of it could bring Ember back.

"Where's Ember?" Devi demanded, her words snapping through the silence as if she had picked the thought straight from Nicu's mind. He didn't move, didn't breathe. Instead, he watched the Wizard as the question struck. Every twitch of Tristan's lips, every simple finger-flex. Would he be honest?

"My best guess? Out," Tristan's brittle smile carved across his face.

Devi stiffened. "What happened to the barrier? The air is different."

Tristan gestured to the sky, his civility fraying. "I'm very proud. Mostly. Our little pet did that. It took some convincing, but thankfully you and the humans scared her enough to send her running back to me."

Devi shot Nicu a half-second glare, which was all the time

she dared to take her eyes off Tristan. Nicu ignored her, focused on piecing together wisps of information into a comprehensive whole.

Ember had run from them. Had reason to. Nicu understood why she had attempted to destroy the barrier, to release them from this place. Yet after the first cracks appeared, she'd stopped. Even healed the breaks somehow. The larger fissures didn't appear until after she disappeared. So why the reversal? And why did her lack of presence cause the greater damage?

"What did you do?" The words rumbled from Nicu's chest.

The Wizard's eyes narrowed, embrittled smile tightening. "Watch yourself, young one. We may still be allies if you are careful."

Nicu allowed his upper lip to curl at that suggestion. His tattoos, long curving lines bent in patterns that never touched, shifted over his skin as it responded to the threat. The Fae Ink caught against the pale blue scars across his form, marks of a Promise broken. A reminder that he had nearly died. That his return came with a cost. That he must choose.

Not this second, though. Now, he needed information the Wizard had.

"Devi," Nicu said evenly. "If I pull him out, can you force him to talk?"

"I can do that from here." She trailed her fingers across her bracelets, brushing crystals as though deciding which one would best bind Tristan's tongue to truth.

"You children honestly think—" Tristan broke off, his attention locking on Devi as she gathered her magic. His jaw tightened, breath dragging sharply through his nose as if he recognized something in her that Nicu did not.

"This is not the moment for insults," Tristan corrected sharply. "We can't afford to delay. Your Fae brethren went after the Council. That means Wist."

Nicu caught it. The strange pause. The shift in Tristan's tone when his eyes lingered on Devi. The edge of the threat seemed to ebb, replaced by something harder to name. Whatever it meant, Nicu marked the reaction and tucked it away for later.

"What of Wist?" Nicu pressed. The Wizard had mentioned him days before, but Nicu had been focused on the Witch Queen, Charlah. He'd thought there would be more time to unravel Tristan's mysteries. But the Council had reassigned him, pulled him from Ember's side to coordinate with Altaya's team.

Now those hunters were reporting back to a man who once urged Nicu to let Ember die.

A force bore down on Nicu's mind, heavy as stone, searing like fire. Ozone stung his throat, salt burned his tongue, as if the very elements twisted to pry him open. Fate and Chaos crowded close, their intent burning through the pale blue scars they'd left on his body after putting him back together. They worked to seize the moment, urging him toward a choice he could never unmake.

But not today.

He braced, kept his head high, emotions neutral, focus sharp. If he knew one thing, it was how to bury secrets so deep even his thoughts could not betray him.

"Only you could manage to balance on such a thin and dangerous line." Words Devi had spoken only moments before. He clung to them, forged them into a talisman.

Tristan studied Nicu for a long beat, then shook his head. "You're still far too loyal to that manipulator." His accusation was well-timed. Nicu internalized the Wizard's words to use against Chaos' intent to force a decision.

"But what matters," Tristan continued, "is that you want to help Ember, regardless. Shall we focus there?"

"So you do know what happened to Ember," Devi charged.

"I have an idea." Tristan spoke with sharp edges on his words. "And a plan."

Devi opened her mouth, but Nicu lifted a hand to caution

her to be quiet. He continued to study the Wizard, whose instance indicated he felt he was running out of time. They just needed to wait for Tristan's own internal timer to urge him into action.

"Have you ever wondered why Ember isn't allowed on Fae land of all others? Why it was never suggested she be imprisoned in Center? Why your orders were not to deliver her to the Council but to manage her out here? Surely you're clever enough to realize this is more than just prejudice."

Devi tilted her head as she listened intently. Nicu remained impassive, waiting for the Wizard to stop his riddles and say something worth hearing.

Tristan thrust out his arm, pointing toward the thriving new growth clawing through the dead ground at the Fae boundary. "You see the evidence, but you still don't understand."

Nicu felt the scars of his broken Promise itch, urging him to demand answers. But he held fast. That had been his old pattern. Obedience, silence, waiting. It had failed him. Now he waited differently. The Wizard's urgency would betray him without Nicu needing to ask.

Tristan clenched his teeth behind tight, white lips. "You need me."

"Prove it," Devi snapped. Her fists clenched, her foot shifted forward as if patience no longer held her in place. "Tell us where Ember is."

The edge of Tristan's posture eased, his expression smoothing into something controlled, almost calculating. He lowered his arm.

"She's done what only the Trimarked Child can do." Tristan paused, though whether for effect or admiration, Nicu couldn't tell. He simply waited.

"Ember Lee has parted the energy trapping us here. She has left our realm and is now in true Gypsum."

2

EMBER

Dreams tangled with pain. A rose floated within a landscape of stars, each of its petals breaking away into a new galaxy.

Nightmares followed. Fae armies hiding in the trees. Witch chants driving daggers into her mind. Winged shadows blotting out a dusky horizon.

Then something in between. A space of indifference where her body felt erased, where every emotion seemed to slip away.

"Do not move." The voice sang with command and weight, pressing down through Ember's muscles. She froze. Fire spread where blood should have flowed, the pain of her shoulder wound sharpening until thought itself crumbled.

"Reyar!" A shout from outside Ember. An unknown name.

"What did you drag home?" The answer rumbled low and resonant, the sound vibrating through her bones.

"Almost there. Do not lose it now." The first voice again, low and resonate. The sound offered no comfort, but it didn't deepen her pain, either.

What were they doing? Were they captors, rescuers, or something in between? Ember's mind scraped for sense, but fear rose faster, hot instead of cold. Heat bowed her spine, her power lashing awake. Razors of energy sliced through every vein without spilling a drop of blood.

"Your Song isn't enough to stop this?" the deep voice asked, surprise edged in its tone.

"Not the time, Reyar! She is—"

The surge broke. From behind Ember's ribs, a cyclone of power tore free, burning every nerve. A windless pressure caught it, twisting upward until it burst from her chest in a radiant stream.

Ember gasped as the tension released, opening her eyes to a starlit night. The aura of power slid like silk across the image, blurring pinpoint stars. Up and up it rose, catching a rainbow glow as crosswinds carried it higher, dispersing the energy into the world as if it had never meant any harm.

"She does not belong here." The deep tones no longer stabbed, but Ember still flinched. Her pain-scattered memories were trickling back into focus with each constricted breath.

She'd helped Tristan. Had grown the tree and cracked the barrier. But he wanted to sacrifice her and she refused to die. Tearing herself from one power, she'd tried to escape, only to discover that crossing the Fae border was forbidden for reasons she never could have guessed.

Rather than landing into Fae territory within Trifecta, Ember had slipped through the Veil and into true Gypsum.

"And yet, here she lies."

The husky voice. It belonged to a woman named Shade. A tall, powerful Fae with thick-soled boots and leather corseted armor. Smokey tattoos lined her left arm, while an inked snake wrapped around her right, the serpent's life-like head resting on top of her wrist. She'd found Ember in this realm, offering shelter and protection against the impossible reality of dragons.

Then something must have happened, but Ember couldn't remember. At first it was only a headache she blamed on stress. Then the burning began, and every other thought fled.

"How did she get here?" The deep voice had drawn closer

and Ember pinched her lashes together. Her left cheek pressed against smooth and rigid leather. With that sensation, more entered Ember's focus. An arm around her torso and another under her bent knees. She was being carried.

And her power had exploded.

Ember gasped, eyes opening to Shade's face framed by the star-flecked sky.

"Fades." Ember tried to speak, though her throat was raw. Shade looked down at her with amused, dark brown eyes, and a crooked smile.

"I am going to assume that is an appropriate slur. Are you ready to stand?"

"Yes?"

Shade lowered Ember's legs first, waiting for them to steady before she removed the arm from around her back. The Fae's movements were careful, if not quite caring. Not exactly the motions of someone whose intent was to kidnap.

"How did you get here?" The question snapped out from the newcomer Shade had called Reyar.

Ember turned toward him, her boots shifting in the fine, silken sand. The desert stretched behind them, white flats disappearing into the dark beneath a star-studded sky, but it was the ruins that held her attention. Broken-down structures loomed, their skeletal remains lost to time, worn smooth by the wind.

Ahead, the city's true heart rose in shadowed layers, still holding onto life where these outskirts had crumbled. The pale pink moon reflected off the sands, casting just enough light to catch the male stranger's scrutiny.

A Wizard. There was no doubt. His eyes, fractured in shades of rainbow tourmaline, gleamed with the sharp facets of a fine-cut gem. A long bronze braid draped over his shoulder, the sides of his head shaved clean and without the deep red dye preferred by Trifecta's coven. His pale linen robes, practical and suited to the desert heat, stood in quiet contrast to the vivid hues worn by the Witches and Wizards she'd known before.

He narrowed his gaze, waiting for her answer.

"An accident," she offered to the best of her knowledge.

"The Veil has been impassable by people for hundreds of years, and you claim pure circumstance?" Reyar demanded.

"How do you know I came through the Veil?"

"You're human."

"She is something else." Shade's voice was soft in a way that set warning bells off in Ember's head.

"Human enough," he interceded, "as she cannot control whatever power she has. Fae Binding Ink marks her with a Witch-made pentacle. That makes her from Terra, most likely from that city trapped in the bubble that locked the Veil."

Ember blinked up at the tall man, startled at his quick and correct assessment of her situation. She raised a hand to the back of her neck, wondering how he saw her tattoo, alarmed to find skin instead of hair. She flinched at the distant memory of raging Veil energy burning through the strands and dropped her arm, latching on to a need to defend herself.

"I've learned some control," she countered, then instantly regretted her claim when both Shade and Reyar turned heavy frowns her way.

Ember had never felt so small, staring up at the incredible beings before her. Nicu was the tallest person she knew, and it hadn't bothered her to stand toe to toe with him. This pair, however, carried more than height. Their bodies were built for battle, their wills just as strong. They were powerful strangers who had helped her, yes, but they also held the ability to abandon her in a world she barely understood.

"What is your name, little one?" Ember flinched as Shade's question echoed her thoughts of being small.

"Ember," she offered, swallowing the desire to fall silent, to watch and listen as these two spoke over her. That approach worked in Trifecta. Here, it was probably wiser to be polite.

"Well, Ember, do you plan on trying to catch fire again anytime soon?" The tick of Shade's lips suggested a hint of teasing, yet Ember refused to let down her guard. Instead, she lifted her hands and flexed her fingers. A gentle pulse of power in her bones responded when she called forward her personal shield, watched as a soft blue light lit her skin, then shifted into invisibility as it settled around her.

"No. I don't know why that happened. Maybe my human body had to get used to Gypsum energy?"

"Or it was this." Shade pulled the two halves of a broken Fae arrow from her waistband. Ember's left hand flew to her right shoulder. More pieces fell together. She'd worn a puffy red coat in Trifecta, but that was nowhere to be found. It had likely been abandoned along with the sleeves of the dark blue shirt she wore that were no longer there, leaving behind tiny threads clotted with dried blood.

"I was shot." Ember's lips trembled against the evidence gripped in Shade's fist. An arrow sent by a Fae. Not Nicu, but the one who stood at his side.

Ember ripped her gaze from the projectile to study her shoulder, only to glance away after a brief impression of torn skin and a deep, red-stained wound. "Why doesn't that hurt?"

"I am blocking your pain receptors and keeping the poison from spreading until we can get you properly healed," Shade offered.

"Poisoned!" Ember exclaimed. Shade nodded as she handed the arrow to Reyar. He sneered at the fletching.

"Terra born and goddess-touched," Reyar muttered, studying Ember. Then, with a grunt, he turned away from them and walked over dry, rocky ground toward the intact city. Ember followed him, taking in the wind-torn ruins around them. The space they tread was wide and empty, likely once a road. Small rocks littered the landscape, but beyond the three of them there were no signs of life. Not even scavengers moved among the crumbling stone of a long-faded time, worn down by ancient winds and stripped of identity, clinging to the memory of what used to be.

"What happened here?" Ember asked.

"Time," Shade answered. "And greed. Gypsum is a broken land. After the Fae reached an accord with the humans and Fate Magic was banned, they acted as though starved. They ransacked their own land's resources for decades, searching for that addictive rush of universal magics. They never found it and the realm suffered. The cultures that survive here do so with the luxury of primal magic and pure grit."

The way Shade said 'primal magic' sent a shudder down Ember's back and she remembered the long shadow of the dragon she'd seen soon after her arrival. She tried to picture the Trifectan Fae in this environment, but the two images clashed, even within her mind. A sense of discomfort settled behind her ribs, though she couldn't decide if it was for her sake or the Fae's and shrugged it away, refusing to think about it.

"And you've lived like this your whole life?" Ember asked.

"Only the last century or so. I can still remember how green this place used to be." Shade's answer was quiet and matter of fact. Ember's breath snagged on the impossibility of it.

Fae existed for centuries? She'd really only known Nicu, Branna, and Edan. They'd grown up with her. So they were mere children in Fae years? How had they come to be her guardians? Maybe she wasn't as dangerous to them as she'd been taught to believe. The thought lifted a weight off her heart, then resettled it on her shoulders.

It shouldn't be a surprise they'd misled her. Yet…

Ember couldn't believe it had been a total lie. Though Shade and Reyar seemed to have brushed off her near explosion, she noted the female Fae remained close and that the Wizard kept glancing back at her often enough to show she had his complete attention.

So there was more to learn. Perhaps these two were more forthcoming than the Trifectan Fae. Or they could be worse.

Ember rolled her shoulders against an involuntary shiver. No matter what this pair thought, Ember was a survivor. She'd gotten away from Brandt. She had fought against the Witch Queen. She had escaped the soul-eating tree. She could figure this out, one way or another.

"Come on," Shade offered. "Let us find you a bed and you can get some sleep. We will figure out the rest later."

"Like getting me home?"

Shade's lips thinned and she shook her head.

"I have only been able to pass inanimate objects through the Veil."

My power can open it.

Ember swallowed that truth with ease. She'd kept it from people she knew for years. Keeping it from a stranger was easy. But should she?

She didn't know enough yet. Until she had a better handle on things, it was a secret worth protecting.

Shade lengthened her stride to catch up with Reyar. Ember dropped her gaze as she passed, hoping to hide any secrets that might be shining through her eyes. But after only a few more steps, Ember faltered. Her breath snagged.

Her feet moved, but only shifted deeper into the sand. There was no sense of the Veil here, no shimmer of blue reflecting her own power. Yet there was no doubt that she could not move beyond this point.

She lifted a hand. Pressed it forward. Resistance met her palm like glass. She leaned harder, weight driving forward as her muscles strained. Blue ripples spread across her skin as if she summoned power, but nothing gave.

This was not the Veil. It was its echo. A reflection rooted in Trifecta, now mirrored here. An imitation Shade and Reyar passed through, but one that held Ember firm. Dark thoughts nipped at the edges of her focus as she fought to keep them at bay.

You'll never escape.

Trapped forever.

You should have let the tree eat you. Then you'd be free.

Boots whispered across the soft sand. Shade stopped beside her and, curious, raised her palm to meet Ember's. They should have touched. Instead, their hands hovered, divided by the invisible wall. Shade's eyes widened.

"Reyar. Come see this."

It took only a few seconds for Reyar's long legs to return him to their space. He studied Shade's hand, then Ember's, and finally focused his gaze on the narrow space between their palms. The corner of his mouth curved.

"Interesting."

3

NICU

Nicu did the math.

Altaya had left ten minutes ago and would reach Center in seven more. If they found Wist or the Council immediately, another ten minutes would pass before anyone could return.

Would the Fae mobilize? Or might Wist come on his own? However it unfolded, the Elder's intent remained the same. Protect the Fae at any cost.

But Ember was not here. What could any of them do against that?

She'd vanished fifteen minutes ago, but that was in Terran time. Time moved faster in Gypsum.

"Are you fading serious?" Devi demanded of the Wizard. "Ember can't leave Trifecta."

"You seem so certain," Tristan drawled.

"She can open the barrier," Devi countered with a dry twist of her tongue. "If walking away were possible, she would have done so long ago."

"Ember may be caught in the Veil's snare," Tristan agreed. "That doesn't mean she's chained to Trifecta. This world is made up of more than one realm."

Devi paused. "Charlah. In the cave, she told Ember to get 'us' out. She'd meant to take Ember with her."

Nicu stiffened. He hadn't known that.

Had Ember wanted to go?

Would Ember be safer in Gypsum, outside Trifecta where she'd been hated, watched, restrained? Might she be freer in that crumbling realm than she'd ever been in this one?

The Promise was broken. He was no longer tied to the Trimarked Child. No magic forced him to shield her.

Nicu grunted at the crush of internal pressure, a solid warning etched with the words: *Passivity isn't a choice.*

His body moved before thought could catch it, his feet directed by a force other than himself. A shimmering figure drifted in and out of sight beyond the closest tree trunks, each thick as stone pillars, easy cover for any who lurked.

Was it the Witch Queen with her long pale hair and soft green gown?

No, this was something different. This person wore black from neck to feet, her hair twisted into a bun atop her head. Once dark, it now gleamed a silvery white. Skin that should have been sun-warmed shimmered strange and pale in the evening sun that filtered between the trees.

"Branna." Nicu stepped forward in surprise. Her eyes, still the same deep brown, were unchanged against the rest of her, which had settled into an otherworldly pallor, pale as heavy mist.

"Oh my," Tristan nearly purred. "So the Fae hid you behind Ember's power, too."

Devi cursed under her breath, but Nicu shoved the sound aside as he searched for the magical tie between himself and Branna. The Fae had mated them, tied their energy together to balance out the dark power of the necromancer and the chaotic mutations to Nicu's magic, allowing him to control others' spells, but not make his own.

Their connection was gone. Had it disappeared with Ember?

Branna scowled at them. If she held answers, she kept them back. She sent an angry glare at the space beside her.

"I will not," Branna snapped. "You can be the one who tells them."

Branna gathered darkness from the forest. Nicu watched the shadows carefully, knowing she'd mastered using them to attack, yet that did not seem to be her purpose at the moment. Rather than send them toward a target, Branna collected them beside her.

The shadows twisted upward, darkening into shape as if filling an empty vessel. They settled into a silhouette Nicu recognized. Wide shoulders, hairless head. Color seeped through while remaining dark and muted, yet the features became obvious.

"Edan," Nicu greeted, keeping the word measured and his voice controlled. Branna crossed her arms and glared, silently berating him for treating Edan's ghost as if he were a live person.

Nicu ignored her, certain there was no other way to treat his departed friend than with the same respect he'd shown in life.

"We need the Trimarked Child." Edan's words were as muted as his form, yet far more distinct. Nicu's shoulders stiffened, pulling against his new blue-tinted scars as he surmised that this timely visit had been an act of Chaos.

"She is as unreachable as you were," Nicu countered. "Is there another way?"

Edan shimmered, showing more emotion in death than he had in life. The effect caused Nicu's gut to twist, and he worked to keep his fingers from curling into fists, his body on offense against whatever Chaos meant to bring him.

"The Watchers are coming," Edan warned.

Nicu heard Tristan's clothes rustle and checked on him

long enough to confirm that he'd simply shifted as if to hear Edan better.

"What are the Watchers?" Devi asked, even as she raised an arm decorated with layered, gem-filled bracelets, a silent warning to Tristan about moving too much.

"Fallen Fae," Branna spat. "Fae who have been away from Gypsum for too long lose their coloring, then their souls." She spread out her fingers to highlight her shimmering skin. Nicu went utterly still, control stretched taut as her meaning sunk in.

"Do you think this pretty shell means you're Fallen?" Tristan asked. His emerald eyes caught the light as he stepped closer, hand half-reaching as though he wanted to touch her. As if he were drawn in by her, and tempted.

"She bears the same marks as the Watchers." Edan's voice was soft. His intent gaze was for Nicu alone. "We must close the dome before they get here."

"Or we break it the rest of the way open and let them go home." Tristan's words brought silence in their wake. Nicu uncurled his fists the moment he realized he'd made them.

"Gypsum is a wasteland." The statement cut through the air as Wist stepped from the forest's shadow. He wore no ceremonial wrap this time, as if the chill meant nothing to him. Instead, simple black trousers and a midnight-purple sweater framed his figure, the deep shade making the white locs at his shoulders blaze like silver fire.

Daz followed at his heels, but it was Altaya who drew Nicu's consideration. They still bore their bow and the quiver heavy with arrows, though they'd stripped away the glaring orange tunic the humans required while hunting. The weapon used to strike at Ember rested easy in their grip, carried like an open threat.

Heat flared in Nicu's chest at the sight of the hunter. Altaya's recklessness had wounded Ember and kept Nicu from halting the Trimarked girl's progress over the Fae border. Had they told the whole truth about their involvement? Did Wist know of Ember's disappearance?

"What lies have you been spinning, Wizard?" The Council Elder demanded of Tristan. Wist's dark eyes hadn't sought Nicu. To hide a secret? Or was his mentor displaying his disappointment?

"None more devious than yours," Tristan responded.

"The Fae do not lie."

"Nor do they tell the truth."

The two men glared at each other, an impasse between those who were not enemies, yet nowhere near allies. After a moment, Wist broke off, gaze sweeping the clearing. His eyes slid over the Helduan sequoia without pause, the scarred, soul-eating giant dismissed as nothing more than an unremarkable addition. Even Edan's shadowy form at Branna's side drew no visible start, only the faint narrowing of Wist's eyelashes.

"Nicu," Wist said, his voice clipped. "Edan is dead, Branna's powers have blossomed, and the Trimarked Child has crossed into true Gypsum. What a spectacular failure on your part. Do you wish you had listened to me now?"

Nicu's throat tightened. He gave no answer, knowing the Elder sought none. The reprimand was precise, his tone cool, yet something in the cadence shifted. Too sharp to be simple anger, too measured to be grief. Fear, Nicu thought for half a beat, before dismissing the idea. Wist never allowed fear to surface.

What was Wist's angle here, then? And only with Altaya as support? The back of Nicu's neck itched where the Trimarked Medallion used to be. But he no longer held it, and if Tristan still claimed it, the Wizard was keeping it well hidden.

"We do not need the Trimarked Child," Wist declared. "Branna, Nicu, and Edan. Return to Center and we'll discuss this among people who can correct this problem."

Tristan broke into a sprint, heading straight for Devi. She lifted her hands and braced herself, yet he wrapped his arms around her anyway and they vanished the moment his feet left No Man's Land.

Wist's jaw tightened.

"Now." His voice was set with an urgency Nicu hesitated to answer.

Branna disappeared, leaving behind the echo of a shout. Without her, Edan flickered once, then was gone.

Wist's deep brown eyes widened, his focus locking on Nicu while he remained rooted in Fae land. "Nicu, we must hurry before the Wizard takes you, too."

Yet Nicu deliberated. There was no external push for him to choose the Fae over Ember. The forceful weight of destiny had lifted, as if the universal powers had taken a solid step back. The absence left him adrift, and when uncertain, he rarely made a choice.

Wist reached toward Nicu, but he would not leave Fae soil. He never had. Their kind claimed the land for a reason. Within Trifecta, the essence of each domain lingered, seeping in through the Convergence and embedding in each sector. The Circle, home of the Witches, pulsed with Heldu's endless flow. The human Town maintained the Terran energy that was locked too deep to affect humans and resisted a mage's hand. And in Center, structural magic saturated each living thing.

Wist would not abandon his place of strength. Yet even tethered to Fae land, his Work could still reach outward. Wist's tattoos darkened his hands and climbed his neck as they filled with power. Nicu stopped himself from stepping back, resolved to not allow Wist to discern the discomfort twisting within Nicu's chest.

The last time Nicu had seen the Elder cast a spell, he had aimed for Ember, but Branna had fallen in her place.

Nicu, at only four years old, had reversed the damage and altered his own relationship with magic forever.

But moving against the Fae would be choosing.

The pressure of Fate and Chaos trickled in, sensing the

shift in his thoughts and foregoing whatever had caused their odd absence.

This is not the right moment. Nicu wrapped the strength of his belief around the thought, infusing it with the power of a truth too potent to deny.

The heavy presence of the universal powers eased back, as if the cosmic forces reacted in surprise. In their absence, Tristan's path surged around Nicu. He did not resist when the Wizard seized his arms and, in a single step, pulled him miles away from the Fae who had always demanded his obedience.

4

EMBER

*E*mber sat on a low chair beyond the white flaps of her dwelling's entrance. With the ruins at her back, she faced the vast desert wavering under the sun. She lifted her shoulder-length hair away from her neck and watched the heat waves dance and blur the horizon, her vision protected by a thick coating of her shield magic. She'd developed the skill after a few days of enduring the bright, reflective light with tear-stung eyes.

She currently lived at the edge of what was left of this Fae city. Shade and Reyar had gathered enough materials to turn one of the shell-buildings into a 2-room home, a space the three of them shared. They insisted it was unsafe for her to be alone, and not just because of dragons. Whether that was true or not, trouble hadn't found them over the past three months.

Still, Ember preferred walking to sitting. She missed the tall redwood trees of Trifecta, their trunks large enough for a group of people to encircle, arms spread wide with only fingertips touching. She craved their encompassing shade and the mountain breeze that wove its way through the ancient giants.

During midday, it was too hot to walk across this desert. Shade had told her it had once been a forest, ages ago. Time, she explained, moved faster on Gypsum than the other realms, and it was further along in the planet's evolution despite the fact that they shared the same physical space.

The conversation hadn't been quite outside Ember's understanding, but it had been enough to cause a slight headache. Whatever was happening to Gypsum, whichever rules bent and broke to make one realm age faster than the rest, she chalked it up to magic. With magic, Ember had learned to take the truth as it stood.

The tent flap waved, and the soft clapping of the fabric drew Ember's attention. Reyar stepped out, blinking into the bright afternoon light, then frowned at her.

"You shouldn't be out in so much sun. You burned to a crisp a few weeks ago."

"Shade gave me a salve before she left."

And what a departure it had been. Shade had been working with Ember on pushing her shield away from her body, creating space between the power and her skin. A shadow had fallen over them, and Ember lost focus, her attention latching onto the image of a dragon straight overhead, gliding in a spiral.

"Fades!" she'd shrieked, rushing to the Fae's side. Shade had shielded her eyes and offered a grunt.

"It's only Yotos."

"Only," Ember croaked, not able to help herself as she tried to fit inside Shade's narrow shadow.

The dragon had a pink belly that nearly blended into the sky, and as it lowered, Ember noticed the upper scales were a darker shade, closer to the deeper tones of autumn leaves. A large green eye flashed far too close for Ember's comfort on its final spiral before the dragon dropped its lids to protect against the thrust of sand kicked up from its landing.

"He's really fine riding them?" Ember's wide eyes turned to Shade as Reyar hopped off the creature's back.

"I told you, the Fae have a special relationship with dragons," Shade offered with a crooked smile.

"But he's a Wizard."

Shade barked out a laugh. "Noticed that, did you? Yes. His goddess manipulation. A Wizard destined to become the Dragon Lord of Gypsum."

Shade strode toward Reyar as if trying to leave the echo of her words behind, never happy whenever there was talk of gods and goddesses. Ember hurried to keep up with her, nervous about the dragon, but having learned to trust these two mages who had taken her in.

Shade held out a hand to Reyar, and he grabbed it, jerking her in for a quick, rough kiss. Ember studiously ignored them, studying the dragon instead, jumping back when the green eye peeked open. The slit pupil extended for nearly half her height and was aimed directly at her.

"Get used to them," Shade warned. "You'll be seeing a lot more soon."

"What do you mean?" Ember spun, her heart skipping a beat as she watched Shade climb up Yotos' side with Reyar's help, though it was clear the siren Fae didn't need it.

"Once upon a time, I ran a circus." Shade flashed a toothy smile. "The Upper Fae, of course, disapproved, but they still came. Everyone loves a little rebellion, even if they don't want to be responsible for it. With a new act, I'm ready to restart and refresh."

"What?" Ember demanded, trying to keep up, but feeling left behind.

"Reyar will get you ready. Stand back now!"

That had been two weeks ago. Ember had no idea what problem a circus solved or what this new act was, but assumed her power had something to do with it. Shade had trained her a little, though Reyar ignored her. Still, they'd provided her room and board and she'd had nothing to trade them in return.

Perhaps this Fae circus would give her the chance to even out her debt.

With Reyar suddenly standing over her in the here and now, Ember rose from her chair. His height made it uncomfortable to talk to him from such a low position. Yet her choice to stand had more emotion behind it than physical comfort. There was something about him, an energy that radiated from him that implied one should stand in his presence. Not for any dangerous reason, though he could certainly be dangerous, but out of respect. Maybe it was the aura of the Dragon Lord. Maybe it was just Reyar.

"Hmm." Reyar studied her for a moment, then arced his chin from her direction to the ruins before walking up the road himself. Ember followed him until he passed the barrier, where he stopped and turned to face her.

The central tower of the inner city peeked above his head, with smaller towers descending from its core. Most of the buildings rose about ten stories to accommodate the heavy population. The tallest spire marked the seat of the government and the shorter ones as temples to the honored deities. Neither Shade nor Reyar spoke about the gods with anything close to respect. Rather they sneered whenever they were mentioned, eyes narrowed and words biting.

"Did Shade tell you her plan?"

"I only heard about the circus as she left."

Which was odd, considering that Shade was the talkative one. Since she'd gone on her expedition, Ember had lived with a silent roommate who came and went as he pleased, never mind the protection he claimed she needed or the help Shade suggested he'd provide. Bringing her out here to talk was unusual, and a little unsettling. Ember wasn't afraid of him, but she recognized a barely tamed wild animal when she saw one. It was best to remain cautious.

"How much control do you have?" He focused on her eyes, but not to meet them. Rather, it appeared he fixed on the shield she used to shade her pupils from the sun, as if he saw the actual energy where most people could not.

"What?" Ember took an involuntary step back at his question. He obviously meant her power, which was something she wasn't in the habit of discussing with anyone.

"When you first arrived, I assumed you had none. Yet you shaped it into a shield. And at a mere suggestion from Shade, you've taught yourself to make sun protection. So what else is possible? Could you extend it from your body, form a sphere around you, bend the light to become invisible, or focus it into an attack?"

Ember blinked against the onslaught of questions, one in particular. Could she turn invisible? The Witch Queen, Charlah, had asked her the same question.

"Shade didn't tell you? She's been training—"

"I wasn't interested," Reyar interrupted. "Now I am. So what are you capable of?"

Ember's inner alarm sounded. Why was he interested all of a sudden? What happened? Ember fought the need to answer him, to let that indescribable power he held wash over her without meaning. He might be a powerful being, but she'd faced off against Nicu enough times that she could pretend, for just a moment, that Reyar was the same.

"Fine," he allowed. "I remembered a dream I had a long time ago."

"Because of me?"

Reyar grunted. "In a way. You're Goddess-touched. It got me thinking, why you? Why now? Then I recalled a Witch asked those same questions in a goddess-manipulated dream."

"Shade used that phrase," Ember frowned. "You were manipulated into becoming the Dragon Lord?"

"I was born the Dragon Lord in Heldu, when dragons are only here," Reyar countered, his rainbow-colored eyes dimming into a bitter matte. "The Goddess Azhirith wanted to tie Helduan energy to Gypsum through me."

"Why?"

"To save Gypsum." Reyar sneered. "But it was in vain. This realm doesn't want to be saved."

Ember looked around at the ruins that surrounded them. To her, these remaining stones were evidence of an ongoing fight against time. The city beyond them a testament to the struggle to conserve resources, gather strength, and survive amidst all this decay.

"Are you sure?"

The question made Reyar pause, and his head tilted in a slight, thoughtful angle.

"Huh. Maybe Shade is right."

"About what?"

"You're an anomaly, Ember Lee. I've spent the last few weeks trying to figure out what god or goddess left you Touched, but I haven't found any connection."

"Because it hasn't happened yet?"

"Because the god hasn't been Made yet."

Ember stepped back, but not from Reyar. She simply needed to move her body, to give it something to do while her thoughts raced.

"I have no idea what that means."

"It means that not only is your power pure potential, but your very existence is, too. Which brings us to my original questions. How much control do you have, and what can you do with it?"

Ember felt as if her brain split in two. One piece of it worked over the mystery Reyar had presented to her, recognizing how out of her depth she was while still trying to understand. The other part of her heard his question, and she lacked the sense to keep her answers to herself.

"It isn't real magic."

"Which is to say you don't harvest magical particles from the molecules of things around you and Work them into spells." Reyar gestured to the ruins. "A bonus in this environment. But power, even raw, can still be manipulated and utilized."

Ember licked her dry lips. She wasn't sure what game he played. Why he simply gave her this information after bringing her out here, asking her questions she was certain Shade would have already explained.

"What do you know about what I do?" she countered.

Reyar's smile was brilliant, softening the edges of stoic features. "You have grown up around the Fae."

Quite an assumption after one counter-question, though perhaps he'd found other clues in the months she'd been under his protection.

"Fine. We know you can create a shield, that Shade was working with you to manipulate it, but you were unsuccessful before she left. Under stress, your energy builds until it releases dramatically. What else?"

Ember's breath quickened, and she took another step back. Reyar watched her from the other side of her boundary, his face settling into neutral lines as he observed her reaction. He remained still and quiet, waiting.

Questions crowded Ember's mind. Many of them cut, creating a physical pain from the internal words. He'd given her information, yes, but it had been presented in broad terms, meant to throw her off balance and gunk up her thoughts, all while he tried to get her to open up. She didn't know enough about this realm, about this person, to even guess at his end goal or the purpose behind his inquiry.

She would have to engage, but she did not have to give in easily.

"What will you do with the information?"

"That's hard to say without knowing what it is."

"What are your intentions? Why did you and Shade decide to stay with me? What do you know about my power and what are your plans for it? What does any of this have to do with Shade wanting to restart her circus?"

Reyar studied Ember for a while longer. She started to sweat under the hot sun and pained uncertainty.

"You are right to ask," Reyar conceded. "The answer is not as clear as you would like it to be."

Ember grit her teeth. Nothing he'd said so far had been as clear as she'd like it to be.

Reyar fell into silence as he stepped through Ember's boundary and led her back to their tent. With a long, tanned arm, he held the flap and gestured with the other hand for her to go inside. Ember followed his silent instructions, breathing in deeply when the cooled air struck her cheeks. Her body leaned into the cold, her brain overheated from external and internal heat, the contrast robbing her balance for a moment and she reached out. Reyar was there to steady her, then to lead her to a much more comfortable chair than the folding one she'd taken outside.

Tan stacks of mortared stone held the interior of the tent up, remnants that once served as support beams. Sun-bleached canvas had been placed strategically to create separation between four distinct areas. Luxury and comfort lined every surface. There was the main room, where she sat in recovery, and then three rooms beyond it.

One bedroom had been gifted to Ember. Reyar and Shade shared another. The third was a stone-and-silver bathroom, complete with a deep soaking tub positioned beneath a gap in the ceiling that revealed the sky, while the high walls ensured shade for most of the day. The main area was furnished with a thick cream carpet, two birch chaises, an abundance of pale metallic pillows, and four low, deeply cushioned chairs.

Reyar had placed her on one of the chaises while she regained her inner equilibrium. He handed her a teacup filled with water, showing calm patience as the color returned to her cheeks.

"Shade and I are rebels by nature," he began. "Shade has delved into magic beyond what the Fae considers appropriate, and flaunts it with her circus shows and by refusing to remove herself from society. I left my realm for this one, to take my place as the Dragon Lord in a domain that was never meant to be my own. The fact that the world is dying doesn't keep me up at night. It isn't mine to save—"

"You said the goddess—"

"Is a goddess." Reyar drew in a deep breath through his nose, as if he'd spoken sharper than intended. His tone softened a beat later. "If she cared to, she could mend it all herself."

Ember lifted her cup, letting the cool water stop her from saying anything she might regret.

"Shade and I were drawn together because we don't bend easily. We don't take on other people's problems or opinions. We only need to live, and even if this realm is dying, she and I have options that others do not."

Ember lowered her cup. "So you'd let the Fae die just because you can walk away?"

Reyar's gaze sharpened. "That's not what I said. There are ways forward the goddess refuses to consider, so Shade and I are left to do the thinking for her."

He leaned back, his voice almost casual. "So whatever Veil parting powers you have aren't actually what I'm interested in."

Ember choked and sat up quickly, dragging air past the water stuck in her lungs.

Reyar smiled at her reaction, his eyes sparkling as he proved he knew more than she'd thought. "What matters to me is what you know about manipulating your own power, and how much you have yet to learn."

"Why?"

Reyar's lips thinned, though Ember couldn't tell if this was due to her question or to some other thought that bothered the Wizard.

"Clearly the gods are not giving up on me or Shade. Your

presence here suggests they're at work again and that you're here to test us, push us in to a corner, or even to take our place. No matter what their plans, our lives should be lived by our choices. Not theirs. Not anyone else's." His gaze sharpened. "Tell me. Have you been told you're meant to be used?"

Tristan's words echoed in Reyar's voice. She flinched as if slapped, but nodded through the discomfort.

"Then let's get you ready to fight back."

Ember studied Reyar, swallowing more water to help soothe the tightness in her chest. His promise rang true, but he obviously spent a lot of time with the Fae. Or perhaps, this was just Reyar as Devi was just Devi. Secretive. Knowledgeable. Slightly dependable. Mostly self-centered.

Reyar admitted he wanted to train her, and she believed him. Yet there was something else he wasn't saying, a truer purpose hidden behind his careful words.

Still, her life wasn't in danger. Reyar offered guidance now, and Shade seemed to be setting up a path that may help later. In a realm she didn't understand, knowing only these two, Reyar's offer was more than she'd ever dared expect back in Trifecta.

Working with Tristan had taught her the value of suspicion. Keeping her guard up would be simple enough, and with this pair, probably respected.

"I can open the Veil in Terra for a short time. Not between realms, but in that physical space," Ember said. "People are able to pass through. Everyone but me."

"Everyone but you," Reyar repeated, a faraway look in his eyes. He seemed to catch his thoughts and returned his attention to her. "What else?"

"I can share my shield." Ember hesitated, then placed her fingertips on Reyar's forearm. A moment later, her power expanded from herself to the Wizard. She took her fingers away, flinching at the slight pinch of a broken connection. Reyar flexed his hands as he examined the effect of her power.

"It will fade in a while, but I haven't timed it. I think it disappears with distance, too, but I'm not sure. I can do this to objects, too, and create a block that stops others."

"And the rest?"

"Someone else suggested I might become invisible, but she wasn't trustworthy."

Reyar nodded, studying his arm a moment longer. With a flick of his wrist, the power cracked, then fell away like a shattered shell. Ember sensed the energy dissipate into the air, her eyes wide on the Wizard in front of her.

"I didn't know someone could—"

"Not everyone," Reyar assured her. "As it turns out, you are an anomaly who has found her way to two others."

Perhaps another of the reasons Reyar and Shade had taken her in.

"Now that we know what you think you can do, it's time to discover what's truly possible. Are you ready?"

Exploring her power had always been a secret, solitary act for Ember. Training with Shade had faltered because she couldn't imagine practicing alongside someone else. She had rarely used her abilities in the open, and never where others might see her slip and assume she meant harm. Then again, this was not Trifecta. Reyar was a Wizard, but he wasn't Devi. And Shade, though Fae, was not Nicu.

What would it mean to her to have true control? To claim the confidence Reyar suggested was possible?

Ember's fingers tapped the cup she held with both hands. She set it gently on the small marble table.

"Absolutely."

5

NICU

*B*eing saved—

Stop. 'Saved' implied he'd made a choice.

Being transported by Tristan was not a comfortable feeling. Nicu's control of movement had been taken away in the effort to keep their momentum smooth. As they came to a stop, Nicu stumbled against the drastic change of pace, though Tristan remained sure-footed and secure.

As Nicu recovered his composure, he took in the landscape. Through the dark, the rushing sound of the river marked their location on a low, flood-cut shoreline with a higher embankment towering above them. His eyes adjusted to the dim light, and he noted the thick vines and exposed roots that wove a tapestry against the compacted dirt wall. The surrounding molecules were saturated with the flowing, organic forms of Witch Magic.

Nicu stiffened and looked between Tristan and Devi, yet neither of them appeared bothered that two Fae had arrived in the Coven's territory without permission.

"He's here," Devi snapped, throwing a forceful gesture in Nicu's direction. She faced Branna and Edan, who stood with their backs to the natural wall, Branna's dark eyes

Tempered

sparking with defiance. "Now tell us more about these Watchers."

The corners of Branna's jaw tightened, and she crossed her arms, leaning against dirt and roots as she added centimeters of distance between herself, Edan, and Devi. Her lids lowered as if in lazy contempt. Devi's own mint-gem eyes flashed with an inner fire as she refocused her attention on Edan's ghostly form, yet it was neither of the two who answered Devi's question.

"They are soul-eaters," Tristan offered, filling the silence Edan left.

Devi spun to face him, her cranberry curls arcing around the shoulders of her fur-lined, berry-colored parka. "And what do you know about them?"

"I've been out in the world," he reminded with a pointed, raised brow. "I have seen them fall."

The silence that followed invited Tristan to explain more, though he did not. Now that they were beyond the Fae's reach, he no longer felt pressured to clarify.

Impatience ate at Nicu's chest. In true Gypsum, an untold amount of time was passing for Ember. He was driven to focus on her, yet everyone seemed more interested in the incoming threat of the Watchers. His temples pounded a steady cadence that sounded like *'choose, choose, choose'*. He held his tongue against the need to control the conversation and maneuver it toward Ember, blaming the impulse on a decade of habit and freezing his thoughts as much as possible to avoid a misstep in his internal fight with Fate.

"The soul eaters want to invade Trifecta." Edan brought the conversation back around, willing to participate considering this secret was a shared one. "After the Convergence, the Veil hardened everywhere. All visiting Fae were trapped in Terra, just as we've been confined in this city. Without being able to return, they turned grey, and in time, their spirits were ejected from their bodies. Then the hunger developed, and they began eating human souls to try to fill the void theirs had left. They did not satisfy."

"So they want to come into Trifecta for what?" Devi crossed her arms, her eyes rising to the sky as she fell into thought. "They can't get back home through here, either."

"The Fallen aren't interested in going home. They want living energy encased in magic," Tristan answered, lips lifted as if he found the situation amusing. Though, the way he looked at them down the angle of his sharp nose, perhaps it was their ignorance he enjoyed.

"They're looking for Fae and Witch souls." Devi restated the information quietly, as if saying the words helped tuck it away into the puzzle she pieced together in her mind.

"You are all too unbothered by this," Edan insisted, stepping toward them as if his ethereal form could drive the point home. "My soul was pushed out by this phenomenon in a matter of weeks. My body is now in the city below us, stripping it of as many human souls as possible while on its way here. Consumed spirits do not move on. Their bodies do not rise again. We need to get the Trimarked Child back and close off Trifecta."

Devi blinked away from her thoughts, looking at Edan with parted lips and wide, focused eyes.

"And you would leave these creatures to continue preying on the humans? Wouldn't it be better to let them come here so we can take care of them?"

"How do you propose to do that?" Edan demanded.

"We get them home, of course," Tristan drawled.

"To a dying realm," Branna snapped, adding to the conversation for the first time.

"Which is the most appropriate place for one who talks to ghosts," Tristan retorted.

Nicu examined each of their faces as they shifted between thought, anger, and uncertainty. He took in the words spoken and noted when others were held back. None of their arguments moved the conversation forward or altered the base of their truth.

Whether he considered the Fae or Ember, two facts were certain. They were running out of time, and Ember's powers were the key to any future solution. He could now focus on getting her back without tipping the scale.

"We need Ember either way." His intercession was quiet, yet gained instant attention. Every eye turned to him with his assessment, though Branna's gaze jerked away again as if she could not stand the sight of him. With Edan's essence standing between them, Nicu could understand his mate's emotions.

No, that claim was incorrect. She was no longer his mate. In spirit, she had never been. Now, even the magical tie between them had snapped, cut the moment Ember fell into Gypsum.

"Bringing Ember back provides options," he continued. "She broke the barrier. Her energy may be what can re-open doors between the realms. Or possibly reseal Trifecta."

"Here we thought she would destroy everything," Devi muttered.

"Don't idolize her yet." Tristan sliced his hand through the air. "Her power might be helpful, yes. But Ember herself will have to be convinced. Her choices may not echo yours."

Edan considered Tristan even as Nicu examined Edan, trying to see what secrets the dead Fae collected.

"So that's why the barrier isn't completely broken." Edan's eyes flickered toward Nicu, warning him to prepare for what came next. "Because she refused to die for you."

Nicu turned and gripped the Wizard's lapel, forcing him to bend at the waist. He wrapped an arm around Tristan's neck, gripping his hands together to tighten the chokehold even as the Wizard's passive defensive spell flared. Having encountered it before, Nicu's tattoos were ready, absorbing the power and turning it null. Yet the Wizard was not without defenses, punching with sharp knuckles into Nicu's groin. Nicu grunted, bending forward while Tristan broke Nicu's handhold and slipped out of the choke, backing up five feet with only one step.

Nicu's entire body vibrated with tension as he held himself back from going after the Wizard. The weight of the universe urged him to follow his instincts, to take down the man who threatened Ember's life. To choose. Though Nicu wanted to destroy the Wizard, he was not ready to give in to Fate yet.

"It was for all of us!" Tristan shouted from further along the river bank. He strode back toward them without fear, straightening his coat as he walked.

Devi's snort suggested she believed him as much as Nicu did. Tristan cared only for the Coven. Only an hour ago, Devi had told Nicu she meant to save everyone. It was comforting to see she would not follow Tristan's words blindly just because they practiced the same form of magic.

"It doesn't matter what we need or even what we want." Devi shook her head. "Ember is the only one who can influence the Veil. Unless she cuts back in on her own, we cannot retrieve her."

"There are tools," Tristan countered. "The star fall knife, for example, though its power is too depleted to be useful anymore."

"And it's with the Witch Queen," Devi spat.

"That's where this Fae comes in." Tristan focused on Nicu. "How much is left of your Promise?"

Nicu raised a brow and shook his head. Tristan scowled.

"Wish Magic, then. That human boy spoke foolishly. Surely—"

Tristan stopped, then stepped closer to Nicu as if they hadn't just grappled, his fingers locked with sharp knuckles pointing outward, his lips thinned into a perfectly straight line.

"Those marks on your skin are blue. They are not of the Fallen. They are not of your Fae Ink, either."

"The Promise broke," Nicu acknowledged, his chin

lowered slightly toward Branna, hoping she could see his apology from her periphery. "Wish Magic depleted along with it."

"He died," Devi offered, as if it were a simple thing.

"He did not." Branna's silvery skin appeared to shift with her agitation, as if the shadows she controlled were trapped under the pale shell.

"Oh, he did," Devi countered with a cutting smile. "And now he owes some powerful forces in the universe... something." The Witch enunciated her words perfectly, her tone lying as flat as a Fae's when there was a deal to be made. Edan studied her as if trying to ease secrets from between the syllables, though Nicu doubted Devi had left room for them to escape.

"Which is even more useless." Tristan grit his teeth, his eyes narrowed into sharp-edged slits as color rose on his cheeks. "Without the Promise and Wish Magic, all connection to Ember is lost. Other options for breaking the Veil will take more time than we can find or make. I have never known a Fae to be so reckless."

Nothing the Wizard said was new to Nicu and was simply his inner thoughts spoken aloud on someone else's tongue. Nicu was the one who disappointed the Fae, unable to stop Ember from utilizing her power. He had failed Ember, proving incapable of keeping his Promise to the letter. Only able to take the cost onto himself. And yet, the universal powers were not done with them, leaving the marks of their contract on his skin. Fate would not send him back if Ember were truly lost.

When he met Devi's gaze, it was clear their thoughts echoed each other, though the excited flush on her cheeks suggested she was closer to a solution. Her face tilted toward the right, pupils slightly expanding to show a glimmer of stardust within their depths.

"I would not write off Nicu so quickly." Devi's smile showed her top teeth, and her eyes snagged Tristan's, delighting in a bit of knowledge she had that he didn't. "You abandoned Ember's mother and then did not stay around to witness the aftermath. You missed when a Fae spell went awry and killed one of their own. How a Fae child reached into the newly born power of an infant before she could be cut off from it and brought back the slain to create a necromancer."

Tristan's eyes widened, and the color drained from his cheeks.

"It was not Ember holding them together. It was Nicu." The Wizard's soft tone balanced on the verge of awe.

"Hmm," Devi agreed. "And then the Fae tried to contain him with the draining energies of Branna, hoping she would also help to dampen Ember through the links. And there you go, Nicu. Our deal is complete. That's everything I've learned from examining your Ink."

This time it was Tristan who cocked his head to the side, studying Devi.

"It appears I have the right people with me." Tristan's lips angled up and he straightened his posture, then reset his hat. Nicu glanced at Edan to see the ghost's eyes widen, giving away that he'd gathered a hidden truth from the Wizard, one that shocked him into reaction. Edan's gaze flickered to Nicu, who raised a brow, but the dead Fae neutralized his features and shook his head.

No matter what the secret was, the information was not important at the moment. Nicu breathed through his frustration, choosing to trust his lieutenant in death as he had in life.

"Branna should go," Edan insisted. "She needs Gypsum's energy before she loses her spirit."

"Perhaps you've missed the nuance because you are dead, young Fae, but this creature is not in any danger of that," Tristan offered. "Her skin is not deteriorating, but cocooned. It's a transition of a different sort, preparing her to accept the full strength of the power she'd been born with. In fact, she may be best situated here."

"I thought you said a dying world was a more suitable home for me," Branna countered.

"Eventually, for certain. But for now, I suggest collecting the spirits of the Fallen. Surely one of them might have an idea about how to fight the Watchers."

Branna glanced at Nicu, then Edan, then away from everyone and lifted her shoulders in a shrug. "I am fine working apart from Nicu."

Nicu kept his face impassive in case she looked his way again. Not because she'd caused him pain, but because the emotion he hid was that of relief. He did not want to hurt her further with internal energies he could not control.

"You will stay, too," Nicu ordered Tristan. "Your knowledge about the outside world and the Fallen can assist Branna." Despite their current rift, Nicu was certain the necromancer would ensure the Wizard remained neutralized.

"I can help motivate Ember," Tristan countered.

Devi shook her head. "We didn't miss the revelation where she fell into Gypsum because she was running from you. You mentioned her character. How quickly do you think she would agree to return if you were the one asking?"

"I suppose that depends on how the Fae are treating a lost human child with the energy of a universe inside of her."

Nicu refused to flinch at Tristan's words, though he couldn't ignore the twisting in his core as he tried to calculate once again how much time must have passed for Ember. Weeks? Months?

"We need to move," he declared.

Devi shook her hands to loosen them up, turning to study the wall of vine-like roots. Nicu sought Branna's attention, but the necromancer refused to acknowledge him. Choosing to respect her silence toward him, Nicu nodded at Edan with meaning behind his eyes.

Branna was now truly Edan's. Nicu no longer had any claim.

Devi grunted as she parted the vines to reveal a long tunnel. Tristan stepped alongside Nicu as he moved to join the Witch, but the Fae held up a warning hand.

"You might be her father, but I am her guardian. Stay here to help Trifecta since your actions contributed to cracking the barrier and allowing this threat to enter. If you continue to deviate, you will no longer have access to Ember, no matter where she is."

Tristan's emerald-gem eyes locked onto Nicu's frozen-amber stare.

"I await the moment when you realize you're in over your head."

Nicu accepted the warning as the Wizard's agreement to comply. He turned his back on Tristan, dismissing him as a threat, and walked behind Devi as she led the way underground.

6

EMBER

"More."

Ember sucked in air through her nose and tried not to tighten her neck muscles as she pushed more power up her arms and out her palms. Her goal was to create a convex oval of concentrated energy between her and Reyar. In the three months of training with him, he'd told her time and time again that her body's tension had nothing to do with the strength of the current, yet her brain had trouble separating the two.

With a grunt and a flexed core, Ember pressed a surge of power through her body. Reyar frowned.

"Not a pulse," he argued. "A steady stream."

Sweat beaded on Ember's brow, making her grateful that her hair had grown long enough to be held off her neck in a high ponytail. She tapped into the source that existed beyond herself, then rolled her shoulders to initiate the relaxation of her muscles.

This wasn't spell work. Ember didn't use artifacts to direct the magic, or an incantation to shape it. She manipulated the power that poured from the core of her bones. The raw material was volatile, yet malleable. In these training sessions, they tested her ability to control and hold the energy. Right now, she attempted a separate shield, held a meter from her body and intended to keep back enemy attacks.

With thinned lips and a negative shake of his head, Reyar extended an arm toward her from where he stood six feet away. Gemstone rings wrapped around each finger of his closed fist, and his thick, leather bracelets were studded with more polished gems. Ember sensed the small, breeze-like energy that flowed from the ground that he stored in his chosen crystals.

"More."

Ember tilted her neck from side to side, shifted her hips in her split-legged stance, and encouraged relaxation within her body. She reached deeper than her soul, searching for the hidden conduit that made her what she was and connected her to the Veil.

A fresh rush of power trickled in. Ember blew out a deep breath as she fed it steadily to the shield before her.

Reyar opened his fingers in a flash. When his energy hit hers, her defenses cracked, then broke.

Ember collapsed to her knees, unhurt, but angry at his apparent ease while she was sweat-soaked and sucking in oxygen.

"You did better than your glare suggests," he assured her. "You would be a challenge for an ordinary mage."

"And where are you on the above-average scale?" Ember pushed herself to her feet, irritated at the gentle tremor that vibrated through her body. She knew it was a sign of using too much of her physical self while casting. If only she could break through that energy-drain barrier.

"High," Reyar answered, his rainbow-gem eyes flashing reflected light in their depths.

Ember swiped her forearm across her forehead and scowled. Reyar approached with the casual confidence that came from knowing that nothing in the universe posed a threat to him. Movements that reminded her she would always be at risk.

"Relax. You are making excellent progress for only three months of training, especially starting at your age."

"Seventeen is old?"

"To learn something that demands full attention while absolute relaxation? Yes, seventeen is old."

"You should know by now that females do not like talking about their age." The musical voice that interrupted them stopped all talk of training. Ember spun to find Shade striding toward her and Reyar. She arrived from the direction of the ruins to reach the makeshift training grounds Reyar had marked out in the wider expanse of the white desert sands.

Reyar greeted Shade with a soft smile. "I take it your expedition was successful?"

"Entirely," she agreed. "In fact, Vaelero is happily shopping at the moment for the new costumes."

Reyar laughed as he pulled Shade close. "Everyone is so eager to flaunt Fae traditions."

"In Vael's case, I think he just enjoys spending my money."

Ember bent to stretch her back in a forward fold as Shade and Reyar exchanged a kiss. She wanted to provide them with some privacy, yes, but there was also something incongruous between the two. Like they were puzzle pieces that should fit together, but didn't.

Then again, Ember had minimal exposure to love and connection. Most likely it was her own discomfort she experienced, so best to avert her attention and wait to learn what it was Shade had been doing while away for so long.

A shadow crossed overhead, and Ember jerked upright, blinking rapidly against the pink atmosphere. In Gypsum, the dragons created sky-cast shadows, not clouds. Even expecting the sight, she couldn't help scrambling back as if a few steps would somehow protect her from the serpentine creature gliding on large, leathery wings above her.

Ember engaged her power, activating a self-defense mechanism that had taken her over twice before. Once here, and once with Tristan. She had more control now, though. Ember breathed in through her nose and rolled her shoulders. She redirected the energy from the destructive blast it wanted to become and poured it into the shield around her skin, focusing on protection from the dragon.

"That is amazing progress," Shade praised. Ember tried to smile, but failed.

"It's just Yotos, right?" Ember asked.

"For the moment," Shade agreed. Ember twisted to ask what the Fae meant, but Shade had turned to Reyar. "You have done well with her."

"This is all the child." Though Reyar's words came as praise, Ember flinched at the moniker, too reminiscent of her Trifectan title of 'Trimarked Child'. "I wasn't sure she was ready to graduate to invisibility. Her power flow has been too irregular insofar."

Wait. What?

Ember looked at her fingers, startled to find them slightly blurred to her sight, as if a thick, pearlescent coating covered her.

"I can see myself. Am I really invisible?"

"To most eyes," Reyar assured her. "How does it feel? Are you overstressed?"

"I'm full of adrenaline, if that's what you mean." Ember flinched as the shadow passed over her again. When she looked up, her increased heartbeat ensured the invisibility shield remained in place. There were two more dragons, both with pale pink bellies that blended into the sky until they crossed the bright glow of the sun.

"I think she is saying you are not that intimidating," Shade teased Reyar with a sly sideways grin.

"If I'd known dragons would be the key to unlocking her stability, I could have used that."

A shudder went through Ember, and she was glad he hadn't had the idea earlier. She shuddered at the image of her standing alongside one Wizard while facing off a handful of dragons as he instructed her to 'relax and let the power flow'.

"You really don't need to fear them," Reyar assured her, clearly guessing her thoughts. "Not with me around."

"And when you're not?" Ember demanded, her hands shaking as the large creatures above were joined by a fourth and fifth. The first arrivals began a slow spiral downward. She remembered how enormous Yotos had been up close, and he'd just been one. She'd focused on his eye, but his teeth had been huge, and she was so small—

"Ember."

Reyar's firm use of her name startled Ember into immediate attention. He'd sounded identical to Nicu in that moment, enough that her pulse slowed and a faint, remembered scent of pine and mist rose from memory.

What was he doing now? How angry was he with her for disappearing? Were the Trifectan Fae searching for her? She knew time moved faster in Gypsum, but by how much?

The distraction of Nicu helped bring her breath into a regular rhythm, and she focused on Reyar's eyes.

Reyar's form blurred from more than the heat and white desert. A mass of colored light, his human height lowered and lengthened until it solidified again into a creature whose head reached her hip. Blue-green scales replaced skin while his skull shifted, extending into a narrow snout even as multiple curving dorsal spines grew out from his backbone along with a newly grown tail. Thick, heavy feet ended in black, pointed claws digging into the sand. All that remained the same were those reflective, rainbow eyes.

Satisfied that Ember had taken in the transformation, Reyar shifted forms again, standing tall and secure before her.

"Appearances can deceive," Reyar informed her. "My second form materializes as a dragonling, but not for lack of strength or rank. There is a level of safety to be found when others consider you small and less threatening."

Reyar's chin lowered, including Ember in that statement. Her spine straightened as she discovered his inclusion brought forth a feeling that tightened across her lower belly, bringing a sense of pride along with improved posture.

"Ember, drop the invisibility," Shade ordered, and Ember responded to the strength of Shade's voice, as if it had been the key she needed to unlock her tight grip on her power. The shield retreated into what she considered its passive form, a thin, protective layer against her skin. Shade smiled in congratulations while Reyar returned to the reason she'd become invisible.

"You are safe from the dragons," he assured her once again. "I guarantee it."

His words an echo of Nicu. A stated promise he could make as the Dragon Lord. As the images of the two men overlapped in her mind, a memory wrapped in pain shook loose from an oppressive pile of greater traumas. A discovery that her old world and the new one somehow overlapped and connected before she'd fallen into Gypsum. High Priestess Leona, hours before her death, holding on to a strand of hemp chain with a matte black ring dangling at its end. Ember had tried to touch it and had been overwhelmed by its power.

Leona's words came back in bits and pieces. Meant for the Dragon Lord's mate, to protect her from the dragon hive mind. Ember's attention shifted to Shade's hands. Had the Fae ever worn the band? Were they searching for it?

The Fae's fingers were naked, but Ember's curious gaze was marked. Shade's forearms clenched, and a snake tattoo twisted down her right arm, pooling into her palm. With a flick of her wrist, the rest of the Ink jerked from her skin, forming into a tangible whip that sparkled with the white-hot energy of lightning.

Ember stumbled back, wide eyes on the flat features of Shade's face.

"You have seen the dragon bone ring."

How had Shade recognized the truth so perfectly and precisely? Was it a shared skill she had with Edan? Did the why matter when it was the consequences Ember faced in the flashing movement of electric Ink?

"Shade. She is not wearing it." Reyar's tone was softer with the Fae, but just as forceful as when he'd used Ember's name. Shade's snake whip snapped with electricity, then she took a deep breath and let the power settle down, the tattoo returning to her arm.

So the ring had been made for her. Or was it? Reyar had emphasized that Ember wasn't wearing the band. Charlah claimed that fate magic had shaped the dragon bone. Perhaps Reyar's chosen mate was not his destined one?

Ember knew whose finger the ring rested on. She'd seen it snap there as if drawn by magnets. Or magic. Ember drew on Nicu's stoic stillness, keeping her weight from shifting between her feet and giving away her trepidation. Though Devi was safe in Trifecta, Shade had contacts through the Veil, ways to pass items and messages. She could cause any amount of havoc with those limited resources.

"Your first arrivals are here." Reyar spoke softly, gently brushing Shade's shoulder with the back of his fingers, his chin lowered as if in apology. Shade's eyes narrowed and her lips curled, the whip curling on itself as if it were a real snake preparing to strike, only uncertain about whether to target Reyar or Ember.

"Train her to fight." Shade recalled her Ink with a snap of her wrist, though the air remained charged and sharp. "We want more than a light show from her before opening day."

Shade spun on her thick boots and stalked further into the desert. Just beyond, a soft cloud of dust rose into the pink sky, followed by excited voices drifting in, and the sound of heavy items being dropped from a great height. The dragons delivered Fae and additional supplies, likely for Shade's circus. Ember had never seen one, of course, though she remembered a picture book from when she was little. Still, she doubted Shade meant to produce red and white striped tents filled with lions, elephants, and high wire acts. What would a Fae carnival look like?

Ember considered her own ambiguous role in Shade's plan. Would it change now? At least she'd told Reyar to continue training Ember, so she wouldn't be abandoned. Proof that they fostered her due to something other than kindness. Not that the knowledge was surprising. Just disappointing.

The confirmation only reminded Ember she needed to keep her guard up. Yes, they meant to manipulate her, but she was able to use them as well. In three months, she'd developed her powers beyond her expectations. For now, the promise of training and safety was enough. She only had to survive Shade's anger.

Ember wiped sweat from her forehead and let out a heavy breath. "How mad is she?"

"She will calm down." Reyar placed a gentle hand on Ember's shoulder, bringing her attention back to the present moment. Ember glanced at him, noting the hard lines around his eyes that suggested he had more questions for her, but he contained them in case they gave too much of himself away. "And she's right. Enough casting for today. Let's work on your hand-to-hand."

A wave of heat left Ember swaying on her feet. "I need water," she countered. Mostly, she needed a place to process and regroup. Reyar's sharp eyes caught both her meanings, and his lips thinned before he gave a nod of approval.

"Then rest. But we aren't done with you."

The warning lingered in Ember's ears as she walked into the ruins, unsteady on her feet for more reasons than one.

"Ember," Reyar bit out, as if he wanted to call back her

name even as he said it. Ember shifted to face him. "When you first saw it. The dragon bone ring. Did someone wear it?"

"No." The word fell gingerly from Ember's tongue. She spoke honestly - no one was wearing the ring when she'd first seen it - but she'd also witnessed what had come after. Reyar's eyelids flinched at the unspoken weight of that knowledge.

"Sometimes I forget that even though you were raised with the Fae, you are still very human," Reyar murmured. "But I was the one who danced around the truth with poorly chosen semantics."

"Reyar?"

"I already knew," he admitted through clenched teeth. "The Goddess of Truth has appointed a Trifectan Witch. I just hoped it wasn't in this timeline."

Reyar let out a grunt and escaped toward the growing crowd of dragons. Yotos' enormous head rose in response to his master's quiet command. Ember turned from him slowly so she wouldn't draw attention to herself, not wanting to become more entangled in whatever chaotic web spun around them, even between the realms.

Dragons. Fate. Magic.

And the foreboding premonition that her training had a purpose beyond mere survival.

7

NICU

Nicu had to walk close on Devi's heels to avoid the roving tentacles that moved in on them, seeking the heat of their bodies and the nourishment of their souls. The thick, arms-width roots hugged the walls, but thinner strands hung from the ceiling in varied thickness, though all supple enough to bend and press against Devi's power, trying to find a weakness in her shield so it could steal their years and add to the cursed sequoia's growth.

With additional soul energy, would the invasive pine continue to break the cracked barrier, or would it bow against what was left of it? It wasn't likely to affect the Veil anymore, though, not if Tristan still needed Ember's power.

Would the Fae approve of Tristan's plan to dismantle the barrier?

Or perhaps they already did. Tristan claimed familiarity with Wist, to such a degree that he felt comfortable advising Nicu on how to manage the Elder. And then there was Wist's reaction himself, when he approached them at No Man's Land. Though his emotions were hard to discern, he'd lacked the intensity Nicu was used to from his mentor. He had called them back to strategize, not to fight.

That puzzle was not his main concern. Any situation leading Nicu's attention from the tunnel was a distraction. He could not deny that his wandering contemplations were meant to relieve him of his current challenge. Staying in this uncomfortable present moment proved difficult with such an unknown future barreling in behind it.

Yet Nicu had honed control his entire life. He separated his thoughts from his emotions and let them run as they would in the background. He focused on each step across the unnaturally clean floor of the cave, on staying a comfortable distance from Devi while remaining safe from the roots. One breath. And another. They continued through the tunnel until it opened into a bulbous cavern.

Devi stumbled at the entrance, her shoulders rising toward her ears as her hands clenched into fists. With stilted strides, she burst past whatever mental block had caused her to hesitate, stopping for the last time at the back wall.

"Do you remember when you forced your Ink from your body to pull Ember from the barrier?"

Absurd question. "Of course."

"Is that a normal Fae skill?"

Ah, this inquiry was not so ridiculous. Nicu delayed responding long enough for Devi to discern the answer herself before giving voice to it.

"No."

"Are you able to recreate it?"

This pause filled with the energy of uncertainty.

"Your connection to Ember is in your DNA," Devi spoke with a brusque tone, as if she were a teacher lecturing rather than a friend explaining. "Which means it's in your blood. And then again, mixed into your Fae Ink. The Veil can be encouraged to soften in places. However, we will need to utilize the inter-body bond you share with Ember in order to get it to part. I can trick it into believing your energy and hers belong together. That they are, in fact, the same."

The unspoken conclusion being that their attempt to cross the Veil must be well executed and perfectly timed. Which meant she had hoped his control was better than he claimed.

Nicu needed to get Ember to save —

Choose a different word. To keep the peace, he might need to protect Ember from the Fae, first.

Chaos was silent against Nicu's mental gymnastics. Perhaps the cave protected him, or maybe the Powers had fallen uncommunicative again, as they'd done in the clearing above. Nicu couldn't know.

"Who starts?" Nicu asked.

"Given your response about your Ink, I imagine we should begin together."

Nicu ignored the implications hidden between her words and offered a nod of agreement.

"This piece of the wall aligns with the Center boundary above." Devi pressed her power against the uneven rock-face and the roots curled and shifted out of the way, providing a triangular section of cleared granite.

"If you need to, place your hands here. I will work around you."

Devi collected gems from her layered bracelets as she spoke. Her lack of interest might be considered polite, but it was more likely she studied him even as she prepared for her upcoming spellwork.

Nicu flexed his hands and willed his body to relax. He did not need to engage his muscles for this exercise, though that's how he had practiced it in his unlit bedroom. Perhaps that's where his progress had faltered.

No time like the present, when stakes were high, to try another strategy.

Nicu pressed his palms against the irregular surface of the cave's rock wall, trusting Devi to keep the roots away. He focused on the Ink, both part of him and separate. Moving the tinted lines over his skin was simple, something he'd been able to do since he'd healed after receiving them.

The Inking began for all Fae at ten years old. Several spirals were marked out on their shoulders and forearms, with six more on the front torso, and four on either side of their dorsal spines. Another set was applied to their outer hips, and then three over each of the quadriceps, and three atop the hamstrings.

As the Ink pressed into their bodies, their blood rose to meet it, blending and testing each other. The spirals unwound over the next few days and carved out their own unique forms as dictated by the Fae's own essence. Every Fae's tattoos were singular to them, like fingerprints. Edan had porcupine spikes. Branna had sweeps of Ink that echoed the shape of a scythe. Nicu's were long waves that ran alongside each other, yet never touched unless he called them forward, as he did now.

One shade darker than his skin, the Ink pooled around the whole of his hands, saturating their power and darkening their hue. Deep breath. He closed his eyes and concentrated, using his years of mental agility to connect his physical form to the wall. They were all made of atoms after all. They all had magic buried within the molecules that created them. He focused on the effortless motion he desired, utilizing the strength of intent. Convincing himself that moving his Ink to the stone should be like causing smoke to rise from a fire.

Devi's low hum encouraged Nicu to ease open his eyes. His tattoos had left his skin and now crept across the rock face, sinking into the convex curves as if they were tiny rivers finding the path of least resistance. A spike of pride warmed his chest, and he worked to keep his breath even against rising excitement.

Devi stepped beside him, close enough that the cloth of their coats compressed against each other. She suspended gems within the vees of long fingers, three in each hand. Nicu didn't study her selection, trusting the Witch's knowledge and skill as she was depending on him. After a grounding breath, Devi pressed both hands against a section of wall that was marked by Nicu's tattoos.

Eyes closed, Devi's mouth moved in the language of Witch magic. Nicu recognized the magical tone of her voice, though the dialect slipped through his mind. Magic itself was invisible, yet sensed. The incantations that controlled it was unique to each mage-race and evaded the understanding of others.

Living in Trifecta after the Convergence had blurred those lines—even more so for those who interacted with the Trimarked Child. Nicu had learned more of Witch spellcraft than any Fae before. The same was true of Devi with Fae spells. Yet for the two of them, it was more than simple exposure. Devi was a prodigy, and where Nicu didn't understand how she saw magic differently, her skill far outpaced and outmatched Witches ten times her age. Nicu could sense all completed spells, capture their essence, and remake them by his will, no matter what type of mage created it.

Systems long since solidified were now softened by the Convergence of the realms by Ember's very existence. Today they applied skills that would have never existed without her in order to find her.

Soft blue light pulsed from the stone, evidence that Devi had connected to the Veil, yet it refused to part. Nicu's Ink resisted integration, becoming dark veins that sunk into the glow without being taken over by it. Devi grunted and leaned her weight against the rock, her elbows bowing slightly from the force. Nicu encouraged the lines of his tattoos to split in half, then into fourths, and again into eighths. Hair-thin Ink spread out amongst the glow, creating a webbing across the awakened power.

"Think whatever thoughts you had when you saved Ember from the barrier." Devi caught her breath at the end of her instructions, redirecting her entire focus on the wall. Nicu glanced her way, startled to find her left eye had turned completely black.

No, not entirely. Specks of light flickered, and swirls of tiny galaxies spun. He'd spotted a hint of this while they argued above, but assumed it had been her magic sparking. Now, though, he recognized their true form, one he'd already observed within the Witch Queen's face.

There was no time to analyze this mystery, only to file it away. Nicu returned to his own task, understanding what Devi asked him to do. She'd asked him to think about what he'd done when saving Ember from the Veil. He had found the tiny spaces between Ember's skin and the raw power, forcing his way between them.

Devi insisted she could soften the malfunctioning barrier between the realms. She would use their physio-magical connection to convince it that Nicu and Ember were essentially the same, or at least close enough to be rejoined. He'd engaged his tattoos to move from surface-to-surface, but they needed to penetrate. Devi wanted him to recreate a moment, yes, but not the one she thought.

Nicu closed his eyes once again and pulled forward an image of Ember. Though he and Ember rarely touched, they'd had two instances of intense intimacy most entities never shared. Their thoughts had bled into one another, their minds connected in ways bodies never could.

It was those moments Nicu recalled, immersing in the memories as if they were events happening now. His tattoos released their connection to the stone, spiraling to wrap around the strands of Veil magic instead. Devi's breath caught and she eased closer to the spellwork, her nose nearly touching the wall.

Yet the power still fought them.

You must choose.

The pressure on his shoulders fell with a gentle, overbearing weight. His bones bowed, and he barely managed to keep on his feet. The earth threatened to crack under him, refusing to allow him the ability to brace.

Nicu was Fae, and the Trimarked Child's guardian. He made choices that left him balanced on a line so thin, only hope held it together. Hope, and his own will.

This was not, as Devi suggested, a choice between good and evil. This was not, as the universal powers suggested, a choice between loyalty and duty.

Nicu wasn't foolish. He knew by now that there was no stopping the world from breaking apart. There was only choosing when, and how much they prepared for it.

The weight of his deliberation pressed into his spine, crushing the air from his lungs, only to break a heartbeat later and flow over him like comforting warm water. It poured over his head, washing away the pressure of choice from his mind. It fed the lines of his Ink, following them from his body and against the Veil, combining forces with Devi's spellwork.

Devi gasped the moment she sensed the change in the Veil. Her fingers curled into the malleable magic, not into the stone but despite it.

"Go first," Nicu ordered. Devi hesitated, but something she saw in the swirl of power convinced her to take that step, and then she disappeared.

Without Devi's steady presence, the spell wobbled, threatening to keep him out. Nicu thrust his Ink forward, holding onto the edges of the pathway they'd created. His muscles no longer relaxed, pressing against the barrier of his skin even as his tattoos held open the passage within the Veil.

Then, with his breath held and eyes closed, Nicu stepped into a world never meant for him.

8

BRANNA

Branna glared at the tunnel where Devi and Nicu had disappeared, hating the very notion of it. Even her ghosts were more integrated with nature than that cave. Magic was supposed to be part of the world, in balance with it. Here, the magic over-saturated everything, becoming too much and forsaking the natural order.

A lot like the humans, actually.

Leaving the cave behind, unfortunately, wasn't an easy decision to make. An uninvited Fae on Witch lands wandering around with an enemy Wizard was likely to be discovered. Without Devi to vouch for them, they'd be detained. Even if they escaped Witch lands, everywhere else in Trifecta held its own risk after Wist had seen her in the clearing. His fiery eyes had met hers with a quiet accusation that set her nerves on edge.

Wist had asked Branna to capture the Trimarked Child for him. Not only had she declined to follow his instruction, but Ember had been lost. And to where? Were they really in true Gypsum? The mess they created was beyond Branna's patience. Tristan had proven untrustworthy from the start.

Why had Ember, and then Nicu, fallen for the Wizard's machinations? It was beyond Branna's comprehension.

As it had been half an hour since Nicu and Devi had ducked into the cave, it appeared they weren't coming back. Branna assumed their experiment was successful. Had it truly taken them to Ember? Did Devi honestly believe she had the power to locate someone lost across the realms?

Branna snorted and shook her head. In the end, it didn't matter. They'd find Ember or they wouldn't. They'd be stuck in their new wherever, or they'd come back. Branna's only concern was that she'd never been this trapped before. Still in Trifecta and planted firmly in Witch land, at least until the Coven's scouts found her.

"Now. What to do until they return?"

Branna ignored Tristan, assuming the question was rhetorical. But then he situated himself beside her, his sharp, weapon-like elbows pressed out as he crossed his arms.

"She is really not Falling?" Edan asked. His semi-corporeal fingers traced a line down her arm. Branna barely detected it, but still shifted out of reach, using the motion to slip further from her unwelcome companions. Tristan was too oily, and Edan was...

Edan shouldn't be dead.

"Not Fallen at all," Tristan offered. Branna's hackles rose against the inclination that he attempted to create some goodwill between them. "The Fallen are grey and dull. Branna is lighter, more pearlescent. Almost shiny."

"Okay." Branna spun on her heel and walked downriver toward human territory, escaping the Wizard on her right and the ghost on her left. Perhaps the Witch scouts wouldn't be so bad after all. Maybe if Wist found her first, he'd arrest her and she would be given her own space, even if it was a cell.

Tristan followed her, his steps smooth and casual, hands tucked demurely into his coat pockets. His small, thin smile greeted her as if he'd only been waiting for her to choose a direction.

"There's nothing to be done about the barrier without Ember." Tristan spoke as if they were in mid-conversation. As if Branna had agreed to listen. "But we can do something about the Watchers. Rather, you can."

"Because you could not possibly get your hands dirty. Coercing Brandt and Ember to grow your tree. Sitting back as Nicu fetches her for you."

"I appreciate that you consider me to be all-powerful, but we each have our limits and our specialties."

"What do you think she can do?" Edan asked, testing the air for secrets that slipped between spoken words.

"Nothing," Branna snapped. "Because I refuse to help this snake."

Tristan studied her for a moment, then focused on Edan.

"Do you know what Watchers do?" The ghost's lips thinned and his edges blurred. He was trying to keep a secret from her. Branna had always seen Edan's tells. Now that he was dead, his fading made his lie by omission obvious.

"Perhaps how you Fall is more important. It's due to your Ink," Tristan offered. "The main ingredient is dragon's blood. Dragons radiate a defensive energy that stop them from using magic. They developed their auras to make magical energies visible within the range of their own strength of spirit. Once dragon blood Ink integrates with Fae blood, the two create quite the chemical reaction. Tattooed Fae can't stray from Gypsum for long. Without a realm filled with dragon essence, the Fae's soul is expelled."

Branna blinked deliberately, absorbing Tristan's words even though she didn't want to, putting the puzzle pieces together the way she'd been raised to.

"Then the bodies try to fill the void by stealing other souls," she murmured, turning to Edan, finding confirmation in his refusal to meet her eyes. "While your spirits wander."

"The Watchers aren't picky," Tristan continued. "They'll go after any soul. Only those souls don't belong to them and so they don't fit. They're burned up, leaving the Fallen Fae hungry for more."

"The consumed souls do not die." Branna's whispered words cut her throat with hidden thorns, and she fixated on Tristan, begging him to tell her she was wrong.

"Correct." The Wizard spoke with a nonchalance that made Branna's stomach churn.

Souls eaten and lost.

"Like your tree," she surmised.

"Worse, in a way. The spirits in my tree are at least still intact."

Nausea twisted in Branna's gut. The subtle touch of Edan tickled her shoulder and she jerked away, not from him, exactly, but from the tragedy of what he represented. What his Watcher body did wasn't his fault. His true self stood next to her, trying to comfort her as the secret he'd wanted to keep spilled from a Wizard's mouth.

But she couldn't accept compassion at the moment. Her sense of loss burned too hot and burrowed too deep. Souls were not meant to be consumed. Energy returned to the universe to be reshaped, remade, and born again, either here or in some distant realm they couldn't even imagine in their current form.

More than that. For most of Branna's life, spirits had been her only friends. Secret words only she could hear got her through the toughest times. As insults were hurled, ghostly voices drowned out the noise with stories of lives well lived. Sometimes, they offered information worth gathering. Sharing some of these stories was how she'd first connected with Edan, and then they'd begun to—

No. He was dead now. Necromancer or not, there were non-negotiable Laws. She refused to contemplate a forbidden romance between herself as a living being and a departed spirit. There was enough tragedy in her life.

"Would it help to know that you're not a necromancer, strictly speaking?" Tristan asked. Branna narrowed her eyes at the Wizard, wondering if he discerned her thoughts. It wasn't likely, which meant he offered the information for a different reason.

"What are you talking about?" she demanded, her words extra sharp, irritated that he'd manipulated her into participating.

"Have you heard of a Shadow Mage?"

Tristan struck without warning, capturing Branna's wrist in his grip. He lifted her arm and shoved back the sleeve of her coat. Edan's presence blurred between them, iridescent and ineffective. Branna called forth her shadows. Tristan ignored the gathering darkness as his fingertips brushed against her forearm. Where he touched, something on her skin moved.

No. Something underneath.

Her grip on the shadows softened, and they slipped back into their natural forms as she stared at a body she no longer recognized. The pearlescent sheen she'd sported for the last few hours had faded and revealed that a dark fog lived inside her.

"What is this?" she hissed, removing her grip from Tristan's, stepping back and feeling for any trace of illusionary magic.

There was none. Only the shifting shades of skin, growing darker with each breath, yet still clearly fluid.

"As I told our dear Nicu, you are merely cocooned. Such a drastic transition wouldn't have been possible without the mate-bond the Fae placed on you. I can't deny that it fooled me to your true nature as well. Irritatingly clever," Tristan ground out, then shook off his darker emotions with a shift of his shoulders.

"The Fae have known this?" The inflection in Edan's voice sounded odd and hollow. His ghostly hand reached toward Branna, though he stopped short of touching her, as if recalling her rejection. His brow furrowed as he watched the shifting of Branna's skin as if he could barely see it with his spirit eyes.

"A secret kept from you as well," Tristan nearly purred. "At least that is some consolation."

"What do you know?" Branna demanded, disliking the Wizard's passive attack against Edan, as if the shared lack of knowledge still somehow left Tristan feeling superior. The Wizard stepped back to grant her the space he'd stolen, a fake apology curling his lips.

"Many things," Tristan teased. "But as we're short on time, I'll give you what you're looking for. Shadow Mages have much in common with necromancers. Speaking to the dead is one. But where necromancers can raise corpses, Shadow Mages can affect the spirit. That makes you incredibly dangerous to our Watcher adversaries."

Branna's heart sank as she realized the depth of Tristan's knowledge in the face of her ignorance. In the end, there was no turning her back on him, and she hated the sudden understanding she gained that explained how Ember and Nicu ended up working with him, and she despised them just a little bit less.

"What can I do?" She avoided Edan's gaze, not wanting to learn what he thought of her now.

"While I'm thrilled to have piqued your curiosity, I'm not sure you're able to understand yet," Tristan mused. "Perhaps seeing them in action first would help."

Branna's cheeks flooded with heat, and she squared off against the Wizard, shadows whipping at her feet. Tristan watched them warily, but refused to step away.

"I will not allow another soul to disappear when it is in my power to stop this," Branna declared.

The corner of Tristan's lips ticked up, though there was no humor in the movement as he prepared his next words.

"You will need to direct your shadows to climb into the Watchers' deep and dark empty parts, and tear them apart from the inside."

9

NICU

A strong hand gripped Nicu's forearm and pulled him sideways the moment he stepped through the portal. The air was dry and his eyes stung, temporarily blurring his vision. He blinked it clear to find Devi peering around the corner she'd thrust them behind.

The heat hit him first. Nicu shed his thick wool coat, dropping it to the ground as he rolled up the sleeves of his shirt. When his eyesight cleared, he took in their bearings. Devi had pulled them between two white canvases. To his right, a row of tents stretched in a gentle arc, creating the smallest of alleys. To his left, a large pathway separated them from the next collection of pale canvas.

"It's silent behind us," Devi murmured, "with quite a bit of noise in this direction. I can't see the crowd, though. Then there's the matter of being a Witch in Fae territory."

Devi pulled back from the gap. She had already used her magic to shift her clothing from her winter gear to a lighter, gossamer skirt the color of her minty eyes and a loose, lace sleeveless top in a milky brown. "Can you sense her? I don't suppose we could sneak between these tents and you would sense which one she is in?"

"Not in the way you mean."

Devi cocked her head, her eyes roving his features as if looking for a lie. "Are you sure? She always noticed when you were about to arrive."

"What are you implying?" Nicu's shoulders stiffened. In his fatigue, he couldn't stop the reflex caused by the suggestion that Ember might use her power.

"I suppose you were never around before she sensed you, so you wouldn't have noted her reaction. Really, though, didn't you realize that she perceived what direction you approached from?"

There were instances that hadn't been true, like when he'd caught her leaking energy in front of that human, Aaron Harwell. Yet he conceded that Ember often anticipated him. He'd thought she had smart quips available just in case, but if she had truly sensed him, that put a different filter on their years of interaction.

"I do not know how she would have done that," Nicu acknowledged. "It does not appear to be a skill we share."

Devi frowned, tapping the toe of her shoe on the ground, creating a soft, whispering sound against the sand beneath their feet. Nicu's attention snagged on the fine grains, his body unexpectedly frozen. Pure white gypsum, the mineral that gave this realm its name. A blanket of crystals that he'd never thought to experience since Terraborn Fae had never been granted permission to cross into their parents' home realm.

Yet Ember had brought him here. He meant to return her to Trifecta. Would she want to come?

One problem at a time. First, Nicu had to find her.

"Would she be a prisoner?" Devi's quiet question held a gravity that pulled his lips into a frown.

"They would not identify her as the Trimarked Child here," he offered. "A human coming here would be odd with the Veil locked but not necessarily cause for imprisonment as she would be considered non-threatening."

"Unless they discovered her abilities."

"Even then. Locking her up would leave them unable to access her power. It makes more sense to keep her close."

"Hmm. Like Tristan tried to do."

Nicu scanned the campsite to transfer his anger-fueled tension into a useful motion. The Wizard's near success was another of Nicu's failures. The Wizard had exploited Trifectan politics and attitudes toward Ember to wear her down and gain her assistance. Nicu's eyelids fluttered at the reminder that her death had been a very real alternative to falling through the Veil, and he had failed to stop her.

He would not fail to find her.

"All we can do is search. Can you disguise yourself?"

Devi snorted at his suggestion. "I could, but they'd see right through it. It's best to put on a glamor that has them simply look away."

Devi indicated she was ready by stepping boldly out into the larger lane. Off to their left, nine delicate, pointed towers stood against the pink-white sky, marking a nearby city. The field of canvas continued behind them, but the buzz of a crowd came from the direction they faced, which showed the multi-faceted roofline of a tent that must be multiple stories high and nearly a half-mile long.

They strode toward the noise, pausing only when they reached the last line of tents. More white sand stretched before them, creating a large gap between where they hid and where they headed. To the right, the canvas-made neighborhood was cut short by the shadow of a deep ravine. To the left, the tents continued for a longer stretch, eventually curving around between the stone-built city and the giant tent before them. Small crowds lined up at five separate entrances spaced out along the length.

Devi clicked her tongue. "Fades."

"Allow me to borrow your power," Nicu requested. Devi

raised a brow. "I can expand your spell. Cover both of us so we can slip in."

"I can do that on my own," Devi snapped.

"Yes, with Witch patterns of magic, and more likely to stand out."

"Or, if they're watching, they'll be looking for Fae spellwork only, and my way is better."

"What are you doing here?"

The unfamiliar voice cut through Nicu's calm, and he spun to face the possible threat. Devi was faster, her cranberry hair flying and fists knotted in defense. They faced a tower of a Wizard, with a long, copper braid that had been pulled over his shoulder, ending at his waist. Rainbow eyes shifted colors as he studied the intruders, his aura exuding a power that demanded respect. Nicu honored that and stepped back, intending to encourage conversation against a being he likely couldn't fight.

Devi did not express the same restraint. She pulled together a spell with more ease than expected as she stood on Fae soil in the Fae realm where magic was severely depleted. Nicu sensed when the power broke its structure and curved into forms more suited for Witches, all drawn by Devi's command.

The Wizard she faced off with took a single step forward, closing the distance to make long-range spells irrelevant. He gripped one of her wrists and tugged her even closer, then his free hand knotted into her hair, jerking her head so that her glare pointed at his greater height. Devi's fingers curled around the stranger's thick braid in a movement that left Nicu wondering if this was a grappling match, or an embrace.

"I am not here for you," Devi spoke through bared teeth with a familiarity more shocking than the Wizard's presence in Gypsum.

How did Devi know this man? Nicu turned over the possibilities, considering that this mage had an artifact, or an enhanced ability to traverse the Veil. His contemplation ceased the moment the Wizard raised Devi's captured wrist and the back of his thumb brushed her cheek. The movement was controlled to the point of being reluctant; the stranger's stoic features betrayed by the intensity locked in his bright, rainbow-gem eyes.

Nicu's questions were futile. There was more between the two than his limited understanding could process. He needed to wait and see if their curious connection would aid or hinder the search for Ember.

"You knew I was here," the stranger condemned.

"Only after I arrived." Devi's eyelids fluttered as the Wizard's thumb trailed her jawline. She blinked the reaction away and fought back with an angry scowl. "You will let me go now."

"Not until I know why you're here. Since it's not for me." The man lowered his head toward Devi, sparkling eyes daring her not to react.

Nicu averted his attention from the pair's antagonistic intimacy. He debated sneaking off while they were so involved with each other, but Nicu didn't want to risk finding Ember only to discover that he needed Devi's help. Yet these two did not appear intent on getting to the point.

"We are seeking a girl I am responsible for." Nicu spoke carefully, uncertain he could find Ember without providing more details. The pair startled as if they'd forgotten his presence. The stranger uncurled his spine, leaving Nicu in the unfamiliar position of looking up to meet someone's gaze.

"She fell through hours ago in our timeline. I am not certain how much time has passed here." Nicu guessed that this man's connection to Devi meant he'd recognize that they'd come from a different realm.

"Any identifying features?" The man released his grip on Devi's hair, the removal appearing part of a caress. He refused to let go of her other wrist, even as she tugged it away, her cheeks as bright as her curls.

"She is a human with a Binding Ink tattoo," Devi spoke. Nicu hid his surprise at her immediate response. He might need to return to keeping secrets from her if she was quick to share them with this stranger.

"How are you responsible for her?" the Wizard asked.

Words failed as a bubble of thick emotions rose from Nicu's gut to his throat, expanding his ribcage with the heat of discontent. He had never had to justify his connection to Ember, or to prove his right to protect and guide her to a path that kept her safe. His tattoos responded to the indignity, growing across his skin, waiting for a direct command.

Multi-colored eyes scrutinized Nicu's reaction even as the Wizard's lips thinned.

"I see." He glared at Devi. "You will stay hidden."

"Because the Fae can't handle a Witch?" Devi challenged.

The stranger's brows furrowed, and he squared his body in front of Devi. "My chosen lady is here."

The flush that had enlivened Devi's skin fled in the wake of his words, turning her as pale as the sand beneath their feet. She jerked her wrist from his hold. This time, he let her go.

"I am not here for you. I'm here for someone far more important." Devi's voice rasped within her raw throat. Nicu couldn't comprehend the connection between the two, but he did not enjoy watching the Witch falter because of it.

"Regardless," the stranger repeated, then stepped back to open the nearest tent flap that hung behind him. "This one will do."

Devi's eyes flashed, and she turned her angry attention from the Wizard to Nicu. Reaching into the pocket of her skirt, she pulled out a thin band of woven cranberry hair and handed it to him.

"I hate to admit it, but he's right. Take this in case you need me. Otherwise, I'll be here until Ember is ready to leave. There's no chance this gnome will come back."

Devi stomped her way inside, then ripped the door flap from the Wizard's grip to close it behind her. Nicu faced the stranger, surprised to find a slight furrow in his brow as he turned from the tent to Nicu.

"What does 'gnome' mean?"

10

EMBER

*E*mber lay flat on her back, her pale linen pants and tunic blending into the soft cloth beneath her. She sank into the thick mattress, her body creating a valley within the overstuffed comforter as she stared at the netted canopy. Her dark hair lie in stark contrast to all the lighter shades, trailing over her shoulders. The strands held memories of hiding her tattoo for years until the moment it was shorn off by rogue magic. Every newly grown inch was proof that what she'd left behind was getting further and further away from her present.

In this new life, Ember had a purpose and a place within Shade's small community. In just a few minutes, it would be time to go on stage to take part in the huge production her foster Fae had put together. The entertainment offered appealed as a distraction and a lure. For the first time in ages, Fae traveled from their broken cities in droves, all drawn to the circus set up in the middle of the desert.

It didn't matter to their spectators if Shade was a radical who used powers they'd once looked down on. Most still did. But the reminder of the days when Gypsum was ripe with magic, power, and status filled the audience with a yearning so strong, they could overlook Shade's faults in order to sit in the stands day after day and dream.

Shade headlined the show with her lightning whip and Siren Song, an innate magic that Shade channeled through her voice in order to manipulate others around her. She used this special skill to enhance the performers, allowing them to complete acts and tricks they couldn't have otherwise. In a world drained of magic to the point it could only be used for bare necessities, the draw of seeing something resembling real spellwork was an opportunity many Fae couldn't pass up. Acrobatic displays pushed the limits of physics. Mock battles raged on the entertaining side of threatening. When Shade told a Fae to swing from one trapeze to another three spots away, they couldn't miss. When directed to throw a knife through a kaleidoscope of ground acrobats, it hit the target every time.

It was a power over minds, and not the natural world. In other times, it had been forbidden. Now, with the realm dying, it was entertainment.

Ember's power was no different. Shade's name might be what drew in the crowd, but they returned again and again for Ember's set. At the beginning, no one had envisioned that a human would be part of the show, nor could they anticipate the danger she put herself in every day. The incongruity of it had become irresistible. Would the human girl continue to survive in her battle against the dragons, or would this be the day she fell to them?

Ember closed her eyes, blocking out the memory of the sound of a crowd's gasps and cheers, jeers, and shocked silence that became so thick, she swam in it. Blocking it out was not possible, not while her senses needed to be fully focused on controlling her power. Unlike the other acts, Ember was not given the aid of Shade's Siren Song. In Ember's battles, a slip of concentration meant that she might fulfill their darkest hopes, where she burned up before them in the dragon's fire.

She'd tried to talk to Reyar and Shade about finding a

different way to pay them back, one that wasn't so dangerous. They'd insisted they wouldn't put her into this contest without full faith that she was capable. They told her that this was why Reyar trained her for so long, and that she was in no real danger thanks to her unique skills and their continued protection.

Only, the battles weren't choreographed, and they kept getting harder. Shade didn't want the audience to get bored, or for Ember to be complacent. Maybe a different collection of dragons and drakes. Maybe Fae snipers in the rafters dropping knives or shooting arrows. Which might not be as big of a deal if Ember knew ahead of time what the new challenges would be.

It was more training in a different form, and one that Reyar and Shade profited from. Granted, Reyar appeared less interested in the crowds and cash than Shade, but he was very interested in her fighting skills. After every match, he walked her back to their tented house under the guise of keeping her newfound fans away. Really, he dissected her fight move for move and planned what they would be working on in their morning practice sessions.

The idea that she had fans was one Ember struggled to wrap her mind around. In Gypsum, not only did Ember not have to hide her power, she even got paid to use it. But she couldn't shake the feeling that Shade and Reyar were hiding something from her. There was a payment coming due for all this goodwill. Nothing had ever come to Ember for free, after all. Not from her mom. Not from the Halfers. Certainly not from Nicu. The unknown cost left her trapped by more than the stupid echo of Trifecta's barrier.

Ember closed her eyes, hands on her belly. She took one deep breath, and then another. She imagined that it was summer in Trifecta and she lay in a thick pile of perfumed pine needles. She imagined the cool summer shade and the warm mountain breeze as she found space away from all the chaos of her life.

And in this quiet moment of safety, Ember allowed a moment to feel the traitorous emotions that were determined to plague her. To admit in secrecy that a part of her missed the familiar essence of pine that heightened her awareness. That she still waited for the sensation of mist across her skin that held an odd combination of irritation and safety. A presence that meant no matter what trouble she got herself into, there was always a safety net with Nicu.

But those days were far behind her. That vigilant version of Nicu was lost in a different realm and time, before he'd abandoned her to the humans. She'd always known he'd choose the Fae in the end; she just hadn't expected that he'd stand by and allow one of their arrows to strike her. Now, no matter the circumstances, she was strong enough not to need him. She was proud of herself for that. Grateful, even.

Yet the long pull of nostalgia tugged at her chest and wound tight in her torso under where her hands rested.

Voices filled the main room of the tent, low and deep. Ember gently tucked away her rebellious reminiscing, realizing it was probably time for her to get up and head in to get dressed for her upcoming performance. She closed her eyes again, looking for a space of emptiness between recalling the past and settling into her present.

Pine and mist.

Ember jumped out of bed.

This was not a memory.

She flung open the flap that separated her room from the main one. Reyar's oversized essence took up most of the large sitting room, but he might as well have been another piece of furniture. Ember's vision darkened, only one focal point gaining her entire attention, as if this person dared to claim to be her whole world.

Nicu.

Here, in true Gypsum. The sleeves of his black button-down displayed corded forearms marked with Fae Ink and new, light blue lines that cut across his skin. Part of her wondered how he'd gotten them. Part of her refused to care.

"Come to drag me back?"

The words snapped from her tongue even as she stomped into the room, the door flap falling into place with a soft thud. She kept her spine straight, her chin up.

Nicu studied her as if he hadn't seen her for a year. Then again, it had been nearly that much time for her.

"Little hybrid." He greeted her with a subtle drop of his chin. Did that mean hello, or had he answered her question with a yes?

The outer tent flap opened, widening Ember's perspective once again as Shade entered. Her brow creased when she saw Nicu, her snake Ink slithering across her arm as if it could gather secrets from the air. Then her entire demeanor changed. Shade sucked in a deep breath as if scenting something sour, her lip curling as she spun to face Reyar, her tattoo bubbling on her arm and sparking with electricity. Nicu shifted, backing away toward Ember, his arms loose but ready at his sides.

Ember's fists tightened as she recognized the stance of protection. As if he deserved to retain his place as her guardian after what he'd let happen.

"Do you think I would not notice your aura shift?" Shade demanded of Reyar.

The crack of electricity left a ringing in Ember's ears and she focused on her two hosts, shock freezing her in place. Ember had only witnessed Shade draw her whip on Reyar once before, and that's when they'd discussed the dragon bone ring.

Nicu had gotten here somehow. Had it been because of Devi? With Devi?

"Shade, she is not here for me." Reyar's tone was soft as velvet. It was not apology enough.

Lightning snapped, and Ember winced at the sound. Nicu took another step back, and his scent filled Ember with memories she did not want. She shook them from her head, keeping her focus on the dangerous couple before her.

"At least you do not lie about her presence. I do not believe for a dragon's heartbeat that she is not here for you."

"She's here for me." Ember stepped purposefully around Nicu. His shoulders stiffened at the movement, and she shot him a glare from the corner of her eye. She was in no danger from the Fae's aggression. Shade's eyes clung to Reyar as if a single glance away would mean she'd lose him forever.

"You finally admit knowing something about the creature who wears the dragon bone ring." Shade's accusation was sharp, but even her anger at Ember could not draw her focus from Reyar.

"The goddess' work, I would assume, bringing more threads together." Reyar lifted his palms to face toward Shade is if in entreaty or apology. "We knew that when we took Ember in. Besides, she is contained. Nowhere near me."

Shade's knuckles whitened as she clenched her fists, body trembling. "You have seen her?"

"And walked away." Reyar's eyes glanced toward the tent flap, his lips softening into a frown. Micro-expressions that might have been missed by anyone other than the Fae and those familiar with their tendency to speak through these tiny muscle movements.

He wanted to go back, Ember realized, but stopped himself. Ember glanced at Nicu out of habit, waiting for his own secret message about Devi and Reyar, what he might have observed. Yet his whole focus was on Shade, his body held in a delicate tension that betrayed his readiness to fight if necessary.

"No," Shade declared. "We have only had Ember for a year. That is not enough time."

"The one who left me Goddess Touched?" Ember asked,

trying to break into Shade's intensity and spread it out to a more manageable density.

"Your Goddess is not yet Made," Reyar reminded her. "This one is Shade's and my atrocity. Yours also likely touched him as well." Reyar tilted his head toward Nicu. Ember twisted to look at her old guardian, meeting his eyes by accident, meaning only to verify what she already knew.

Eyes of liquid amber, lighter than any other Fae in existence.

"And Devi's are pale green," Ember murmured.

"Do not speak her name," Shade growled. Though the warning was for Ember, she continued to stalk Reyar. For his part, the Dragon Lord remained still, allowing the enraged Fae to close in. Thunder filled the living space. Nicu stepped closer to Ember, attention refocused on Shade, his own Ink expanding its borders.

Ember shook her head, hoping he'd see the movement from the corner of his eye. A subtle distraction hadn't worked. It was time to remind Shade of her duty toward this grand enterprise she'd put together.

"It's almost time for my performance," Ember announced to the room. "Vaelros won't be happy if we have to rush costume and makeup."

"And I will take Ember's visitor to watch," Reyar offered, the unstated promise that he would not be returning to Devi.

Shade's whip trembled for a moment, her lips thinning as she worked to reclaim her actions despite being flooded with fury. She turned and ripped her eyes away from Reyar, then strode out of the tent. Reyar let out a sigh with her departure, the lines around his eyes softening as he looked between Ember and Nicu.

"Your guests do not change our arrangement," he told her. "As brave and reckless as it was for them to find their way into Gypsum, finding a way out will not be as easy."

"I did not invite them." Ember spoke firmly, her features

purposefully neutral. Reyar's eyes flicked from her face to Nicu's, a small smile on his lips.

"He said he had one been responsible for you. I can see the resemblance now."

"Still responsible," Nicu challenged, and Reyar's smile deepened.

"Ember?" A reminder to head out toward her performance. An invitation to respond.

Ember squared up against Nicu. She let her eyes run from the top of his head, down his thin braids, over his buttoned shirt and pleated slacks, then back up to his eyes as if dismissing everything she saw. Then she turned toward the exit Reyar held open for her, leaving Nicu with whatever thoughts were trapped behind his stoic facade.

"Allow me to lead you to the viewing area," Reyar offered to Nicu, though they both heard the demand through the veiled invitation.

"You do not have to follow them anymore."

Nicu's words stopped Ember in her tracks. It was so like him, assuming he was the stronger one. Assuming he was right. Without looking back, she shook her head, the strands of her hair falling just past her shoulders with a light, feather-like touch. A reminder of her new growth inside and out, making her strong enough to stand on her own.

"I can slay my own dragons."

11

DEVI

Devi heard the flap fall behind her. She didn't need to look to know Reyar hadn't followed her, yet the rapid rate of her heart suggested her emotions weren't so sure.

Stupid overpowered Wizard.

Stupid heart.

He had rainbow-colored eyes, just like the dragonling she'd met in Trifecta. She hadn't made the connection in her dream. Was it a dragon trait? Was he able to shift forms?

Given how sweet the dragonling had been to her, Devi doubted they were one and the same. And Reyar hadn't suggested he'd seen her outside a shared dream.

No, she decided. They weren't the same. No matter the truth, it was nicer to believe.

To distract herself, Devi observed the tent. It was a simple six-foot by ten-foot rectangular space with a ceiling high enough that most people could stand up straight. She was surprised to find only the tiny kitchen stove in the corner appeared to be activated by magic. At the center, a luxurious futon was angled into a seat, though it could flatten out and comfortably sleep two people. A small dresser rested in the opposite corner from the stove, and then the back part was partitioned off. When she checked, she found other simple magics tied into the bathroom appliances.

She recalled how deep she'd had to reach into the earth when she had pulled magic to confront Reyar. This was worse than Terra with its thin and fragile magic tucked so deep into cellular structures that most mages couldn't access it. This was a world where magic was supposed to thrive, yet it had been mined to near extinction.

Devi plopped onto the couch. Working on the problem of Gypsum's disappearing resource could be the distraction she needed while stuck in hiding. She spared a moment to hope she wasn't invading someone's rented space, or that they wouldn't suddenly burst in to find her loitering. If they did, she'd just blame Reyar. It was about time he suffered consequences for his thoughtless actions.

Not thoughtless, actually. Unfortunately, Devi had a strong suspicion he meant to protect her. His chosen lady was here, after all.

Devi knotted her fists around the unforgiving dragon bone ring on her left middle finger, all thoughts of Gypsum's magic problem dissolving. Moisture pricked her eyes, and she pressed the palms of her hands to her eyelids as if she could push her tears back in.

She did not want them. She did not want this. She did not want—

Him.

Fading fate.

}|{

Three days ago in Trifecta

Devi stared at the dragon bone ring, a dark slice across the pale skin at the center of her left hand. She'd taken refuge in her warehouse, but the Coven wasn't respecting her space as usual. To escape, she'd gone deeper into the building than usual, climbing a few stairs to the raised office. Windows lined the upper half of the walls that overlooked the loading platforms while leaving most of the interior workspace closed off from view.

The small room stank of vermin, dust, and years. But at least it was a place to study in silence, to no longer be bothered by the Coven demanding her presence because her mother had been killed less than twelve hours ago.

They acted on their grief, denying Devi hers. Well, she would take the time she needed, with or without their permission.

For once, though, looking through her notes did not draw her attention. She'd experienced too much in the last few days to be able to refocus her thoughts where she wanted. And at the center of all her confusion was this ring.

So then, she would focus on the ring.

Devi slipped it off, though it fought her progress, as if it were physically tied to the base of her finger and did not want to let go. Once past her fingertip, Devi held the small circlet between the pads of her middle fingers, right at the height of her mint-green eyes. As she twisted it, she noted that the ring didn't reflect any of the soft light that filtered in through the windows. Instead, it seemed to consume it so that only its black surface remained, untouched and unchanged no matter its environment.

That absorbing nature made it difficult for Devi to delve into its creation and capture the threads of magic that caused it to claim her. She brought the ring closer to her eyes, then gently lifted it away as it became blurred. As her focal point shifted, she noticed the strands running through the ring's center, and her breath held. The spiderweb of magic was delicate, so fine that she gained an instant respect for whichever mage created the Work.

With more effort than she was used to, Devi zoned in on

the power, using her senses to follow the strands and struggled to discover the heart of the spell. That her mother didn't want her to be near it was a warning. That it stuck to her like glue was a symptom.

If time passed, Devi wasn't aware. She found her consciousness separated from her form, lost in a void of thought while she dove into the structure of the spellcraft. The magic-made spiderweb spun around itself, creating a three-dimensional funnel of complex passageways. Whether she shrank or the magic grew didn't matter as Devi placed herself within the Work, discovering small drops that looked like dew clinging along the length of the thicker strands of power. Devi approached one of these cautiously, startled to see a miniature scene within. A watercolor depiction of white ground and pink sky, and a single, blurred figure within.

Devi walked from drop to drop, wondering how these images had been captured in so fine a spell, wondering what it all meant. She startled when one image showed a dragon swimming through a crystal-clear pool. When a separate drop displayed a version of herself, she gasped and leaned in closer. The vision revealed her floating in nothingness, a brilliant red light twisting before her. That one unsettled her so much that she spun away, leaving it behind so quickly that she didn't stop before accidentally running into another of the mysterious drops.

Devi stumbled from the shadows of her mind into a deep, narrow canyon with red-rock walls that swept up on either side. Thick, blue-green grass tickled her ankles as she waded through. When she saw the crystal-clear pool, her eyes widened, searching for a dragon's form in case she'd walked into the image where she'd seen one swimming.

"This isn't a safe place for a dreamer."

The voice drew her attention to the right. Shimmering as if he himself had just arrived, the man settled into a solid form. He lay stretched out in the grass, his torso propped up by his elbows, his golden-brown face tilted toward a bright, sunless sky. A long copper braid coiled on the ground beneath him.

Devi wasn't used to being struck dumb at the sight of someone, yet it was something other than his physical form that drew her. An addictive energy radiated from him along with the sense that he was much older than he looked. He held a treasure trove of knowledge and experience she could only imagine as a young Witch trapped within a small bubble. His scent held a subtle promise of questions answered and knowledge gained.

Despite his being a stranger, she took a few cautious steps closer, unable to resist the allure. Could he be a being of knowledge? Had she entered into this realm because of her never-ending quest to discover all there was to know?

"What about a seeker?" Devi countered, testing her theory. "Someone looking for answers rather than rest?"

"Then I'd say you're in the wrong place."

"Oh." Devi's lips pursed and her cheeks puffed out against a hard exhale. "Then I don't know why I'm here. I was just…"

Devi lifted her hand, staring at the dragon bone ring wrapped around her middle finger. She wrinkled her brow, not remembering putting it back on. Thick, warm fingers wrapped around her wrist, pulling her hand down to be level with his scowl.

"No." The man's denial lashed through her mind, and Devi flinched at the force. She tugged her arm, but he squeezed to keep her still. "This was not meant for you."

"It seems to think differently," Devi snapped. She used her free hand to draw a glyph in the air, intending to show him exactly why he shouldn't hold her captive. He raised his glare to hers and then.

And then.

Devi found her whole self reflected back from the depths of his eyes. All her strengths presented as a strong, stable foundation, and all weaknesses as beautiful imperfections that helped create her unique shape. She saw the same in the man before her. A core of independence that demanded he act on what was just, even if it wasn't fair. Scars showing where failure had tested that strength, and where he'd survived despite the odds. She knew him now for the first time, only to realize she'd known him for longer than they'd both lived. To find that it wasn't knowledge or spellcraft she'd been searching and longing for.

It was him.

"Reyar." His name was a shape her mouth had always longed to make. Devi's heartbeat deafened her ears, and the breath in her lungs left her lightheaded and free.

What was happening to her? She didn't have full control of her movements or thoughts. Her right hand abandoned its spellwork to touch his cheek. Her eyelids lowered with a heavy softness and she swayed toward his form. There was no room for logic or hesitation. The surrounding air thickened, urging her to close the inches between them. There was no shame in the taking since he was hers to take, to do with as she would. He was her Dragon Lord.

"No," he said again, though this time his husky voice lacked its original insistence. "This cannot be. You are not my chosen lady."

Devi's heart froze, and its chill burst through her body. She blinked against the haze his closeness had caused and stepped back. He released her wrist, folding his hands onto his lap where he still sat on the grass. His eyes were no longer tunnels of belonging, but sharp, iridescent gems that struggled to focus on the pool while continually finding their way to her.

"I don't understand." Devi stumbled away, rubbing her forehead. "Nothing like that has ever happened before. How can I know you? How can we—"

Her eyes focused on his lips, derailing her questions. She tore her attention away and focused on the clear water.

"A spell," Reyar answered. "A mistake. A goddess's attempt to control us and force us to her will."

Devi took a deep breath, wrestling through the mess of emotion to drag her logic to the forefront. His claim made sense, though part of her didn't want to believe it. Surely this was a power so strong even she couldn't control or fight against. A knot of discomfort settled behind Devi's ribs, and her hand rose to cover it.

"To do what?" she asked.

"If I explain, will it help you fight this? Help you see that what we feel isn't real?"

Devi's heart shattered and sliced through every internal organ, causing pain bright enough to blind her with a flood of fresh, crystalline tears.

This intense knowing wasn't real?

"You're sure?" Devi flinched at how small her voice sounded.

"There is a goddess. Azhirith. She thinks her truth is equal to fate and has decided to intertwine our lives, for ill or nil."

"But… why? Why us?" *Why me?*

"Gypsum is dying. There are two ways to save it. She wants to use us for one of them."

There was a part of Devi who wanted to know more. To know what he meant about saving Gypsum. About the role the goddess wanted her to play and what other options Azhirith was ignoring.

But her brain wouldn't work, wounded from the destructive truth that he didn't belong with her after all. She closed her eyes. A rustling alerted her to Reyar's movements. Was he leaving? Her palm pressed to her aching sternum, and she was desperate to understand how he had the strength to go.

Then fingertips brushed the side of her neck, parting her heavy curls from her skin. The fear of his leaving unwound within her, leaving behind a warm welcome she longed to believe.

"This isn't real." Devi tried to use the reminder like a talisman, yet the knowing wasn't enough to overpower the feeling. She swallowed a sigh as she felt his body heat close in.

"I didn't think so." His breath flowed over her cheek. "But this feels different from what I expected. It's like—"

My soul is your soul.

Devi could only hope those were the words he'd refused to say.

"I have to wake up," Reyar told her, even as his nose brushed lightly against her own. "I have to figure this out."

"Will you come back?" Devi asked.

"I have another woman waiting for me, one I have pledged loyalty and love to. I do not intend to allow anyone else to dictate my life path."

"Right." Devi cleared her throat and opened her eyes wide, turning her face from Reyar's closeness.

"Yet." His fingers tightened around the back of her neck, a steady pressure that didn't hurt, as if his body willed something his mind fought against. His fingers pressed against her jawbone, turning her toward him until all she could see were his rainbow eyes.

"I think I will come back after all. If you wait."

Reyar disappeared, taking his tender touch and powerful presence with him. Devi sucked in a deep breath of air. She fell to her knees, lost in the rapid beat of her heart.

What in Convergence was that? Who was he?

Who was she, that she settled deeper into the grass, a soft smile on her face, waiting at another's request?

}|{

Devi trembled with the effort to push the memory away. She'd waited for what felt like days in that dreamscape, and awakened to find a mere hour had passed. Yet she didn't doubt that if he'd wanted to come back, he would have done it in that time.

She'd been a fool. Of course, once he woke up, the spell he'd talked about would have lessened. He would have opened his eyes to his current lover's and been reminded of what was real and what was magic.

Devi was tangled up in a different way. She didn't have the anchor of a real relationship to keep her in place. All she had was the memory of him.

With a hard shake of her head, Devi resumed her pacing. This was only a digression. She needed to be out looking for Ember. She would use Nicu's own stoic control as inspiration to see Reyar in the real world. She just hadn't expected the pain of abandonment to be drowned out by what was clearly a very strong goddess-strength spell.

The tent flap opened with a hard thrust that let in the desert's outer brightness. Devi faced the entrance, startled when three Fae entered, all in light leather armor. Then the center one nodded as if she was exactly who he expected.

"Search the Witch."

The two Fae flanking him strode toward her, each of them grabbing an arm. They didn't frisk her or pat toward pockets. Instead, their grip dug into her forearms, pressing her gems deep into her skin. They raised her hands, though they only needed one.

"She wears the ring."

Devi's stomach sank. Her eyes locked on the Fae remaining by the door, holding the flap open.

Had Reyar arranged this? Had he really acted as if he'd wanted to protect her only to send guards after her?

The Fae at the door raised his free hand, formed in a fist. His tongue twisted on Fae words that her Witch ears heard as gibberish. When his fingers jumped open, his spell hit her full force against the forehead, casting stars across her vision.

Numb energy trickled from the point of contact into her

brain and down her spine. With each heartbeat, the empty chill spread through each of her limbs, and Devi's only defense was stripped away from her: her magic.

"Let us go," the one at the door spoke. No further explanations. No verbal threats or goading.

The two Fae who gripped her moved her toward the door. Devi jerked at her arms, though she knew her strength was no match for these two, especially without access to magic. They dragged her out into the open, then toward the tall structure of the main tent and toward whatever spectacle the Dragon Lord and his chosen lady had planned.

12

NICU

Nicu followed close behind Ember. He had not missed her parting quip about slaying dragons. Every thought fled his mind at her announcement except for one.

Not with him around.

Ember's legs were shorter, yet she was quick as she strode purposefully from the ruins and across the sands to a well-hidden flap in the main event tent. It closed between them, and Nicu rushed to catch it open, but a hand gripped his shoulder and stopped his forward momentum. Nicu took a deep breath through his nose, turning to face the one called the Dragon Lord.

"You walk a perilous line between the Witch and your Fae," Nicu accused him, intending to throw him off enough to loosen his grip. Instead, Reyar smiled.

"It sounds like a position you're familiar with. Yours likely being ... Ember and the Terra-bound Fae?"

Instinct set Nicu's features into a neutral state, but even that was a tell for the strange Wizard before him. Reyar's smile grew, then he released his grip only to pat Nicu's shoulder in a heavy slap.

"Come on. Ember will be head-deep in her costume change and make-up. Non-performing staff uses a different entrance. You're not technically an employee, but I promise we'll have a better view than from the stands."

Nicu recognized an order when he heard one. Though he preferred to follow Ember, she was likely out of sight from the entrance at this point. Following Reyar wasn't ideal, but it would satisfy his need to be within reach of Ember.

She appeared different, and not only because her hair was six inches shorter. Her defiance was honed, more focused than her previous pattern of fighting everything presented to her. Where she'd argued with him in Trifecta, she had followed his suggestions when she thought he wasn't looking. He hadn't had to be concerned with her words as her actions were all he cared about.

Now she'd defied him and followed through. She'd directed his actions with Shade and managed the situation as if well practiced.

Shade. The muscles in Nicu's forearm twitched as he recalled how easily her Ink had slid off her skin, becoming a weapon on its own. Even on Trifecta, stories of Shade were whispered in the shadows. The Fae who defied tradition and order. Who chose her own path with power and force.

Yet now she directed this circus. One Ember was a clear and important part of.

Nicu had missed something. There was more to learn from Shade and the Dragon Lord. Why had they taken such an interest in the Trimarked Child? Her power was the obvious answer, but also just part of it. What did they want to use her for? Did Ember see it, or was she as easily manipulated here as she had been with Tristan?

"How long has she been here?" Nicu asked, wondering how much information was free and where it would start to cost.

"We celebrated her birthday nine weeks ago."

Shade had said Ember hadn't been with them a whole year yet, so this would be her only birthday in Gypsum, making her eighteen years old. That placed them mid-August here on Gypsum. It would still be November of last year in Trifecta.

The time flow benefited him now that he was in this realm. More time here would not exponentially increase the danger in Trifecta. It appeared he would need that time to convince Ember to return, and to manipulate a way out of her current living situation.

Reyar led Nicu around the tent to a different hidden entrance. They stepped behind a soft white canvas that muted the eye-watering brightness of the outside environment. The area they entered was a narrow stretch between the opaque outer canvas and a transparent inner curtain. A three-level scaffolding took up the majority of the space with folding chairs on each level, all facing an egg-shaped arena that they were at the narrow part of. On the longer curves of the tent, over a hundred rows of stands angled up and away from the rocky surface of the central stage.

"This curtain has a one-way view and blocks sound from our side." Reyar pressed his palm against the cloth to show it wouldn't move against his force, proving it was more of a barrier than expected. A warning for Nicu to stay put. "We'll go this way."

Reyar gestured to the stair that zigzagged up the back of the scaffolding. They rose to the top level before the Wizard suggested they take a seat. Nicu breathed deep, fighting his physiology, working to release the tension his muscles wanted to hold. To clear the thoughts crowding in with questions he could not answer and refused to ask. Why so high? What exactly did Ember's performance entail?

All would be answered soon enough.

The Fae controlling the lighting flashed shadows across the stadium. It appeared to be a signal for the audience to find their seats. The generic cacophony of thousands of voices condensed into an excited buzz. After a minute, top sails snapped into place, blocking the light from the bright sun without the use of magic.

Mirrors were employed to capture outside light and focus a spotlight below them and to the right. The entrance's flowing curtain flew forward into the stadium. From between the billowing folds, Ember stepped through and out.

Thick dark lines painted her face with detailed green scales that had been drawn from the side of her nose to her hairline. Sapphire-blue lipstick echoed the extensions added to her dark hair. Her suit was made of small dragon scales, cut and tailored tight to her form, leaving no room for hidden weapons. She carried nothing else, keeping her posture tall against the boos and the cheers, which seemed equally intermixed. Nicu scanned the floor and all the available spaces for doors, trying to piece together what they expected of his little hybrid girl.

The answer came when the floor to ceiling curtains parted at the opposite end of the tent.

Nicu burst to his feet when the light brown, giant snout poked through, exhaling a breath so hot and strong it blew specks of sand into the air. The edges of his tattoos expanded as the giant beast entered the space. Its body seemed to go on forever, each step vibrating the ground as it moved closer to Ember, who stood nearly flush with the invisible curtain before them.

Then smaller lizards wove in and around the giant creature's feet. Tall, serpentine humanoids with wings as long as their arms and with cream-colored scales. The wings were not likely big enough for them to take flight, but they were clearly dangerous with curved spikes at each joint.

Nicu strode to the front of the scaffolding. The distance was not too far as long as he cushioned the fall correctly. There would be a way in once he hit the ground level. With one foot over the air, a hand shackled his left bicep and reversed his momentum, jerking him back to the center of the platform.

"Don't think that you're stronger than me just because you're Fate-Marked." With Reyar's warning, Nicu glanced at the blue scars across his skin. Yet this was not where Nicu's strength came from. Nicu jerked his arm away, only to be caught in the vice of Reyar's grip.

"Do you really have so little faith in her?"

"Against dragons?" Nicu clenched his teeth as he swallowed the bark in his voice. "I assume they are under your control then, Dragon Lord. That she is in no real danger."

"They can be, but they're not." Reyar bodily forced Nicu back into his chair and where Nicu allowed the forced movement, he also recognized he was out of his league with this Wizard whose strength so casually trumped Nicu's own. "And of course it's dangerous. The dragons are sentient, but they're still pure animal. That's why people come to watch. The odds for Ember are way better than they were at the start. It used to be a million to one, everyone was so certain she would die."

"And now?"

"They're closer to a thousand to one. Quite an improvement. Of course, Shade keeps increasing the difficulty."

"Why?" The question was sharp and short, its meaning long and deep.

"She wanted to get stronger. We're more than happy to help her do so."

Yes, but for what reason? Reyar's partial answer was at least confirmation that they had a concrete plan for the Trimarked Girl, one that went beyond simply entertaining the masses.

A shimmer of magic swept across the arena between the floor and the spectators, made visible for effect and, likely, for reassurance that the audience would be safe from whatever happened below.

At the end of the field, numbers flickered into existence and read 30:00. The crowd hushed at their appearance, a heavy sense of waiting descending within the enormous tent. A hidden bell toned, its vibration breaking through the silence as the clock started to count down.

The crowd roared in response, many rising to their feet with fists thrust into the air as the large dragon opened its mouth. A deadly cloud of twisting orange, yellows, and white moved with silken undulations overtaking every inch of visible space.

Aimed directly at Ember.

Reyar's grip around Nicu's upper arm tightened in anticipation of his reaction. Nicu didn't allow the Wizard the satisfaction of feeling pressure against his restraint and maintained perfectly relaxed muscles. He'd regained control over his immediate reactions and observed through the filter of logic.

Clearly, Ember had done this before. Clearly, this was an expected beginning. And sure enough, once the blaze burned itself out, Ember stood in place, encased in skin tinted light blue.

"Is the arena set to show spells, or does each caster make them visible?" Nicu ensured calm filtered through his words, simply a spectator asking about backstage secrets.

"It's an effect of the dragons, actually. They cannot cast magic themselves but have some ability to neutralize it. To truly erase a spell takes an enormous amount of energy and so they developed their powers to work passively, making magic visible and allowing them to escape the spell's trajectory. Sometimes the easiest defense is avoidance."

So this, at least, was not part of Ember's education. And Nicu learned something else. His skills and Devi's were not likely known and therefore would not be expected.

Nicu watched Ember break into a run, heading toward her opponents, her shield expanding until it formed an elongated bubble around her, thinning out as it went. Moving in would limit the lizards' ability to fire off such a strong attack again, yet this strategy opened her up to physical attacks from the drakes. Though Nicu didn't spot any weapons, the dragons came equipped with natural defenses that were capable of causing damage to any opponent.

Nicu flicked his eyes toward the numbers in the sky. The countdown read 25:37 and was likely marking the duration of this fight. So she didn't have to win. She just had to survive.

Ember reached the large lizard who lifted its head and vulnerable eyes out of her way while raising the leg she aimed for, as if dodging. Nicu's eyes narrowed, shifting from the large lizard's head to its clawed paws, all larger than Ember, but also very difficult to maneuver in the space provided by the arena. Cavernous before the dragon entered, now the space felt crowded.

Ember switched direction and picked up speed. The smaller drakes guarded the second front leg. They were each two feet taller than Ember's small frame. She lifted her arm to block a clawed attack trying to reach her from above. Her shield shined slightly, becoming darker just at the point of contact and the reverberating energy caused the drake to ricochet away.

Another drake looked to take advantage of her shifted resources, edging around and aiming an assault at her lower back. Again, the energy of Ember's shield shifted, concentrating just before the strike. Then again as a third assault reached for her leg. Reyar nodded in firm approval.

"She's been working on that one. It's the first time she's successfully redirected defensive energy so quickly."

Only three of the six drakes attacked Ember, the others taking up defensive positions around the large lizard's leg. Without warning, Ember switched direction and ran past them all, taking an arc just beyond their reach. Was she running away?

Then Nicu noted her goal. The thick spear of the dragon's tail curled along the far edge of the arena floor. Ember leaned into her sprint, arms extended out, palms pressed toward the tail. Blue Veil energy flowed out in a faded stream until it caught the tail spine closest to her. It gained purchase and encased the whole spike, sinking down into the ground even as it spread over more of the dragon's tail. By the time she was within reach, half the tail tip was covered. When her hands made contact, her power instantly covered four feet of the tail while pooling on the ground.

The drakes were right behind her. With visible effort, Ember yanked her hands away from the dragon. Her power had locked the tail into place even while she maintained her shield. It shrunk once again to cover her like a second skin. She twisted and evaded sharp clawed grasps, and ducked under the taller beings, using her small stature to her advantage. The last drake shifted tactics and lowered its stance. Instead of trying to grab her with its clawed hands, it wrapped both thick arms around her.

Blue light flared around Ember until she was barely visible. It coated the drake from head to toe, then pressed into the space between Ember's body and the drake's arm. She ducked out while the drake itself remained rooted to the floor as if turned into a statue.

21:09 on the clock.

"Can they nullify her power?" Nicu asked. Reyar's grin took up half his face.

"They haven't found a way to, yet. She produces the raw energy of the Veil and dragons have always been restricted by Veil borders."

Nicu watched the race below him as it became a game of defense. Drakes worked to block Ember's access to the dragon as the clock ticked down into the seconds.

"Why is the circus here and not in the city?" Nicu asked. Reyar declined to answer, yet Nicu gathered a few more puzzle pieces, starting with their location of arrival. The ravine that likely matched the Pine River in Terra. This place must correspond with the same space in Trifecta, merely a Veil parting away.

Tempered

The timer announced the end of the match. Cheers and jeers filled the air even as Ember's power flickered out around each of the lizards. The large dragon backed out of the now opened tent flaps, the drakes following suit. Ember turned and walked toward their end of the tent, her eyes raised as if she saw Nicu through the one-way curtain.

Or, if Devi were to be believed, as if she sensed exactly where he stood.

Nicu watched her on her way in, looking for any hitch in her stride or any hidden wound she worked to shelter. All he discovered was a familiar, stubborn line on her lips, and pale gray eyes that sparked in challenge.

The Fae would not approve. Rather, the Trifectan Fae would not approve. Nicu had worked his whole life to keep Ember contained, to keep her threat level as near to zero as possible. All of that had been destroyed in the months she'd lived here, in true Gypsum. That she was trained by Shade, of all Fae, would only taint her more in the eyes of the Terra-bound Fae.

How could he take her back to Trifecta as she was now? He knew without a doubt she'd no longer be content to follow his lead. That she'd work to find her own place in the world. Deserved as it might be, such a thing was also dangerous.

The Trimarked Child might have learned how to fight dragons, but Council Elder Wist was not as tame.

"You've made a mistake." Nicu swallowed his claim, careful to keep the words only between him and Reyar. "You don't know what she is."

"We know exactly what she is."

Nicu turned to find Reyar ready to lock stares with him. There was no hesitation hidden. No doubt of his knowledge.

"She's not so easy to use," Nicu warned.

Reyar's lips ticked up. "All it takes is a shared goal."

Was it one Ember already agreed with? Was it time for Nicu to leave her to her choices and their consequences?

Is this your choice?

Pain stabbed between Nicu's temples and his heart squeezed as he fought against Chaos' attempt to take his thoughts and make them final. He swallowed his doubts and fears, determined that there was more data to collect and more truth to weigh. How could he possibly make a decision until he discovered what Reyar and Shade meant to accomplish? Would Ember be better for the fight, or the Fae of Trifecta? He was nowhere close to knowing for certain.

When the battle within him eased, Nicu found Reyar studying him with arms crossed against his chest. Nicu glanced down to find a soft glow fading from the blue scars he carried, then met the Dragon Lord's scrutiny.

"Barely broke a sweat," Reyar noted, his voice laced with a new thread of admiration. "Stronger than I thought. That's good to know."

Nicu's fingers twitched toward fists as the Wizard descended from the platform. He allowed his hands to clench for a moment while there was no one to see, struggling in the face of his deficiency. In that one small battle with the Fates, he feared he gave away far more than he'd gained during his conversation with the Dragon Lord.

13

EMBER

*E*mber allowed herself a smile as the tent flap closed in around her. She stood within a cocoon of quiet in a closed-off room between the dressing rooms and stage prep areas that provided the performers a moment of stillness before and after a performance.

The number of drakes had been raised from four to six today, but it hadn't mattered. In fact, Ember had been particularly clever, rushing for the tail first. She'd never attempted to pin down the tail before because in such a small space it was relatively useless as a weapon. Yet binding the dragon's rear end near its front had hindered the movement of its back legs far more than she'd anticipated, making them much easier to go after.

Take that, Nicu, for thinking she needed to be saved. Ember's grin grew along with the electric energy that surged through her frame. She rose onto her toes, arms above her head in a full-body stretch that honored the work it had done and the success she'd gained.

Still in costume, Ember turned toward stage prep, where the scents of pine and mist were strongest. She'd known he was watching. Knew he stood high, probably on the scaffolding. She sensed he had dropped to her level now as she pressed through the split canvas and she met his stare directly, taking note of Reyar standing behind him and to the left. A guide and a guard, much like what Nicu had been for Ember her entire life.

Good.

Nicu openly studied her dragon-scale costume and the elaborate paint on her face. His hands were mostly relaxed, hanging at his sides, but she noted how his fingertips twitched slightly. Perhaps a normal movement on anyone else. For Nicu, it gave away how uncomfortable he was, how he wished he could take her in his grip and force her to see his point of view.

After nearly a year without him, she didn't care anymore. No longer in Trifecta, she didn't need to follow his every rule to ensure the verge-damned Fae didn't appear in the woods and fire arrows at her until she was dead.

As if he read her thoughts through her glare, Nicu lowered his lids with deliberate care, and a frown flickered at the edge of his lips.

So he thought she was being naive.

"That was an excellent showing," Reyar approved, and Ember tore her eyes from Nicu's silent communication to her trainer. "The two extra drakes didn't faze you. And the way you froze them. Brilliant. Unfortunately, it was a little too clear today that we have tipped the odds of these battles in your favor. We'll have to fix that immediately so the spectators have a reason to stay in their seats."

Ember nodded in understanding, appreciating the minimal warning. Usually, they didn't give her hints about when they would increase the difficulty. Ember imagined there would be something particularly challenging tomorrow. She'd have to pay attention to any changes in her training, then, to try to gain some insight.

Shade's voice filtered in. Startled, Ember turned toward the arena as Reyar did the same. The Siren Fae wasn't due to be on stage. Usually a transitional act came in, tumbling and goofing off while engaging the crowd as a way to space out large acts and give spectators a chance for a break.

"Our security has discovered an uninvited guest!" Shade's siren voice amplified itself for the audience, many of them stopping in their tracks at the revelation. Some reversed their exit to regain their seats while others loitered in the aisles as if waiting to see if this was something worth staying for.

"Reyar, what is she talking about?" Ember asked.

When he didn't answer, she turned to find that he had adjusted his body to face Shade head on, his lips curled to bare his teeth, fists clenched as if holding himself back from using his strength against her.

Ember had never seen Reyar so angry at Shade. Only the other way around. And those times were about—

"Shade went after Devi," Ember whispered, eyes wide.

Nicu strode toward the curtain Ember had exited from. He thrust it open to find a group of Fae watching Shade, their movements frozen while they murmured to each other about this unexpected twist. There had been no warning, then.

At that moment, the opposite end's curtain billowed forward. Devi was led to the floor, surrounded by six security guards. She walked with her chin held high, shoulders tight, and fists knotted. Reyar's body jerked as if under two unseen, opposing forces, his cheekbones reddening even as the color drained from the rest of his face.

"She is powerful." Nicu dropped the curtain and returned to Ember's side, eyeing Reyar's reaction. "She will be fine."

"You haven't seen Shade fight." Reyar's voice strained, pushed through a throat too narrow. He took a step back as if through deep mud. "She's a damned fool." Reyar's lips curled away from his teeth. Without him saying more, Ember wasn't sure if he was referring to Devi or Shade.

"Let us teach the Witch a lesson, shall we?" Shade's whip slithered from her skin, snapping with white lightning.

The room darkened, with a single spotlight on the Fae at the center of the arena. Devi remained just outside the circle of light as the security guards withdrew. This would be a one-on-one fight. The crowd fell silent, now certain this was worth their time. Shade's smile curled on tight lips, her anger loud enough for those in the highest seats to understand.

Shade opened her mouth and began to sing. Reyar took another step back, though smaller this time. Ember's ears only caught part of the tune, and she looked to Nicu.

"She's a Siren," Nicu spoke, eyes wide. "She's calling Devi to her."

"Ember," Reyar growled. "Pin my legs down."

"But you can break—"

"Then you'd better keep the power flowing."

Binding Reyar caused her far more anxiety than her face-off with the dragon and drakes. Ember moved past Nicu to reach Reyar, startled when the back of Nicu's hand brushed hers.

Let me help you.

Ember jerked away, glaring at the Fae for daring to enter her thoughts. She did not need him for this. Didn't he just see her battle? She shook off her reluctance and approached Reyar with confidence. Ember placed gentle fingertips against his lower back, then breathed out even as her power melted over his legs, connecting to the floor and locking him in place.

Reyar wrenched against the bindings the moment Devi stepped into the light. Her hair shimmered like rubies as it flowed around her shoulders, the curls wild and untamed. Her hard, mint-gem eyes focused on Shade, her hands tight fists at her hips.

Shade's tune shifted, and her whip flickered. Reyar jerked, but Ember's power held. Across the stadium, they watched as Devi grit her teeth and stopped her footsteps, proving herself stronger than the Siren Song. The Fae's whip hissed as she slashed it through the air. She stalked toward Devi, long muscular legs eating up the space. The Ink whip shot out, growing to cross the distance. Devi turned to run at the last second, evading the first lash. Thunder rolled when Shade called the tool back to her.

"They took her magic." Reyar's torso tilted as he fought against his binding. Ember felt his pull against her power and increased the flow. "This is more than a trap. It's a test."

"What do you mean?" Ember asked.

"Devi and I are Goddess-Bound. Shade is testing what that means. How far she can go before I intervene, whether I want to or not."

Ember studied the Wizard, gathering pieces.

"And you don't want to help." Though Ember said the words as a statement, she couldn't hide the question in them. On the surface, Reyar's reluctance was clear. He'd asked her to stop him from moving, after all. Yet, the doubt in her voice was enough to draw Nicu's attention, his gaze bringing with it a hidden question as they both studied the Dragon Lord.

"It's more complicated than that." Reyar's volume was barely above a whisper, a secret he didn't want anyone to know. "I refuse to be manipulated by a goddess throwing a temper tantrum because she didn't get her way. I'm sure Devi would feel the same."

How did he know what Devi would feel? Had Reyar met her before? How? Where?

The crowd gasped and drew Ember's attention back to the fight. Devi panted with effort, the edges of her clothing shredded with evidence of the biting whip. So far, there was no damage to her body, but it was clear Shade was toying with her. The Fae warrior tested her lover to see how his devotion to Shade weighed against the Goddess-Bond to Devi.

Reyar surged forward with a sudden movement. Ember winced when her shield cracked against his force. "No," he growled, which could mean anything. The storm in his eyes suggested it meant everything.

"Little hybrid."

There was a slight lift in the way Nicu called to her, as if there was a question in his tone instead of a command. Ember glanced to see that his tattoos had expanded and twisted along the back of his hands.

Ember shifted her eyes pointedly from Nicu to Shade, asking if he could manipulate her power from here. Nicu's lips thinned, and he shifted closer to her side, his movement implying that if he were capable of that, it would already be done. Perhaps Shade's power wasn't close enough to the magic he was able to manipulate. Maybe they were too far away. The result was the same.

For any other reason, she'd say no to his request for collaboration. But this was for Devi. And Reyar, she realized with a wince as another of his jolting motions cracked her shield further. Ember split her power and lifted her hand toward Nicu, releasing the raw energy into the air. The movement was enough of a distraction to pull Reyar's attention their way.

She and Nicu were about to give up a secret. Once upon a time, that would've made both of them hesitate, but Ember had learned there were some people worth spilling secrets for. What had happened to make Nicu feel the same?

A question for another time. With the molecules of magic now available to him, Nicu grasped on. He stopped in surprise at the strength of her power, sparing her only a glance before his features shifted into stoic acceptance and he twisted the energy to his will.

"What are you doing?" Reyar's question was ignored. Ember focused on accepting Nicu, on opening up and agreeing to his use of her power. Without her permission, it would hurt. She'd learned that with Tristan and with Devi. Yet Nicu had never used her power without permission. There was trust in that, and her energy flowed toward him like it recognized an old friend.

Nicu didn't have to chant to refocus the power. There were

no lyrical sounds slipping past her human ears. His tattoos absorbed the specs of power, darkened as they filled, and then wove into a spell that left through his fingers. The magic ignored the physical space of the curtain before them and rushed in twisting lines of a heavy breeze as they drove toward Devi.

Ripples of magic crashed as Nicu's spell hit the invisible barrier around Devi. Shade called out in anger, glaring toward them. She jerked her attention back to Devi, who stood with arms crossed defensively in front of her bowed head, eyes squeezed against the back blow of two clashing spells.

Ember fed Nicu more power, and the strands of magic began to tint blue with the added concentration. Reyar rolled his shoulders and stopped fighting his restraints as he studied how Nicu worked, and how Ember supported him. A sharp cracking sound snapped through the arena. Nicu's spell had done its job, cracking through the barrier around Devi. He grunted with the effort to retrieve the magic before it could harm Devi's physical form.

Devi uncrossed her arms and swept Nicu's spell to the side. Ember reclaimed her power and severed her connection with Nicu even as his Ink settled into place.

Shade lashed out with her whip. This time, Devi didn't work to avoid it. She allowed it in, let it wrap around her forearm. She grimaced as the lightning within flashed, blinding everyone in the arena for a fraction of a second.

When the lights returned to normal, the two opponents stood face to face. Devi's fist holding the whip was raised between them. Shade glared at the Witch's grip. Minutes passed in stunned silence. Then the Ink melted from Devi's hold and twisted onto Shade's arm, the head of the snake resting on the back of her right hand.

The audience stood without applause, hands covering mouths or gripped together in shock. There wasn't a sound from within the arena as dust motes sparkled within the spotlight surrounding the contestants.

Shade's lips moved, but only Devi heard what she said. After a tense moment, the two broke apart and then bowed toward the stands. Confused, slow applause exploded into cheers as the pair exited the way they'd come, through the doors opposite Ember, Nicu, and Reyar.

"Thank you." Reyar addressed them both, his thought-softened gaze moving between the two of them. "If I'd had to step in… well. The result would have been much different. That said, I should track them down before Shade decides to try something out of sight. You will both stay with me. Within my view at all times."

Nicu raised a brow and glanced at Ember as if to imply he'd been correct to be suspicious. Ember ignored him, accepting his silent communication as proof that he didn't really know her, didn't realize that her entire life was about figuring out how to live in peace with daily, deadly threats.

Her ex-guardian could think whatever he liked. Ember fell in beside Reyar as if they were leaving the arena like any other day. Let Nicu stay where he liked best. Out of the way, in the shadows, expecting her to simply obey his edicts. Leaving her to find her way on her own.

14

EMBER

As they exited the tent, Reyar's part of the conversation trailed off. His attention was pulled around the long side of the arena. As they passed the corner, both his steps and his words stopped. A small group headed their way, led by the black-haired Shade, who was flanked by fiery Devi.

Ember ignored Nicu as he stepped closer to her. She wished he would give her space but recognized that he had placed himself in this position in case they needed to act on Devi's behalf again. Reyar's eyes flickered over both of them.

"Devi still has her magic." Reyar's proffered information sounded friendly, though the stiff line of his shoulders suggested it was an order to stand down. Ember nodded at Reyar to show she heard, but didn't relax her guard. Nicu pretended not to see, as if his full attention was on Devi and her escort of Shade and three other Fae guards.

It was about time both of these men realized she didn't take orders from either of them.

Shade's eyes locked onto Reyar, who couldn't tear his gaze away from Devi. With a deeper twist to her scowl, Shade jerked her attention to Ember and Nicu.

"Nice to know I'm outnumbered. At least the odds are

even," Shade hissed as she shouldered her way past Reyar. The Wizard sighed, slipping in between Devi and Shade, trying to keep his steps close to the Fae but incapable of stopping the slight drift toward Devi. The three Fae guards watched Nicu and Ember warily, yet passed them with the intention of staying on Shade's heels, probably just as ordered.

"It is a strong spell," Nicu murmured. "That he can fight it is impressive. That Devi can is astonishing."

"Then you haven't been paying attention." Ember enjoyed the sharp turn of Nicu's head as he looked at her with eyes barely hiding their surprise.

What had happened to him to make him lose so much of his precious control? Ember let herself look at him, truly see him for the first time since his arrival. He didn't appear much different, except for—

"What happened?" The question left her before she fully took in the changes to his dark skin. She'd taken note of the faded marks before, but hadn't realized how extensive they were. Tiny blue scars criss-crossed his forearms and neck, their trajectory suggesting they'd appeared all over his body. This was not Fae Ink.

"Has it been so long for you that you can't remember?" Nicu's eyes were suddenly flat, and he pulled down the Fae curtain even she couldn't see through. "Our Promise was broken."

Ember's fingertips fluttered as if they wanted to fall into their old habit of tapping on her thighs. She recalled the moment he spoke of. She'd been running from the humans when her breath had cut off for no apparent reason. Nicu had stared at her from a distance, his feet firmly in the forest while her spirit was being torn apart.

She'd thought he'd caused it, but if he had scars when she didn't...

Her curiosity pressed up, bringing a confused sense of compassion.

But no. He'd found her again. He'd seen Tristan attack. He'd let the Fae shoot her.

It had been his broken Promise, too. Maybe these marks were exactly what he deserved.

"Ember!" Reyar's voice thundered toward them, a sharp reminder that she and Nicu were supposed to remain close to him. The distraction of Devi hadn't been enough to make him forget about them.

Ember trailed the group, and Nicu adjusted his stride to match hers. They didn't have far to go between the arena and their home, so it wasn't long before they passed the three guards now stationed outside, two looking out as usual to keep spectators away. The third was a new addition and stood a few feet away, watching the door.

The air within the tent was a few degrees higher than Ember was used to. She felt it instantly, given that she still wore the full body suit from her performance. The props and costumes manager, Vaelros, would not be happy she hadn't returned with it right away, but then again, the Fae could take it up with Reyar if it became a true issue.

"Why are you here?" Shade demanded, her irritated growl suggesting it wasn't the first time she'd asked. The Fae stood at the center of the room, towering over where Devi sprawled in one of the full chairs, clearly having taken the seat without permission. Reyar stood off to the side, his hands once again knots of forced control.

"Reyar?" Shade demanded. "You told me you soul-bonded with her. What is her purpose?"

"I don't know," he answered, shooting Shade a narrow-eyed glare against her snort. "Whatever brought her here happened after that event. I only have access to her memories from before."

"Then just—" Shade turned her back on both Reyar and Devi, her eyes and jaw squeezed shut. Clearly she desired the information, but she didn't want to follow through with her initial, intuitive suggestion that would likely have put Reyar and Devi in deeper contact than she wanted to encourage.

With Shade facing away, Reyar drifted a step closer to Devi who tilted her face away from him in order to study the nails of her right hand even as her left arm stretched out across the chair, palm up, fingertips in the Wizard's direction.

Nicu's assessment had been correct. The spell was incredibly strong, drawing the two together despite their best attempts to show otherwise. The emotions flooding the room had to be the reason for the increased temperature. Shade, desperate to hold on. Reyar, torn between desires he couldn't separate from magic. And was Devi like Reyar, or did the spell affect her differently since she didn't have an outside relationship?

Whatever the answer, there was pain in this room. Looking between the three powerful magic users within the space, Ember found her stomach fluttering with nerves. What would Shade do if Reyar gave in? What would Devi do if he didn't? What would happen to Reyar if he continued like this?

Ember's own torn, tumbled emotions had backfired last year when she'd been avoiding the Fae and misread the humans as a possible safe space. Her desperate need for escape had led to her running toward Tristan of all people. Believing Tristan of all the liars. Helping him, thinking all would be okay, only to discover he was yet another being willing to sacrifice Ember's life in order to reach his goals.

Powerful magic users experiencing strong emotions were not safe beings to be around.

"Is there a way to break it?" Ember asked. Shade's eyes snapped open, glancing between Ember and Nicu.

"Like if you combined your power with your old Fae friend? You might be able to snap through a mid-level Fae spell, but a goddess's is still far beyond your league. And don't think we won't be talking about your trick with him, either. Clearly, you kept a few of your known abilities to yourself."

Shade focused on Nicu, eyes narrowed as she latched onto the second newcomer.

"Perhaps you will be more forthcoming and tell us why you and the Witch have tumbled into Gypsum."

"For the Trimarked Child." Nicu's answer was simple and obviously incomplete.

"I assume that is Ember. But why?" Shade demanded. "Why, when your Trifectan leaders tried to bind her? When you let them shoot her in the shoulder with a poison-tipped arrow?"

Nicu's breath pulled in long and deep as he put on his stoic mask. Either he hid the answer or he hadn't known.

Ember dug her nails into her palms and caught herself before she asked for clarity. She refused to be left hanging on for his response. She certainly didn't want him to know how important the answer was to her, how it might rewrite how she saw her entire last year.

"There may be a way to end this." Reyar's addition to the conversation pulled everyone back to the discussion about the connection between him and Devi. Even Shade turned to face him again.

"And why have we not tried it yet?" Shade asked through her teeth.

"Because she wasn't here." Reyar spoke slowly, caution in each word and each breath as he worked to keep his feet still, which were many steps closer to Devi than Ember had last noted and put him only a foot away from her chair. The crackling along Shade's snake tattoo showed she noticed as well.

"We can petition Azhirith to end this. To show her that we are resisting and offer our suggestion of another way."

Shade rocked on her feet, her eyes flickering to Ember, then Nicu, then returning to Devi before giving a sharp shake of her head.

"That damned goddess never sways from her alleged

truth," Shade countered. "And fighting what? You are practically crawling into her lap as we speak!"

Devi stiffened at the suggestion and jerked both hands in against her ribs, limiting her own reach toward the Wizard. Reyar simply shrugged and took a generous step away.

"Yet I'm not, and your back had been turned for minutes."

Shade twisted her right wrist as if she longed to feel the whip in her grip. The effort she exerted to keep her Ink in place likely rivaled Reyar's to maintain distance between himself and Devi.

"Fine," she bit out. "We will go to Azhirith's temple. Remind her of what the Fae already know. Truth has many faces. She can pick a different one."

"You can't come," Reyar warned.

Shade extended her whip, no longer able to deny her need for it.

Reyar lifted his palms as if in surrender. "If any of this is to work, if we're going to keep ahold of all our options, then you must stay here with Ember and continue her training. See if what her ex-guardian brings can be of help."

Ember held her breath, eyes on the whip rather than on the people. The hair on the back of her arms stood on end as electricity primed within the room. She pulled up her shield, wrapped tight around her body. Nicu stepped closer to her, and Ember wondered if she should shield him as well, or leave him to whatever energy Shade chose to unleash.

"And without me?" Shade demanded. "What do you think will happen?"

Reyar allowed his eyes to fall onto Devi, and the lines above his cheekbones softened even as his lips thinned.

"Certainly, we'll be touching. A lot."

Devi sucked in a breath and sat up straight, glaring into the empty space of the room, refusing to look at anyone as color rivaling her bright hair flooded her cheeks.

"Given how long it takes to gain an audience with Azhirith,

I'll likely kiss her within that time as well." Ember's cheeks warmed at Reyar's casual assessment, and she imagined they matched Devi for color.

Devi stood at the announcement, her hands slapping against her thighs.

"Right. Well. When are we leaving then, because clearly this needs to be over as soon as possible?" Devi strode to the center of the room, bravely taking up space next to Shade with her arms crossed, as if the Fae would somehow protect her from Reyar's stated expectations. A dramatic move that told Shade *'you can keep him'* as loudly as if she'd spoken.

Shade studied the Witch from the corner of her eye, then gave a sharp nod.

"Yes. Fine. It is not like I can stand another moment in the same room with both of you. Go to the city. Petition Azhirith. Get this damned curse over with so we can actually move forward."

The back of Nicu's hand brushed against Ember's, and she startled with the contact, breaking it immediately. When she settled, Nicu touched her again, the combination of skin and Ink forging a connection between them.

They mean to use you for that plan.

As if she needed the reminder. As if she cared.

They can think whatever they want as long as they help me get stronger.

With that, Ember ripped her hand away and moved to Devi's side.

"Stay safe," she offered. Devi met her eyes and produced a crooked half-smile. The Witch surprised Ember by reaching out and wrapping her in a tight hug. As she leaned away, her fingers trailed down Ember's arms to grip her hands.

"I plan to."

Devi left the tent, head high and steps determined, as if the entire trip were her idea. As if she were the one who waited for Reyar.

Ember shifted out of the way as Reyar and Shade said their stiff goodbyes. He leaned in for a kiss, then adjusted at the last minute, pressing his lips to her cheek rather than her mouth. With a frustrated growl, he strode from the tent as if Devi was inches from disappearing from his life forever.

"Well." Shade's word came out as a heavy sigh. She looked down at her whip as if surprised to see it was there, then let the Ink slide back into the pores on her arm before focusing on Ember.

"Return your costume to Vaelros before he burns our house down to retrieve it. Your friend can stay here. We will get to know each other."

Ember nodded and turned to follow her instructions. She wasn't worried about Nicu with Shade. He would hold his council, like always. She would make demands and spin out words that gave little to nothing away. Besides, Ember needed her regular clothes back. Her dragon scale costume didn't have pockets, and she needed a safe place to carry the small gem Devi had slipped to her.

15

NICU

Nicu studied Shade for a moment, but it was clear her thoughts were elsewhere. As he'd been given no further instructions or restrictions, he walked toward the exit of the tent.

Black Ink wrapped around his torso, white-hot electricity taking small nips through his clothing as a warning.

"You may have been her shadow where you come from, but here, Ember is free to move without a constant guard."

Keeping his hips facing forward, Nicu slowly twisted his upper body to gain sight of the Fae. She stood in a split-leg stance, the whip trailing from her hand to rise in a low arc until it connected with him.

This was a skill Nicu wanted. Could he learn by observation, or would he need this woman's help? No matter, it was not wise to offend her as she could easily restrict his access to Ember.

"I was not her constant companion before, nor do I plan to be one now. I was going to see Devi off."

Shade's eyes narrowed, and the lightning flashed, arcing away from him as he was not the target of this particular surge of emotions.

"Interesting that a Fae and Witch are such friends."

Nicu decided not to note that she and Reyar were the same. "The Veil has trapped the three races together for twenty Terran years. Both Devi and I were assigned to the Trimarked Child."

"To do what, exactly?" Shade's grip tightened on her whip as the outer corners of her eyes narrowed. Her mood had shifted yet again, and she made no move to hide it. Was this a dissimilarity between Terran and Gypsum Fae, or was his upbringing via Wist the part that was unique? Maybe the difference was all Shade.

"I was to guard against her impact on the Fae. Devi was to study her access to power and assess if the Trimark Tattoo was doing its job."

"The Binding Ink? It is merely a decoration on that girl."

"It did what it was intended to do. At least until its physical counterpart broke."

"Who was the fool who put that much control into a breakable object?"

"It appears Ember's Wizard father had coordinated the unprecedented circumstances of Ember's birth. Recent events suggest he had done so in order to break the lock of the Veil."

"Yet the Ink and the physical counterpart are Fae."

"Council Elder Wist organized that after he was unable to end the threat of the Trimarked Child."

The glow from the whip burned so bright, the light within the white-walled tent seemed to dim in shadow. Nicu kept his eyes on Shade, blinking slow and measured to clear out the protective moisture. The heatless blaze only lasted a few seconds before the Ink retracted between them, setting into the shape of a snake wrapped around Shade's right arm.

"End Ember as a threat," Shade repeated. "You say that so casually as if you would not care. Despite your tone, you found a way to traverse the solid Veil in order to track her down."

"I was four at the time of his attempt." An explanation

more than a defense. Nicu delivered the statement without hinting at how he may or may not feel about the situation. It was not her business, but his neutrality also worked to avoid the pressure of his inevitable choice.

"And you are his protégé. Controlled emotions. Constant relaxed posture. Too scared to give anything away."

"I would not assign fear where appropriate caution resides."

"A reluctant student, then, but an apt one. Leaving us with the last question regarding your loyalty." Shade studied him as she weighed thoughts he couldn't begin to guess at. He waited her out, observing the different twists to her face, learning her physical ticks with the intention of eventually figuring out its language.

"Go say goodbye to your Witch. At the arena tent, turn left to find her. Do not go backstage. Do not pursue Ember. She will return here, and you should as well. Wait rather than chase."

Nicu exited the shared home now that he had her permission to do so. The three Fae guards had disappeared, and he was left alone to untangle what he'd learned from Shade.

Could she mean to help him by giving him advice to wait? To what purpose? Or was her warning simply to keep him from wandering where she didn't want him? Such a simple explanation felt unlikely, even for a Fae not trained in hiding her thoughts and emotions as part of communication.

And the way she spoke of Wist. There was a familiarity in her words. How much, he couldn't be sure, but that connection had shifted something in her, made her willing to allow him to travel freely within the realm, even if under strict orders.

Though the questions held weight, Nicu shelved them for a moment. He was not drawn to conjecture and making up stories. There was not enough data to make connections to real answers. He would continue to speak only when necessary, and to gather as much information as they let slip.

Following Shade's instructions, Nicu rounded the arena tent toward the left. The desert was completely alien to his limited terrain experience. He judged that the heat would be a problem. Though the landscape was flat, the shifting sands on the ground made for uncertain footing. There would be a period of adjustment, and Nicu imagined hours of training were ahead of him. Ember did not appear ready to return to Trifecta, and he refused to sit idle when he needed to prepare for the need to run.

Nicu's fingers twitched as he passed the entrance he'd seen Ember use earlier, but ignored the one Reyar had escorted him through. Now wasn't the time to push limits, and he doubted a costume change was the right venue to continue a conversation. The suggested path took him to the side of the arena he had yet to see, opposite the field of tents where he and Devi had originally appeared.

Nicu's steps faltered without his permission, and he stopped at the sudden sight of dragons. He'd known they existed, having heard the stories from the Gypsum-born Fae. He'd seen one adult in the tent and the smaller drakes as well, but he'd been more focused on his conversation with Reyar and Ember's actions to truly take them in.

Out here in the open, the reality of the animals hit differently. They were not penned, or chained, or guarded by any of the Fae. Six large creatures like the one Ember had faced stretched out under the soft pink sky, tails curling lazily from bodies lounging comfortably on the rock and sand. Their bodies were like small hills rising in pale shades of tan, though one was a faded green while the largest was the most bold with a dark red coloring that lightened at the tips of each scale.

Drakes congregated in groups between the larger lizards. An odd combination of reptile with the bipedal ability of a man, it appeared that when they weren't fighting in the arena, they preferred to move around on all fours. Their coloring was much more uniform, nearly as pale as the sands they walked on. Though a few lounged as smaller copies of the adult dragons, most moved about as if restless.

"What do you mean, we're riding one of those?"

Devi's voice cut across the distance, breaking into Nicu's perusal of dragons. He cleared his mind with a deep inhale, reminding himself he had a purpose. Noting the direction of the drakes' interest, he trusted their silent directions rather than the echoing sound of the Witch's disgruntlement.

He found them standing near the front right leg of the red dragon. Devi's hair had been tied up in a mess of curls atop her head, her hands firm fists against her hips.

"The city is right there." She gestured with a sharp point of her finger. "Why do we need to fly?"

"It's faster," came Reyar's curt reply. "Stop being afraid."

"So what if I'm frightened?" she countered. "Well intentioned or not, I'm the same height as that beast's tooth. One tooth!"

"Which you will be more than safe from since you will be riding on his back." Reyar faced Devi, the dragon lounging behind. Its bright green eye was cracked open, the edges of its lids curled into a shape that, on a mouth, would be considered a smirk.

"Do not forget I am the Dragon Lord. You have nothing to fear as long as you're with me."

"Except that you might decide it's easier to drop me from the clouds rather than to ask a god's favor."

Reyar's skin darkened, and his lips thinned. He closed the distance between him and Devi, a hand reaching up to form a physical connection, his eyes melting from fury to concern.

Devi spun away from the movement before he could make contact and took stiff, angry steps in the opposite direction. In the process, she caught sight of Nicu and adjusted her stride in his direction as if she'd meant to approach him all along.

Even without Shade's emotional conflict about Reyar

leaving with Devi, Nicu was of the same mind that it would not be good to share space with these two for long.

"I would do almost anything not to go on this trip." Devi's growled words were edged with frantic energy, her curls dancing as if moved by her irritation. "He says it could take a week to be granted an audience, and that's if the god is in a good mood. Can you imagine!"

Nicu understood that her anger had little to do with the time she would have to wait, but rather with whom she would be doing the waiting. As always, he allowed her to expend her excess energy without interruption so she would get to the point she truly wanted to convey. As expected, Devi gave herself a visible brushing off, then looked at Nicu from the corner of her eye as if sideways words were the only way to share confidences.

"He made me prove I could leave the area. He didn't give a reason, but it isn't hard to figure out why he would want to know if I could pass a particular point in this world just because I come from Terra."

Nicu nodded and stopped his attention from drifting toward the tent where he assumed Ember was. So she was still contained within the Veil's borders somehow, though there was no evidence of the bubble barrier in Gypsum. With Devi able to pass, the defect likely wasn't here at all. What did it mean, then, that the Trimarked Child was still trapped? Would it matter to getting her back home?

"I am only going on this stupid trip because of the timeline difference." Devi raised her voice with the next statement, leaving her confession between them. "Ember was here for nine months while it was mere hours for us. And because it's my chance to be rid of him."

Devi bared her teeth, her shoulders rising toward her ears as if she used them to keep herself from looking at Reyar.

"I will ride his fading dragon, and I will petition whatever god I need to, but I will not forget why we're here. Be sure to do the same."

Nicu raised a brow. Was she worried that he'd feel so at home here in the land of the Fae that he would discount his life's duty and forsake his oaths? Never mind the weight of the choice given to him by Fate and Chaos.

"I will endure."

"Oh my." Devi's lips twitched into a smile and her shoulders relaxed. "Was that a teeny joke, Nicu? Yes, fine. Let's both survive this fading place and then get the verge home. You know the Trifectans can't do anything without us."

Nicu allowed Devi a small nod and curled his lip. Her grin was brilliant, and she kept it plastered to her face as she turned so Reyar could see it—more of a show for the Wizard than genuine emotion, it seemed.

"Don't worry about me," she raised her voice again. "I'll be back before you know it, even if I have to make my way on my own."

As Devi walked away from him, Nicu lifted his gaze, intending to study the red dragon. Instead, his attention was caught by Reyar's focused glare. The Wizard's eyes flickered between the two, a twist of doubt angling his lips into a frown as if he was deeply concerned with the apparent affection Devi displayed for Nicu.

Those two had a tumultuous time ahead of them. Nicu only hoped his onward task would prove easier than theirs.

16

DEVI

*D*evi lifted a thick curl to her nose, breathing in the remnants of her vanilla and lavender hair oil. The faint floral scent almost covered up the musty air trapped beneath Yotos' large frill. They nestled underneath the leathery underside of the dragon's collar, which was held aloft to make room for them in one of the few places along the spine that wasn't interspersed with patterned spikes.

She sat deeper under the frill than Reyar, both to keep out of the wind and to block all proof that they were, in fact, flying. However, finding a comfortable position was impossible as Devi straddled Yotos' vertebra, leaning forward and bracing her hands. She shifted sideways but had trouble holding herself up there, too.

Reyar had somehow managed to balance cross-legged where the dragon's neck widened toward its shoulders. Devi would accuse him of magic if he hadn't made it clear that there was to be no spellwork while flying for risk of a long, spiraling crash to the ground.

At least this wasn't a horse. She wasn't being forced to touch Reyar at all during this ride, or to be bounced along. The gliding flight was smooth for the most part, with the dragon flapping its wings every now and again to keep a steady hundred feet or so from the tops of the ruins.

"This trip is less than twenty minutes, and the times you've shifted has been at least double that number," Reyar drawled. Devi's answer was a solid glare, and the Wizard sighed.

"Devi, I do not mean to offend. I just do not want you to wear yourself out."

"Are you suggesting I'm not strong?" she demanded. Sure, most of her life was spent behind a desk studying, but she hadn't neglected her health.

"Of course not," Reyar countered.

"Because I am incredibly capable," she assured him. "I am brilliant and cunning. I problem-solve in creative ways, able to find solutions simply because I don't accept stated restrictions without testing them for myself. My magic ability is incomparable, as I see things no one else can."

"Of course," Reyar offered, though it fell flat as a peace offering. Devi pursed her lips.

"You know it's because of me that we crossed the barrier. I manipulated the threads of connection from Nicu and sent them searching through space and time for Ember. Then, I carefully reconstructed them to ensure Nicu and I arrived as early as possible so the time gap between us was minimal."

Devi ran out of breath at the end, turning her head as she sucked in air. It was not her habit to defend herself or to explain her process, yet she found herself unable to hold back when faced with Reyar. Her tirade wasn't from a simple desire to explain herself. Magic was the one thing she understood. It was her anchor when nothing else made sense. Yet she couldn't deny the yearning hope that her explanation would impress Reyar enough to...

No, that brand of hope was not worth feeding. They would figure out this goddess-created connection, cut the strings that held them, and he would return to Shade. That's how magic worked, after all. These particular strands were simply beyond Devi's current level of understanding.

"Devi, are you goddess-born?"

"What did you say?" Devi straightened her spine, not sure whether to lean forward or away. Reyar's question echoed the Witch Queen in a memory closely tied to the moment Devi lost her mother. Leona had denied the phrase too quickly; her exclamation meant to pull back the Queen's words rather than calling them false. Devi did not want to think about Leona, did not want to remember the pain of watching the life fade from her mother's eyes. However, this new information offered insight that she didn't have, possibly unlocking not only Leona's secrets, but Devi's own understanding of herself.

"I assumed your light irises meant you were god-touched. You, Ember, and Nicu. But Ember's deity doesn't exist yet, which makes me wonder. Devi, are you the Goddess?"

"Obviously not," she snapped.

"Not now. Then. Time has—"

"No meaning." Devi finished the sentence with Reyar, her breath caught in her throat.

How many times had she thought those exact words? How often had she felt as if hours, or days passed while in deep meditation? How she would pose her questions and gain answers that appeared as if from somewhere else.

How her mother Leona would stare at her in fear even as she asked, "Is this teachable?"

How a dragonling with the same color eyes as the man in front of her had found her twice, both times when the dragon bone ring was involved.

It had not escaped Devi's notice that no other dragon on the field outside the circus had rainbow-colored irises. Nor did any of them have the distinct gem-like appearance unique to the Witch and Wizard race. If the dragonling was somehow him, it must be a future version of Reyar, then, she decided.

The one sitting in front of her would never seek her out, just as he hadn't returned to the dreamscape as promised.

"I can't break the bond between us," she offered as if that might be the only reason he would care to ask about her potential power.

Reyar's lips thinned and his fists clenched against his knees as if he were stopping himself from reaching for her. The jostling of the dragon left her clawing against its scales, squeezing her eyes shut against the force of the long, slow spiral. When the movement ended in a soft drop, Devi swallowed a panicky squeal.

The brush of Reyar's hands on her shoulders brought instant comfort. Devi raised her eyelids even knowing she'd be lost in his gaze. Reyar leaned close, his breath tickling across her skin as his pupils dilated. When his cheeks flushed, hers heated in answer. Reyar's fingers slid down her upper arms, soft lips thinning as he worked to ease away from her.

"If I thought you could break our connection, there would be no need for this trip. Goddess-born is not goddess-made."

"What's the difference?" She was breathless again, caught in a tangle of what could, should, and would never be.

"A choice."

Reyar pulled further away in slow-motion reluctance and climbed down Yotos' arm, which was extended like a handy ramp. They had landed in a large clearing of sand between ruins in better shape than the ones they'd left, bordered by a forty-foot high stone wall that looked as if it had been through a war and was just inches from crumbling.

Devi sucked in a deep breath of air, hoping to cool the burning in her gut. She shifted her attention from Reyar's descent, pushing against the memory of rainbow-gem gaze that peered at her with something gentle. She did not want to see him soften toward her. She needed to keep the walls up. Because at the end of this, he would have Shade, and Devi would have her books and magic.

It had to be enough. She could not allow herself to crave more.

This was just a spell.

Liar.

Devi grit her teeth against her inner voice. One moment of seeing into someone's soul should not turn her entire world upside down, not when every other interaction with him had been of anger and denial.

"Do you require help? We need to get into the city to find a place to sleep before it gets dark," he called.

With a hard shake of her head to clear out the cobwebs, Devi picked her way down the dragon's appendage. At the bottom, she swayed as a burst of lightheadedness took away her vision, and she stiffened when Reyar's hand wrapped around her upper arm.

"Our choices are all that matter." His words sank into her consciousness, thick and weighted. "Whatever situation we're born into, and regardless of what forces get in our way, it is our decision what to do with it."

Devi thought about stepping outside of his touch. Instead, she met his concerned gaze with what she hoped looked like defiance.

"What are you cautioning me against? Why?"

Reyar's awareness dropped to where his fingers curled around the skin of her biceps. His thumb rose and brushed against the thin lace hem of her sleeveless shirt.

"The god-born can fabricate new magics. Sometimes they are so strong, what they produce becomes accessible to other mages. Most of the time, their skills are theirs alone. God-made power is so much more than that. It's more than borrowing and shifting molecular structures. It's creating from nothing. Changing the very fabric of the universe. But the sacrifice."

Reyar's grip tightened, and he lifted his gaze until it connected with hers. He wanted her to listen, and Devi leaned into his grip to prove that she was.

"To choose to be Made, you would give up everything that makes you a person. Emotions. Connections. Family. Even your world and your realm. These things are not for beings who deal in pure power. That desire to run after Ember? To work with a Fae to get her? All of this?" The fingertips of Reyar's right hand traced the ridge of Devi's collarbone. His left arm wrapped around her waist, a gentle pressure bringing their bodies into light contact. "Gone."

Yet what he promised her with that physical connection was a lie. She stepped back, gripping his wrist and pushing against his hold.

"You're manipulating me."

"I'm trying to help," he defended, though he let his touch slide away, taking his heat with him.

"By promising what, Reyar? That if I stay, then you will? To imply, for the first time, that what is between us is more than magic?"

"Of course not. I want you to understand. Gods are abominations, more-so than any other beings since they have the power to change everything while lacking everything necessary for proper consideration."

"Oh, I'm sure they consider a lot. Just not what you think is important."

"Devi, they destroy lives—"

"Stop!"

Devi's voice cut across the sands without an echo, simply fading into silence.

"Thank you for the information. But please don't package it as a desire to help. I recognize that our ability to make our own choices is essential. That's why I rode this blasted beast to get here. Because you—because we agree that we should not be manipulated. Once this connective magic is gone, however, what is left for you? For me?"

Reyar retracted, holding his arms lightly at his sides, his

lashes flickering as if he wanted to look away, but found it impossible.

Magic or choice?

It couldn't matter.

It made sense that he didn't understand the attraction toward not feeling. To live deep within magic. Tied up in knots of spellwork and desire, Reyar would want to keep her from claiming that opportunity. But Devi did see the draw of knowledge, and power, and an eternity of learning and creating.

Not now, of course. She had things to do. People to save. Ember, for one. Then there was the threat of the Watchers.

She was only on this trip because she had time. Although they'd been on Gypsum for most of one day, mere portions of a second had passed in Trifecta.

Later, though. When she was done. When she wasn't needed, maybe then she would seek out this unique form of freedom. She'd forget that her people feared her even as they expressed their demanding needs. And the pain of losing her mother would no longer scar her sense of self.

Most importantly, Devi could escape every ill-fated memory of Reyar.

17

EMBER

*V*aelros, the costume manager, would never yell at Ember. However, the twitch at the corner of his eye was as impactful as a gunshot. The way he smoothed the wrinkle-free silken scarf wrapped around his hair suggested he'd like to iron out a few of her personality's wrinkles.

He glared down at her even though she'd been out of costume and wearing a sturdy cotton robe for over twenty minutes. She wasn't being allowed to leave until her ensemble had been fully checked over, as if taking it for a brief trip outside was more dangerous for the dragon scale material than her mock-battle activities.

Finally, the assistant stuck with the job of examining every seam declared the suit in good repair. Vaelros grunted at the announcement, then released Ember by walking away himself. The assistant followed up with a quick, apologetic shrug, then ran off, probably to take the garment for cleaning and to get their own break from Vaelros.

That left Ember in her changing cubicle, a small room within the tent that had been incredibly tight with three people inside, but now allowed for space to breathe. Ember eased off the uncomfortable backless stool. Behind her, her change of clothes hung on a clothing rack. She dressed quickly, aware of the sounds of performers rushing around outside. She wasn't really alone here, only separated for privacy.

Story of my life.

Ember shoved the thought away as she tugged on her shirt, careful with the hand that gripped the gem Devi had slipped to her. It had been a challenge to keep it safe between her fingers while the costume had been stripped from her and she'd been shoved into her robe. Thankfully, Vaelros wasn't interested in seeing if she hid anything other than an unexplained fracture in one of the dragon scales. The assistant was also preoccupied with not becoming Vaelros' next target.

Holding her breath, Ember listened to the sounds outside to ensure no one needed her changing room. When no impatient grumbling filtered through the canvas, she exhaled slowly and opened her hand.

The moment was anticlimactic. The gem was, in fact, just a normal gem. It was a pretty black with a reflective polish that allowed the tiny silver specks within to catch the light as she shifted it. There was nothing else about this stone that told her why Devi had snuck it to her.

Ember gripped the gift, then tucked it into her pocket. She wished the assistant had left behind something for her to sew a smaller, hidden pouch inside her clothes, but that kind of mistake would heavily incite the costume manager's anger. Ember would have to find something else and be thankful the pockets in her linen pants were deep and the cloth thick enough to hide the small addition.

As soon as Ember opened the flap, she paused, surprised to discover Shade waiting outside, leaning on a tall stool. Movements slowed, Ember let the door close behind her. Though Shade had been her initial rescuer, Ember had spent most of her time with Reyar. Given her connection to Devi, she wasn't entirely sure where she stood with the powerful Fae. Ginger steps took Ember closer to her patron who stared deep into the prep space past makeup counters and racks of clothes as if she'd started by watching Vaelros pass, and then her attention had gotten lost along the way.

On any other day, Ember would think Shade had decided to check in with the performers, or might be preparing for her own surprise entrance. Shade didn't have a specific program or obligation to show herself. Not knowing when the infamous Fae would present herself was all part of the circus' appeal.

Today, however, everything had changed. Devi and Nicu had appeared from Trifecta without Ember's ability to open the Veil. Reyar had left with someone Shade considered to be a rival, and Nicu must be—

Where was Nicu? Ember scanned the busy dressing room lined with more private changing rooms on either side of her. A row of back-to-back makeup tables through the center leading to the costume racks, with only a few of them currently occupied. Wherever her ex-guardian was, it wasn't here.

"Shade?" Ember called, figuring it was better to check in rather than to leave without saying hello. The Fae drew out of her distraction. A soft smile grew on her lips but barely touched her cheeks and steered clear of her dark eyes.

"What do you call that Fae who claims you are his responsibility?"

Arrogant. Irritating. Never in the right place at the right time. Until he was needed most. Though that probably wasn't what Shade asked.

"Nicu."

"No title? No reverence?"

Ember crossed her arms and looked to the right, shaking her head along the way. Shade's laughter pulled her attention back.

"Many women would love to have that man on their heels, no matter the reason."

"Until he speaks."

"Oh, darling, do not kid yourself." Shade clicked her

tongue, then stood up in a surge of energy. "That Witch, though. It is interesting that they came together. Are they involved?"

Ember lowered her eyes, knowing her answer wouldn't be what Shade hoped for, but also not able to lie. "Not beyond a competition over who gets the most information about my power."

"To what purpose?"

Ember opened her mouth to respond, then swallowed the empty air. She thought she had an easy reply. Perhaps she had one a year ago, but then she'd gotten stuck in Veil energy and needed to be rescued. Then, Charlah had ravaged the Halfer population in Trifecta. Now they'd both found a way to break through an impenetrable barrier to find her.

"It used to be that they were making sure I wouldn't be a danger to their people."

"Used to be," Shade repeated, her eyes narrowed, and she silently asked for more.

"That was before I saved Devi from the Witch Queen and a soul-eating tree. And before I—" Ember paused again, not entirely certain what the right answer was here. "Nicu was working with the Fae the last time I saw him. And then he saw my power feed that soul-eating tree."

"The Helduan sequoia." Shade nodded as if another puzzle piece fell into place for her. "So you know Tristan, too."

"What?" Ember asked. "You know about the tree?"

"I believe I once told you we figured out how to pass nonliving things through the barrier. I was, still am, involved in passing black market items through the realms. Tristan ordered a Helduan seed probably four hundred years ago."

Ember's eyes widened to the point of pain, and she took a step back from Shade. The Fae saw it and waved her hand as if Ember's fear was nothing but an annoying fly.

"I had no idea what his intentions were. For all I knew, he wanted something to remind him of home while stuck in Terra.

That tree does not eat souls within its own realm. It's rather ordinary, actually."

But had she known what it would become if planted in Terra? If she had, would it have mattered?

"What do you know about Tristan?" Shade asked.

"He's my father," Ember answered, still distracted by her dark thoughts of Shade's intentions. She flinched as her brain caught up with her slip, grateful that wherever Nicu was, he hadn't been there to see her lack of control.

"Huh." Shade clicked her tongue, the sound of another puzzle piece finding its right place. A group of twelve Fae pushed through into the dressing room abuzz with post-performance energy as they exchanged high-fives and well-intentioned jabs. Shade frowned and blinked at their intrusion as if she'd forgotten where they were.

"Come with me," Shade ordered, and she cut a path toward the arena tent's exit.

Reservations or not, Ember wasn't in a position to offend the woman who housed and fed her. Her gut twisted in a way it hadn't for almost a year, a return of the old pain of knowing aid only came if she had something of herself to give. Here, she'd thought the exchange was in her favor, at least in the short term. Was she about to find out the truth of the cost? Would it be more than she could afford?

"Ah, there he is." Shade's voice drew Ember's attention to find Nicu standing at the edge of the ruins as if waiting for them. "I trust Reyar and his... dragon left?"

"Mmm," Nicu answered simply, his flat eyes focused on Ember as if calling out her inattentiveness. She had fallen so deep into her own thoughts she hadn't noticed where Shade was leading her, much less that they'd been approaching Nicu. Ember gripped the hem of her tunic, hating to acknowledge that the Trifectan Fae was right.

"This way, children," Shade directed, either uncaring or not noticing their brief exchange. The Gypsum Fae led them back to their tent. Once inside, Ember chose a lounge chair so that she could face them both without the risk of either one sitting too close. She needn't have bothered as both the Fae chose to stand. With a sigh, Ember realized she'd inadvertently given up an equal footing, visually at least.

"The three of you coming here has been enlightening in ways I realize you do not understand. I am sure you would both like answers, but suffice it to say that I am beginning to think Azhirith's plan has more parts than this ridiculous connection between Reyar and that Witch. So, in an effort to help you recognize and, hopefully, to escape whatever trick she is trying to play against fate, I am going to train you both."

"Train us?" Ember demanded, sitting up straight and gripping the arms of her chair.

"Playing against fate?" Nicu asked at the same time, and it was his question that gave Shade pause. Her eyes tracked the blue lines that climbed the column of his neck, and a wide, catlike smile curled her lips.

"Oh, yes. And as that is the part that broke through your stoic facade, I am assuming you have some skin in this game, too."

"I am mutated," Nicu countered. His words were flat, yet his fingertips twitched as if fighting against curling in. "I cannot use magic as the Fae do."

"I have seen what you can do," Shade reminded him. "You are not like most Fae in many ways, Nicu Coccia."

Nicu's chin tilted down and his eyes narrowed, darkening in a way that reminded Ember of redwood shadows and secrets that slipped between the trees. Pine and mist invaded her sense. She caught a lungful of the scent, then held it as Nicu spoke in the same quiet, affected tone he'd used when telling bullies to leave Ember the verge alone.

"How do you know my last name?"

"There is only one family line known for its random mutations." Shade's snake whip shot from her arm without the usual show of slithering to the floor. It cut through the air in an instant strike. Ember's power surged with an instinctive response to the appearance of a threat, coating her skin with a light blue shell.

Nicu stood firm, though every muscle in his body tensed. The twists and curls of Nicu's Ink flowed down his forearms, darkening in its concentration. He lifted his arms in a defensive X, presenting the solid Ink as a shield. The whip hit his fisted hands and instead of striking, was sent back toward Shade with the strength of a ricochet.

Ember's lungs burned, yet she couldn't let go of the air. Her eyes strained as she struggled to keep both Shade and Nicu in focus. Shade calmly reclaimed her Ink, her chin slightly lifted.

"I would imagine your mother was Saedtha."

Nicu nodded. Ember remembered how to breathe even as she coped with the idea that she now knew the name of one of the Fae women who had died beside her as she was born.

"In that case, welcome to Gypsum, great-nephew."

18

DEVI

Yotos had landed well within sight of the gates but still a generous walk away. As Devi prepared for the trek across the soft sand, Reyar turned to the dragon.

"I don't know how long we'll be," he said. "I'll call when it's time."

In answer, Yotos stretched his body out, tucking his wings in and resting his large head on the sand, eyes instantly closed. A small smile curled Devi's lips at the sight of the giant beast sleeping as if it were a tiny child, knowing beyond a doubt that he was safe. She tapped the scales on one large, curled toe as she passed. A small purr vibrated from the dragon before he puffed out a heated burst of air, knocking a cloud of white dust from the ground.

"Quite a different attitude," Reyar noted as he kept pace at her side.

"Jealous?"

The instant flush on Reyar's cheeks suggested he might be, but he ignored her question by deflecting. "These are the dragon gates. They're the least guarded, but we'll still be questioned on the way in. Don't be surprised."

"Who is there to keep out?"

"Resources are scarce. Not all cities are maintained well."

"We're only two people."

"On a dragon," Reyar elaborated. "Which is why this is the least guarded gate."

Getting in was as easy as Reyar suggested, especially as the Wizard was instantly recognized as the Dragon Lord. Devi remained silent and followed Reyar in, overwhelmed by the noise and the height of solid white bricks that surrounded her.

The entry was a tall arch, but not a deep one. The space opened up slightly beyond, but only for a road that appeared as if it might follow the whole of the outer wall. Across from the entrance, hundreds of buildings sprouted, easily four stories and more tall. Handcarts were pulled along the street, some Fae with their heads down, others shouting that they were open for trade. They crossed the circle road and moved between the buildings, dodging more people who came in and out or were clearly on their way to somewhere important. Devi was jostled more than a few times in just as many seconds as she struggled to hide the absolute shock she felt at experiencing such massive congestion.

"How many people live here?"

"Millions," Reyar answered. "And they're all equal parts denial and desperation, so stay close."

Reyar stepped in next to her, his touch trailing from her elbow to her wrist before he wove his fingers between hers and gave them a light squeeze. She peered up at him, certain she'd find he'd be looking for a way through the crowd. Instead, she met his eyes.

"This place is a maze that's easy to get lost in. We're headed to the red temple district, which is right under the closest tower."

Devi looked up, following his directions. It was impossible for her to tell how far away the tower was or how long it might take them to reach it in this type of crowd.

"Don't worry. The crush should thin out for some of our walk. It will likely return once we reach the district, though."

Reyar led them unerringly through the streets. Though most of the Fae avoided them, a few stared at Reyar with mouths agape, steps faltering back, hands twitching forward. He ignored it all, keeping them on track until the red tower became too tall to comfortably look at, and they finally stood within the courtyard surrounding it. Stepping into the more open area, Devi could see this space was rounded like an eye, with the tower at its pupil. The buildings appeared carved from white stone, some with simple geometric lines and others with bass relief faces and scenes laid out like stories to be read.

People lined up at the different entrances, most of them waiting to get into the tower. In the shadows between, ragged Fae bent and bowed, their eyes staring out hungrily. She stopped when she noticed that at least one group of them were children, skin drawn taut across their cheekbones as they squatted between two temples along the outer curve. Reyar noted the direction she stared, then tugged her gently forward.

"I know," he spoke softly.

"Who's helping them?" Devi asked. Reyar shook his head, his frown deep.

"According to the Fae, their gods. But in reality, there's just not enough livable space and barely enough food. The magic that's left is used sparingly for necessities. That's why Shade's circus is so popular. There's enough magic mixed in with illusion that the Fae don't mind forgetting what parts are real."

"What about all the money the circus is making? What about you?"

"Cultures come and go all the time."

"You do not mean that," Devi hissed. Reyar sighed.

"I am not a god, Devi, and I have no desire to become one. And as I am, I cannot fix a species' failure to care for their realm."

Devi wanted to fight back, to argue more. Even small

things could help. But there was a weight on Reyar's shoulders when he spoke about being unable to change things. And there was the essence of him that lived inside of her from when they touched souls. He'd fought this battle before, for a long time, she realized. They hadn't listened to him then, and it was too late now.

"That's Kamél's temple." Reyar redirected the conversation, pointing to the tower whose entrance was marked by curved arches and rounded windows inset with prismatic glass. "She's the Goddess of Vision and Possibilities, which is why so many flock to her. I haven't ever known her to visit her temple, though. To truly get to her, you need to go to her star."

"Star as in outer space?"

"The universal plane, yes."

Devi blinked, the tickle of excitement within her chest igniting her curiosity. She promised herself to investigate this new discovery as soon as she could sit down with one of her notebooks. A pledge was all she had time for as Reyar directed their path toward one of the simple temples. The entrance was presented with simple pillars supporting a thick white slab that covered the seven steps leading to paneled doors, unadorned by anything other than the oil that kept them polished.

"This is Azhirith's temple, then?"

"Mmm," Reyar agreed.

"Why doesn't this one have a line?"

"Because very few people want to face the Goddess of Unyielding Truth."

They reached the top step, and the small door opened to reveal a Fae dressed in black from head to toe, wrapped in a thick robe that gave nothing away about the person's identity. Their hands tucked into opposite sleeves, their elbows bent and resting against their sides. Even the slit in the cloth at the eyes was narrow and shadowed.

"Purpose." They spoke softly, their voice devoid of expression.

"We request an audience with Azhirith at her convenience," Reyar offered, his tone far more polite than Devi had anticipated. "The threads she's woven have bound us well. I come not in defiance, but with a proposal I hope she'll deem worthy of exchange."

The acolyte stood still as a statue for a moment, and then gloved hands emerged from their large sleeves and the palms opened, cradling a polished black shard that absorbed the afternoon light. Reyar dropped his hold on Devi so he could gather the artifact with both of his hands.

Dragon bone. Devi reached for the matte black ring on her right middle finger. Reyar never spoke of it. The hand he held was the one without it, as if he didn't want to feel its reminder. Or maybe she was making up stories.

"You will know when Azhirith is ready for you. Please bide your time nearby." The acolyte turned with silent footsteps and passed through the white marble door without allowing them to gain a glimpse inside the temple.

"That's it?" Devi asked.

"For now," Reyar agreed, lifting up his tunic to expose a hip bag where he carefully placed the piece of dragon bone.

"And you think you have an argument strong enough to change the mind of a goddess?" Devi asked, still thrown by Reyar's show of reverence to the acolyte.

"There are many ways to solve a problem. Using people who are willing has a higher chance of success. She'll understand that." Reyar readjusted his tunic, then reclaimed her left hand. "Are you hungry?"

"No." Devi spoke quickly and quietly, unable to get the faces of the starving Fae out of her mind.

"Let's find a room then."

The walk through the city was slow given the crush of people, and it made it difficult to judge distances. Still, Devi was certain it was at least five times larger than all of Trifecta's territories, and possibly more. Her feet hurt in ways she didn't know they could after such a long time on uneven cobblestone walkways. It was a relief when Reyar finally led her up the stairs of a place called the Impish Inn. At first, it appeared they wouldn't get a room, then Reyar showed the dragon bone artifact and made sure the Fae had a nice, long look at his rainbow-gem eyes, and a key was reluctantly passed across the counter.

The room they rented was on the fourth floor of ten, and Devi was grateful it wasn't higher, her thighs burning after today's dragon ride, city walk, and this last stair climb. She changed her mind about food on the landing and asked their guide if they could order dinner with her. With a meal on the way, Devi waited impatiently for Reyar to unlock their room, uncertain of what she'd find. Given that the manager was reluctant to rent to them, did that mean it would be the tiniest of spaces? One bed or two?

Relief warmed Devi's muscles as they walked into a pleasant sitting room with a couch and two chairs, decorated in pale peach and rich shades of green. One door was opened to display the edge of a bathtub, and two other doors promised not only separate beds, but separate rooms.

Thank the gods.

Sleep would wait until after food, though. Devi made her way to the couch and fell across it with a heavy sigh, closing her eyes as she took in the sweet scent of sun-warmed polished wood.

"Aren't there any Witches here?" Devi asked. "Other than us?"

"Some," Reyar answered, making soft noises across the room, moving things around perhaps, but she was too tired to open her eyes. "Visitors who got stuck, so they're very old. Some of them have settled in with Fae families. Most keep to their own and tend to live close together."

Reyar fell silent and Devi took that as permission to rest. Even her curiosity about how the people here continued to live in such harsh conditions became mute. Her breath caught when the foot of her couch dipped with what could only be Reyar's weight. He shifted her legs until her feet were on his lap, and he peeled off her shoes. Devi pushed herself up onto her elbows to demand an explanation when he opened a small glass bottle to pour the cool oil over her heated skin.

"Oh," she breathed, collapsing back. No matter what was between them or how much Devi wanted to fight a connection that could never be hers, her feet hurt. She was not above letting his magically induced need to care for her result in a massage.

"I'm sorry," Reyar murmured from the end of the couch. Devi sighed, relaxing into the firm press of his thumb against the arch of her foot.

"For not even kissing me?" she teased him, cracking open an eye to watch his reaction. "And you promised Shade."

His skin didn't darken as expected. His eyes remained soft and locked on hers.

"You don't deserve this."

Devi puffed out a sigh. "Of course not. We only deserve what we work for, not what falls into our laps."

Reyar's brow twisted. "How are you doing this?"

"What?" Devi's teeth ached with the force of the word. "Trying to relax after a remarkably hard day?"

"I cannot stop thinking about you," Reyar rushed, twisting on the couch and placing a hand on each of her calves, pressing up the hem of her long skirt. "I must be near you. I must be close. Yet you aren't as affected. You came to this couch, not into my arms. If you decided to touch me in any way, I would not be able to keep my own hands off you. So why is it harder for me?"

"I assume your goddess gave you a more potent dose." As if to highlight her strength over his, Devi shifted until she sat up, legs curled beneath her. The truth was, Devi recognized the same pull she saw in Reyar's eyes. Falling into his arms would have been so much sweeter than collapsing on the couch. It was easier for Devi to turn away because she was used to avoiding barbed affection. To ground herself in a need for knowledge. To rely on books and thought as her only willing companions.

Reyar clearly didn't have the same practice. Living with his lover. In constant contact with dragons who, if Yotos was a reliable ambassador, absolutely adored him. Self-denial did not appear to be in the Dragon Lord's vocabulary.

Supporting her assumption, Reyar knelt on the couch, one hand on its back as he leaned over its length. He hovered as she leaned backward until she collapsed, and he held himself above her supine form. Devi's breath caught at the sight of him poised over her. The fading red light of the afternoon painted the copper strands of his auburn hair as he slowly lowered toward her.

"You would deny me?" The fingertips of Reyar's free hand brushed over the freckles on her cheekbones, his breath brushing her lips with temptation. Devi's heart raced. She wanted nothing more than to grab his braid and pull him closer, to find out what it felt like to touch the fine hairs of his brow and test the texture of the tendons straining at his neck.

But Devi hated running, and there was no way she would be chasing him.

"As long as you plan to return to her, yes."

Her words were as much an answer as they were a challenge. How badly did he want her, in truth? He claimed weakness, but was it chosen, or forced?

The skin at the corners of Reyar's wide eyes wrinkled. His mouth opened, then closed, as if there were too many thoughts to choose from. When his breath entered her lungs, Devi gasped.

"I mean it," she whispered, trembling when she realized that the very edges of her lips barely brushed against the heat of his. "Our choices are all that matter."

Reyar stiffened, then pushed himself up, his arms fully extended as he stared down at her, skin pale and eyes surprisingly damp. Devi's own eyes stung with added moisture. She lifted her left hand, fingers trembling, wanting to reclaim her words. To pull him in. To take what she could in this moment and hold on to it for the rest of her life.

A knock sounded at the door, and a muffled voice announced that their dinner had arrived. Reyar jumped up and went to answer. Devi ran into the nearest bedroom, throwing the lock, hoping Reyar found those kids from the temple's courtyard to offer them the food she wouldn't be able to eat.

19

EMBER

*E*mber sat on her hammock chair, adjusting the attached umbrella and pulling in her legs to make the most of the provided shade. She'd decided to haul it with her on their fourth day of training despite the awkward size. Since Shade's attention split between her and Nicu, there was more time to rest than usual, and sitting on the hard sand had quickly lost its appeal.

Training was becoming her second favorite time of day behind performing, because it provided the most distance between her and Nicu. The stagehands had expanded their makeshift home by adding enough canvas to create a third bedroom. Unfortunately, that left her in close proximity with Nicu. Shade hadn't been in the tent much before, but with Reyar gone, she showed up to sleep, then woke them all up as soon as possible. They trained outside the dragon fields, which had the added benefit of making their magic visible so Shade could judge the whole process.

Ember was always first, practicing her energy flow while Shade called out physical exercises of her to slip through. Jumping jacks for five minutes. A twenty-second sprint, then somersaults, which were horrible with sharp, pointy rocks hiding beneath the otherwise soft sand. Jump up for jacks again only to dodge the unannounced flick of Shade's lightning whip. Before, Reyar had Ember train with a few drakes, but Shade had taken that part out even though Ember still encountered them in her daily performances.

Once the Fae was satisfied with Ember's ability to maintain a solid flow of energy to her shields even while having to move unexpectedly, Ember was told to have a seat. It was shorter than her training with Reyar, but with an intensity that never stopped, even for corrections, and Ember was always ready and willing to take her break by the end.

Then it was Nicu's turn. On the first day he'd worked with Shade, she'd announced him an utter failure, and not because of his lack of skill, but because he lacked willingness.

"You think keeping secrets is your power, but it is just another wall to hide behind. You think you can learn without acting, make decisions without moving, when all that does is leave you stranded. An easy, stationary target ripe for the picking when the only way to success is to meet the enemy on the ground."

Shade's lightning had ignited from her whip, sparks jumping away from her body and her hair rising due to its force. Ember had been so shocked at Shade's show of power, she'd instinctively opened a channel of magic between her and Nicu, coating his skin with a film of blue. The Siren Fae's electricity died down, the flow clear with the dragons lying only a few yards away. She shook her head at Ember, though her anger had melted into a soft smile. The lesson had been over for the day.

On day two, Nicu acted as if he'd taken the Siren's message to heart. Ember hadn't been able to relax as she'd done the previous day, pinned to the edge of the training field on her own accord as she watched her guardian and patron train.

She'd never seen Nicu's tattoos leave his body. Devi had told her back in Trifecta that he'd pushed them off arms in order to save her from being trapped in the Veil magic.

At first, he'd thrown his Ink without purpose. His brow had been creased with concentration so strong, Ember found herself studying the folds in his skin, part of her surprised that he wasn't carved from stone after all. Shade had grunted in approval with Nicu's attempt even as her whip struck his separate tattoos. They instantly retracted back into his pores.

Where Shade only offered shouted corrections to Ember, for Nicu she stood close while in conversation. Their words were technical, and some of them so seeped in Fae magic that they blurred in Ember's mind. At first, she watched each match carefully, trying to discern exactly what Shade was teaching and follow Nicu's progress. After the third day, she realized the context was beyond her, and she'd grabbed her folding hammock chair.

After that first time, Nicu had carried it ever since, and they took turns resting while the other trained. She didn't say anything to him. He didn't speak to her, not with Shade's ears focused toward them. Their Fae instructor's rant on the first day was enough to make Nicu a better student, but he certainly wanted to keep other secrets.

"Ember."

Her body reacted to the unexpected call before her brain did. She was on her feet and walking toward Shade. Nicu's frown was fleeting, but it was enough. He thought she acted without self-control. It irked her to realize he was right and wondered if there was a way to keep her reaction time while also engaging her active attention. It wasn't a skill Reyar or Shade showed interest in her learning, yet with Nicu's presence, it suddenly seemed like an important piece to incorporate.

Anger twisted in her gut, and she breathed through it,

shaking out her fingers as if to loosen them while she truly fought to keep them from becoming fists of irritation. Why was it always Nicu who made her think? That made her consider? That made her remember it wasn't safe to trust?

"Stand across from me and next to Nicu."

Ember shifted her attention between Nicu and Shade as she took up a defensive position. Nicu's frown accused her of being far too complacent if she'd been so caught off guard. She cycled through the excuses. She hadn't slept well since he had arrived. Couldn't keep her thoughts from the thin canvas that separated their beds. Shifting between imagined scenarios of him dragging her back to Trifecta to face another slew of Fae arrows for her inflated transgressions.

He hadn't tried to confront her, though, and her anxiety grew in the vacuum. She didn't expect explanations, but certainly he'd lay out his argument for her to do as he wished. Yet he'd clearly decided to bide his time. Was it solely for Devi, or for some other reason?

"Ember, feed him energy. Focus on defense. Nicu, try again."

Ember hesitated, and Shade's whip sped toward Nicu. He raised an arm, darkened with Ink. It blocked her lightning but not the physical force, pulling a quiet, involuntary grunt from his chest.

Fade it all.

Ember gathered her energy and bowed it out in front of them first, then opened a conduit to Nicu. The power fluctuated between her two focuses, thinning and thickening instead of remaining steady. Ember grunted in frustration, sure she'd gotten this split right the first time when she'd tried it while holding Reyar back in the arena.

"You are a conduit, not the source," Reyar had told her months ago. "Where a mage needs access to harvestable magic and time, you don't have a resource challenge. You don't even have to shape the spell, just the energy. You are faster. Your access is unstoppable. That's what makes you so unique. All you need is the strength to direct it, and the force of will to control it. Now, keep the flow steady."

Stamina. Ember relaxed her shoulders and pulled in a deep breath. She ground through her feet, a psychological aid Reyar claimed she wouldn't need one day, but was a good method for training.

The shield first. She strengthened it just in time for Shade's next attack. The connection with Nicu was slipping, though. She tried to remember what was different about this experience from the last. There'd been a deep desire to help and protect Devi, and to follow the desperate request of her teacher. But it had to be more than that. She refused to allow emotional motivation to be the reason she was good at this.

"I can help," Nicu offered. "I can pull."

Ember flinched away from the idea. Nicu noticed, offering a small nod as if to say it was her choice.

He wasn't wrong, but this was different from simply letting energy free into the air for him to collect into his tattoos. Ember remembered the pain of being drawn from. How Tristan had tried to claim her power. How Devi, in her grief, had pulled blindly. How it hurt, even when she gave permission.

Shade's next attack had more force behind it as she tested the strength of Ember's shield, and as a silent push to get her mind back on training.

Ember took a deep breath. This was Nicu, and that might be the difference that mattered. There was no denying that they shared a connection. That somehow she always knew what direction his pine and mist scent came from. That he'd found her across the realms.

"Okay."

Nicu's magical touch felt like warm water. She gasped at the simplicity. Somehow, his gentle pressure opened up something in her. An understanding of how the power originated deep within her bones, but also from the universe itself. She understood how it flowed, not through her veins, but through channels of energy that pulsed through her body.

And then it was easy. Her shield strengthened into a rich blue, darkening their view of Shade. Nicu's tattoos flowed from his wrists, wrapping around each other in two thick ropes. They sped toward the shield, and Ember opened a small window for them.

Shade's whip lashed out. Ember pulled back enough energy to add more transparency to the shield without losing too much strength. Nicu's ropes avoided the single, serpentine flash of the lightning whip. He gripped Shade's wrist with the rope from his left arm, the second wrapping around her throat.

The three of them stood staring at each other for a moment. One of the tan dragons had raised its head, a large, sea-colored eye focused on them. Drakes stopped pretending to do small jobs around the dragons and stared, waiting to see what happened now that Ember and Nicu had captured Shade.

The female Fae broke the silence with a deep laugh. Lightning crashed, blinding everyone who dared to watch. Hot, heavy energy flooded through Ember's body, and she gasped, stumbling back. She withdrew her connection to her source, instinctively needing to limit the power flowing through her fragile human frame.

Nicu let go the instant she pulled. His involuntary vocalization started high, tinged with pain, then lowered into a forceful grunt. Ember blinked her eyes, trying to regain functional vision around the spots of white.

Shade's thick boots stood three feet away, having closed the distance while they recovered. Her Ink whip flickered at her feet, a small spark dancing along its length.

Ember reached for her power.

"Stop."

Shade's command once again controlled Ember's actions

before her brain caught up. Ember grit her teeth, glaring up at the Fae.

"You are close to burning out like a bit of tinder," Shade cautioned. "Apparently you absorbed my lightning instead of letting it bite you and Nicu. Very impressive. Very foolish. We will have to cancel your presentation for the day."

"I will walk her to the tent," Nicu stated. Ember studied him from the corner of her eye, wondering if he was actually worried about her, or if he intended to switch his strategy and start campaigning for a return to Trifecta. Either way, Shade was not inclined to humor him.

"You were also impressive, but are far from burned out," she told Nicu. "You can practice with Mize." A Fae on the edge of the field tossed a scale brush to a nearby friend and presented himself with a wide, open smile. Nicu's jaw tensed for only a moment, but he nodded to indicate that he would follow her instructions.

"Bath time, Ember." Shade offered her a hand, and Ember gripped it on her way up. Shade kept a hold of her until they were out of hearing distance, then she released Ember from her grip. Apparently, Nicu wasn't the only one who wanted to speak to her privately.

"I did not know you could do that," Shade murmured. "But I had hoped."

"You hoped I would burn myself out?"

"No, of course not. I hope that if others could use your power, you could use theirs."

Shade watched Ember take in the information, the Fae's smile widening along with the understanding in Ember's eyes.

"Next time, take his tattoos."

"I can do that?"

"You will not know if you do not try. It will surprise the scales off him if you can. Teach him that he cannot always be in control of you."

Ember smiled at the idea of surprising Nicu for once.

However, what Shade was talking about... it was like Tristan trying to steal her magic. Or maybe Devi was a better example, since Ember had at least wanted to help the Witch. Part of her wanted to do what Shade told her. Her body already imagined the motions of what it might feel like. But taking without permission was stealing, and seizing someone's magic was an intimate, devastating act.

"Where I see and commend your hesitation, it is not a bad thing to take when necessary," Shade offered. "Perhaps you are right and now is not one of those times. You two do seem companionable, if not friendly."

Ember grunted a noncommittal answer. Shade shook her head with a large smile.

"I did not lie when I told you I was impressed. Reyar said you were special, but I did not fully appreciate what he meant until we started working together. I wish I had continued training with you sooner."

"It's been amazing to learn from you."

"It has, but be fully aware that we are learning from you, too, Ember. I meant it when I said 'training with'. It honestly gives me so much hope."

Ember's cheeks heated under the praise, and she looked toward the ground. A foreign warmth filled her chest. She took a deep breath, not to dispel it, but to encapsulate it. To hold on to the feeling for as long as possible.

"Reyar thought there might be a way for you to help us. To help Gypsum. I was not so sure, but you have changed my mind. Is that something you would be interested in, Ember? I know you cannot leave here, that you cannot see what is going on inside the city and others like it. But maybe... Come on."

They'd reached their tent, and Shade pushed inside, a low trembling in her fingers. Ember followed, surprised to meet Shade's wide eyes and relaxed features. She hated being in this tent, but now, with whatever ideas danced within her head, she was excited.

"Please sit down."

Curious, Ember sat on the couch, startled when Shade plopped next to her. The surface of the round beechwood table shimmered, pulling Ember's attention.

"Gypsum was once as rich as Heldu, but as you can see, our Fae realm has been severely depleted. Despite our long lives, we did not give much thought to finding ways to elongate the lifespan of our domain, to protect our resources. Or perhaps it was our power that fooled us into thinking we could fix whatever came along. We are Fae, after all. Powerful. Gods walk among us - are born from us - and perhaps that instilled a belief that we would be saved."

As Shade spoke, beautiful images flowed across the table. Landscapes thick with vegetation, flush with water. Streams filled with fish and waterfalls provided majestic backgrounds to flying birds. Fauna raced between trees and hid in the tall grasses of the plains.

Then paradise faded. Leaves browned and fell. Animals thinned in body, then in numbers. Slowly, the colors dimmed. As if all No Man's Land spread across the whole of this realm, so many living things vanished, rotted, and turned to dust, exposing the stone beneath.

Ember glanced toward Shade, who regarded it all with pained lines around her lips and eyes, watching something she'd lived through on repeat.

The images disappeared.

"Now, anything that lives does so within one of our remaining cities. The Fae found that our magic was not enough to save the whole realm, but we could maintain parts of it. Even the edges of those, though, are starting to fade and break away."

"Why don't you leave? Find another realm? Maybe the Witches—"

"We cannot, even if we wanted to."

"But the Fae in Trifecta—"

Shade interrupted again. "From what Nicu tells me, the bubble in the Veil allowed for Gypsum and Heldu energies to seep through, but only in limited portions of Terra and only within your small city." Shade stood, shaking her head.

"Our magic requires that we stay with the dragons and the dragons stay in Gypsum. At least for now. It is believed they could leave, find another planet, but passing through the Veil is a near impossibility for them. They can certainly live in this realm longer than we will. It has not mattered to me, honestly, because of Reyar. As the Dragon Lord, he goes where the dragons go. They care for him as he cares for them. I would remain with them."

Shade's voice broke as uncertainty cut through the story she'd believed for so long. Ember's fingers curled in her lap. With Devi here, there was no longer a guaranteed safe escape for Shade. Even if Reyar cared enough to take her along, if Devi was also part of the bargain, Ember couldn't see Shade agreeing.

"Then you came. You beautiful, powerful conduit. You are growing so fast. Learning so much. Reyar and Devi have their path. We hope it works, but we cannot know. I have another idea if you are willing."

Ember opened her mouth to answer, but Shade raised her hand, halting her response.

"I am not ready yet. You are not either. I have some research to do to make sure it is safe. But if it is possible, would you think about it? Would you consider saving Gypsum? It would mean you could stay here, too. With or without Nicu. It would be your choice all the way through."

Ember's breath came with short, heavy motions of her chest. Her choice of a home. Her choice of company. Her own control of a situation.

"Of course," she agreed, her voice thick.

Shade's smile lit the room as if her own lightning shone

from within. "Wonderful! Just one more thing, then." Shade leaned over and wrapped an arm around Ember's shoulders.

A soft hum sounded in Shade's chest. A gentle song laced around the next words that slipped out of her mouth.

"When Nicu is ready for you to leave, remember all the reasons why you shouldn't trust him. Do not let him sway you."

20

NICU

Nicu faced off against his new sparring partner, Mize. They'd gotten used to each other over the last few days as Shade had declared Ember required additional rest, though she did not deem the same need for Nicu. Also, the Siren Fae felt he no longer needed her direct instructions and that he could hone what he knew with another Fae.

The shift didn't quite feel like abandonment, but it was close. He was not worthy of instruction without Ember, it seemed. Their enforced separation also raised suspicions. Frustration gnawed at Nicu's gut, not believing Shade's reasons for a moment, but also lacking the required information to unearth her true goal.

Redirecting the erratic emotional energy into something productive, he flushed his tattoos and directed them toward his wrists. Against his palms, the separate curves spun into thick ropes, growing longer and expanding beyond the space they took up on his skin.

"Time to fight," Mize challenged. The Fae wore bracers shaped into elongated shields that he could move with ease while allowing his hands to grip a pair of dirks, long daggers perfect for close combat. Nicu had no intention of getting within range of the Fae's attacks.

Nicu resumed the offense, though he did not give it his full focus. Day seven and no Devi. She must not have had her audience with the goddess yet. How much more time did Nicu have to convince Ember to return home?

If future days echoed the last week, that would continue to prove difficult. He'd been watching Ember carefully, watching for a sign she'd be willing to listen rather than default into defiance.

Nicu did not make the mistake of assuming Ember's automatic protection of him during training suggested a personal warmth. Shade was powerful, and it was in Ember's nature to protect. He recognized the same instinct when it had come to her mother, where even though Susan was infected by the Queen, Ember insisted on keeping her close and as safe as possible.

Mize's blade slashed across one of Nicu's tattoo-formed ropes. The Ink parted with the cut, leaving a dashed line. Nicu grit his teeth and chased the severed piece, willing the molecules to stitch together and restore itself. As they connected, his control slipped and his tattoos rebounded, settling into the pores on his skin as he worked to catch his breath and slow his heartbeat.

"Nice!" Mize called as if Nicu's retreat was somehow a victory. The Gypsum-born Fae slid his dirks into their sheaths, then unstrapped the bracers as if that had marked the end of their practice session.

In many ways, Nicu's new sparring partner reminded him of Daz, a Terra-born Fae he could almost call a friend. They both wore optimism like a shield and preferred physical activity. Where Daz was a Fae Weaver, Mize's job was to help care for the dragons.

Nicu followed Mize as he put away his gear, diverting

slightly from the weapons cache to the adjacent storage space that held everything from brooms and hammers to foot-long files and metal-bristled brushes. Grabbing a bucket, two brushes, and one file, Nicu stepped back outside just as Mize re-emerged.

Mize's smile acted as thanks, and he grabbed the file from Nicu. They made their way to one of the smaller dragons decorated with milky-brown scales that deepened into a darker fawn along the spine and wing ridges.

"Is this your only dragon," Nicu asked, "or your first?" He'd held on to his curiosity for the last few days, unsure if Mize was also meant to act as Shade's spy. Though he hadn't found any evidence to support his worry, Nicu wanted to remain on guard. Asking about the Fae's job, however, was innocent enough, and might even lead to a deeper conversation where Nicu learned something important.

"Are you kidding?" Mize asked. "It would be suicide to have more than one charge."

"Because they are territorial?" Nicu asked, though he doubted the premise of the question given that another dragon lay only twenty yards away.

"Because they are big, selfish animals," Mize replied. "They are not aggressive to the Fae, but they are still dangerous. Do not let their ability to communicate fool you."

"I was not aware they could," Nicu countered.

"Oh, yeah. A type of telepathy that is basically limited to 'I am hungry' and 'sure, I will fly you to Berjchan today'. But that does not make them tame. And as big as they are, accidents happen. The only one who can claim any real control over the dragons is the Dragon Lord."

Nicu dropped the bucket and pulled out a scale brush, using the chiseled end first as Mize had shown him, easing apart scales and scraping sand at the same time. The dragon's head raised slightly, turning to peek at him as he worked. With a heavy, hot breath, it flopped its head back down but kept a slitted view of him.

"There, see?" Mize pointed as if the dragon's movement had spoken volumes. Clearly, to the caretaker, it had. "Torus knows you're not me because of how it feels when you work. I have been working with him for years, learning his cues, where he prefers I start first. Where I should not bother with at all. That is his tail tip, by the way."

Mize patted one of Torus' thick toes. The dragon raised it up, revealing a black talon as tall as the Fae.

"Basically," Mize continued, "taking on another dragon would be taking on split loyalties. I would never be able to get to know them as well as I should to be a good caretaker. I would risk losing them both."

"Losing them?" Nicu stopped his work and focused on Mize. A pressure he hadn't felt for days fell onto his shoulders, holding him in place.

"Yeah, the agreement between Fae and dragons. We care for them, they do not eat us, and even protect us. You think Torus needs his scales cleaned every day? Not a chance. But he likes it. He likes me. And it is an honor as a Fae to be chosen by a dragon, to be an ambassador of the race as we hold up our end of the pact."

"So, no one takes on more than one dragon?"

"There are exceptions. Older Fae who know their dragon so well that they are able to learn a second. Sometimes potential caretakers will start with a few just to see how they click. But eventually, you have to choose, or you lose both. Losing a dragon marks you as incompetent, and you will not be chosen again. A few Fae still fail out of caretaking, but the wise ones realize from the beginning. No split loyalties amongst dragons."

The pressure let up, allowing Nicu to return to his task. He flipped the brush and began cleaning out the smaller channels lining the surface of the dragon's scales.

"What happens," he asked slowly, "to those that fail?"

Mize was quiet for a moment as he finished smoothing the peeling edges of the dragon's keratin claws. He stepped away, and the tip of the claw sunk back into the pure white sand.

"Before, they simply found a new trade. It might be difficult given that they had proven fickle, but not impossible. Now, though... Now being a caretaker is one of the few positions of security. We cannot let the pact fail, especially as the realm is dying. We need the dragons for so many things. Protection. Ink. Entertainment," he offered, waving his arm toward the arena tent.

"What is life like for the other Fae?"

Mize clenched his fists, turning to glare at the city and its collection of towers.

"Hard."

Nicu gripped the brush in one hand, taking in Mize's words, wondering what he might see if he made the long walk to the city at the center of the ruins. Assuming Shade would allow it.

Mize shook off his dark thoughts and reclaimed his smile, tapping Torus' next toe so he could get to work on the other claw.

"Hey, enough of that, though. We are the lucky ones, so we shouldn't waste it. There is going to be a bonfire tonight, out by the rose garden. Want to come?"

"What roses grow here?" Nicu questioned, and Mize shook his head.

"You will see when you arrive."

"Hmm," Nicu answered, noncommittal. Mize's grin shifted so one side was higher than the other.

"Ember's coming. And Shade won't."

Nicu's movements froze, and Mize's laughter filled his ears in a way that made heat climb up his neck.

"It is not what you think," Nicu argued. Mize only laughed harder.

"That is what they all say," he teased. "And yet, she is still the reason you will be there tonight. Come on. Let us finish Torus, and we can get ready to meet your lady."

Nicu's lips thinned and he shook his head, redoubling his effort on the next scale, glad that Ember wasn't around to hear Mize claim that she belonged to anyone but herself.

21

DEVI

Devi had never walked so much without a clear destination. She was becoming like Ember, but instead of roaming the Trifectan forest, Devi explored city streets. The shadows were the same, with the buildings rising tall and stark against the pale pink sky. The smell was worse, saturated with sweat, excrement, and decay, the last of which was a pure mystery since there didn't seem to be anything organic left to rot.

Yet as hot and uncomfortable as she was out here, remaining in her shared suite with Reyar was not an option. The weight of his eyes was on her as she moved through the room. The heat of his attention seeped through the walls, as she tried to sleep or when she took a bath. Even when he wasn't there, his scent was; a dusky desert musk that invaded her lungs and dug into her skin to the point where she wondered if she'd absorbed enough of him that her own perfume had been erased by his.

The air out here might not be fresh, but at least it wasn't addictive.

As intimidating as the city had been on her first impression, Devi discovered there was a simplicity in its design that made the main roads easy to travel. Most of the streets were laid out in a grid with the exception of the Wall Road and a few shortcut passages that all seemed to focus around the towers themselves.

There were a few small park spaces at each intersection, corners taken out between the buildings and the street. Some had been turned into alternate places of worship with makeshift altars and scattered offerings of little value, making the locations look more like trash heaps than shrines to make wishes. Others held tents for the overflowing population, but there were a few she discovered that had been left with the skeletal remains of fruit trees that somehow stood despite their dry, brittle state.

Once she had a handle on navigation using these park spaces as landmarks, Devi allowed herself to meander without direction. She kept clear of the temple square because of the crowds, and made sure that she didn't wander too far in case the activation of the goddess' artifact sent Reyar searching for her. Devi had noted one particularly large grove of trees on her third day of exploration, and detoured from the street to walk beneath the crooked gray branches, imagining them as they must have been once upon a time.

Then one of the Fae children sprinted past her, letting out a squeak at the sight of her colorful skirt amidst the monochrome park. He spun even as he stopped, eyes wide as he looked her over from head to toe.

"Am I too late?" he asked, breath short and lips trembling. "Is it all gone?"

"Is what all gone?" Devi asked, trying to keep her movements soft and her voice kind. "I'm not sure what you're talking about."

"Service," the Fae child answered, then he blinked away his fear. "You're a Witch and you don't know about it?"

"I'm newly visiting," she answered, and the child let out a

deep, shaky breath. Without another word, he turned and continued his headlong rush through the park.

Curious, Devi followed the young Fae to the corner he disappeared behind. When she entered the intersection, she noticed a line of people curving around a building a few doors up, and disappearing into an alley space. Everyone in line was Fae, dressed neatly if not well. As Devi approached, the sweetest smell she'd encountered in days reached her nose.

Fresh bread.

It was a food line.

Devi decided that getting into the queue was not for her, even to satiate her curiosity. Food was something she and Reyar had plenty of, and clearly those here didn't. She waited, though, ignoring the curious stares of the Fae as they drifted through the natural motions of waiting. Eventually, some of them started to leave.

"I'm sorry," a velvet voice called from the alley. A Wizard stepped out with a basket clasped in his hands, his hair a startling, natural black. "We are out for the day. Please take your ticket so we can make sure you receive the first portions tomorrow."

Though there was some grumbling and a few tears from one of the small girls, the remaining Fae calmly took their tickets, and shuffled out of the way. So this was a common occurrence, and everyone understood the rules. Devi ran the numbers through her head, realizing that they'd fed nearly one hundred Fae, and then had to turn away a few dozen more.

It was truly unacceptable, but given the state of their resources, Devi could only find gratitude for the Wizard who offered the Fae at least a little boon. The Wizard sighed as the last Fae family left, heading in Devi's direction. The bright swirl of her rainbow skirt caught his attention, and his sapphire eyes twinkled as he approached.

"Oren," he introduced himself simply and without further greeting.

"Devi," she responded with a raised brow, a challenge in her look.

"Are you from the River District?"

"Just visiting," Devi countered, then because she couldn't see the harm: "Waiting on a goddess."

"Ah." Oren watched her for a moment longer, then stepped back and gestured toward the alley. "Would you like to sate your curiosity then?"

Devi debated the wisdom of following a strange Wizard down the narrow passage. She'd done the math, and there were still some Fae inside, likely finishing up. Devi was curious to know how and why this Coven was feeding them. And Reyar would hate the very idea of her interacting with others.

"Thank you," Devi agreed, and then followed Oren in.

They entered a small courtyard. Lines of tables and benches took up most of the space, with a small, perpendicular line of counters that were currently being cleaned of eating implements and whatever had filled the large, iron cauldrons.

"You feed them."

"Yes," Oren answered, continuing to keep his answers simple as he let his eyes rove over her. Even here she stood out. This Coven wore colors long since bleached by the sun, while hers were bright and new. Their hair was left to its natural tones, and hers retained the vivid cranberry red she preferred. Her entrance claimed everyone's attention. She let it roll over her as if none of it mattered.

"You grow the food?"

Oren answered her by leading her out of the courtyard and into the back building. They climbed an unfortunate number of stairs to reach the roof, where Devi struggled to catch her breath, even as her shoulders fell.

It was barely a garden. Raised beds took up as much space as possible, with narrow walkways between. The dirt was pale and tired. Leaves drooped, small and struggling. Witches and Wizards had a natural talent with plant life, and if this was the best a whole coven could do, Gypsum was truly entering its last days.

Devi wove her way through each aisle, her fingers combing through lemongrass, petting heads of lettuce and fluffing up carrot stems. And with every step she reached beyond this rooftop and the building supporting it to the earth below. She dug deeper than she thought she could, threading tendrils of power up and up through miles of hot rock, then cooled crust, all to add the promise of vitality to this modest garden.

And that night, for the first time, she fell asleep without tossing and turning, exhaustion chasing Reyar from her mind.

That had been three days ago, and she'd shown up every day since. She came earlier now, helping this charitable Coven set up stacks of silver bowls, towers of copper cups, and haul out gallons of soup created from the roof garden that had suddenly started producing a healthier, plentiful crop.

Devi kept up her work. She tweaked the spells on the cauldrons, managing to scrape together sufficient power so they duplicated their contents by ten percent. She repeated the spell on each of the silver bowls, frustrated that despite her skills, there wasn't enough magic to maintain the spells for more than one service. Still, it meant that more Fae could be served, and each of them was a little fuller than they would have been otherwise.

Though the Coven never caught her spellwork spoken in soft whispers and behind their backs, they clearly noted the changes had arrived with her presence. They greeted her with smiles and open arms, providing her with whatever she needed. Even the Fae began to smile at the new, vibrant Witch who had come to help them out.

After her third service, Devi said her quiet goodbyes and slipped through the alley with a smile, noting how full the basket of vouchers was today, meaning fewer Fae had been turned away.

"Devi," Oren called just as she emerged onto the main side-

Tempered

walk. She twisted to meet the Wizard's sapphire eyes, and he gestured for her to return. If they were going to talk, then she definitely preferred the slightly cooler space of the shaded alley, so she stepped back inside.

"The Coven and I were hoping you would stay a little longer."

Devi glanced at the sky, not that she could exactly tell the time by the sun. "How long?" she asked, wondering if they needed some more assistance with cleanup, or if he wanted to take her up to the garden to see if she might produce any more hidden miracles.

"Forever?"

Devi's eyes snapped to Oren's and her lips parted in surprise. His grin sat crooked in his oval face, with strands of black hair framing sharp cheekbones. Warmth radiated from his sapphire irises, his mouth curved upward as an invitation.

"No." She answered simply. Oren's lips flicked down, but then his smile returned.

"Okay," he accepted. "But for a while? Once you meet your goddess, you could stay. I've seen that you care about what we do here. We're all aware that you have a special touch."

A question lifted his brow, but he was wise enough not to ask it. She hadn't engaged much with the group other than in the most utilitarian sense. Yes, she wanted to support their cause, and she hoped she could find a way to leave something behind that could last for more than a day. But she couldn't stay.

"I'm sorry, Oren," she murmured.

Oren's eyes danced over her face, and Devi's heart stuttered as she realized she'd missed something very important. This Wizard hadn't been observing her just to check for signs of magic use. He was paying attention to her because he found her attractive.

"Can I have a chance to convince you?"

Oren leaned in and Devi struggled to hide how her breath came in quick spurts. Objectively, he was handsome. Their ideologies appeared to match, since they were both here, feeding those that they could.

He wasn't Reyar.

Which was the best argument yet. Maybe if she let him kiss her, maybe she could develop an attachment outside this spell, one like Reyar's relationship to Shade. An anchor. A place to return to when Reyar left her in a world that was falling apart.

Oren leaned in.

No.

Devi's hand rose to his chest, pushing him back. Oren's brow wrinkled with confusion.

A gentle force gripped Devi's arm, tugging her out and away from the shadows and into the sunlight. The extraction was painless, smooth, and left her pressed against Reyar's very rigid, very angry side.

Oren stumbled a few steps backward, his eyes wide and his face pale as a very real dragon's growl emerged from Reyar's chest. Devi felt its vibration, and she jerked her gaze to his face to find his brows twisted in feral fury.

Laughter burst from the depths of Devi's stomach, and she hugged herself against the unexpected force. Oren's eyes flickered rapidly between Reyar and Devi even as the Dragon Lord turned his furious visage from Oren to her. Watching him shift from enraged to confused sent another bubble of giggles through her. Devi waved the air in front of her face, as if she could brush them off.

"What do you think you are doing?" Reyar demanded.

"Volunteering," Devi answered, gulping in oxygen to get ahold of herself.

"That is not what I saw," he growled, his hand slipping behind her neck.

"I-it was nothing," Oren stammered. Reyar's sharp glare cut off any other attempt at speech.

"You would kiss her as if it were nothing?" The growl emerged again, and this time, Devi didn't find it so funny.

"And so what if he would?" Devi slapped away Reyar's touch. "Or maybe it did mean something to him. To me."

Reyar's skin flushed, his fists tight at his sides as his prismatic eyes flashed with razor-edge facets.

"You do not get to say that to me," he declared.

"Really?" Devi asked. "And since our first meeting, how many times have you kissed Shade? Made love to her? It is you who doesn't have the right to come in here and interfere with my life. My choices."

"A choice, Devi? Or a reckless decision because you're not getting your way?"

Devi's hand snapped out and up, aiming for Reyar's cheek. He caught her wrist, managing to stop her attack without hurting her. His lids flinched and his lips flattened, as if his words were the reckless decision he was suddenly regretting.

"Ah." Oren spoke from halfway up the alley. "Thank you for all your help. We understand why you can't stay. I'm sure we will manage from here." Then the Wizard was gone.

Devi jerked her wrist from Reyar's hold and pushed out a frustrated shriek that sounded eerily familiar to Reyar's own growl. She spun on her heel and stomped away.

She wouldn't be able to return after that. Even if they let her in, it wouldn't be the same. The Coven would look at her with suspicion. Caution would guide their interactions as they worried if the Dragon Lord would show up again, and there was no mistaking that he'd been recognized. Everyone in this fading city seemed to know him or know of him. It had to be those rainbow irises, imposing height, and copper hair. No one else looked like he did.

"I'm not sorry I stopped him from kissing you," Reyar grumbled as he caught up with her.

"What about taking away the one thing that I have actually

enjoyed doing since stepping foot into this realm?" Devi demanded.

"One person's effort won't be missed. That Coven will be fine."

Except he didn't know she'd been casting on the cookware and the dishes. She'd had to refresh it every day because this verge-forsaken world couldn't sustain such a simple spell. At least her Work in the garden seemed to be holding, but then that coordinated with her magic and her kind's natural ability to manage plant growth.

"It's been a week," Reyar offered softly. "I'm sure Azhirith will see us soon, and we'll return to your Terran friends."

Devi ignored him. He didn't understand. She'd already told Oren she wasn't staying. She just wanted to leave them with something.

"I'm sorry." Reyar's words left a deep ache in Devi's skipped heartbeat. In those two words, he recognized his lack of understanding, apologized for not digging deeper, for not allowing this connection between them to deepen by asking about simple, everyday things.

Devi hummed, the only answer she had the energy to provide. Then, Reyar's gentle touch wrapped around her forearm, his fingers tickling the skin until they interlocked with her left hand. He refused to look at her, as if he didn't want to acknowledge his lack of control over the motion. And Devi kept her breathing as even as possible, as if his touch wasn't the highlight of her entire existence.

22

EMBER

*E*mber clung to the scaffolding with one arm and leg wrapped around the bars, leaning out carefully as she replaced the color gel that had melted a bit during the day's show. Though she wasn't currently training with her power, there was still plenty to do around the circus, and it was better to keep busy with small jobs than to risk running into Nicu.

Once the sheet was secured, Ember pulled herself back onto the scaffold's landing. Working at this height meant traversing a ladder, but she'd done this job often enough that the stacked rungs didn't hold the same intimidation they'd held when she'd been introduced to them. Ladders certainly hadn't been something she'd ever come across in Trifecta, especially one that reached so high.

Some of the performers would slide down by gripping the vertical bars of the ladder, but Ember wasn't that skilled, or that brave. One step at a time was good enough for her, and then when she reached the larger landing, she switched to the stairs.

On the ground, Ember stood awkwardly for a moment. Though she had worked with the circus since it started, she actually didn't know many of the performers well. Vaelros' was the only name she truly remembered. At first, she'd figured that it was just because she was Shade and Reyar's protégé, and that the time she spent training was the reason it was difficult to get close to anyone. But it hadn't escaped her notice that Nicu didn't have the same reception. He knew at least a few of the dragon caretakers' names, along with the dragons.

So she'd started trying harder. To put faces to tasks, to listen as the Fae spoke to each other and catch their names through eavesdropping. Yesterday she'd been brave enough to try one out, thanking Nami after they'd finished wiping down the makeup stations. Nami had looked startled, then smiled shyly, and the next thing Ember knew, she was having lunch with a group of the female Fae. She hadn't had much to say, but it had been nice to be invited, and by the end she'd had another invitation to tonight's bonfire.

Ember had been equal parts excited and nervous all day. She tried to remember as many names as she could and use them, and found that it made working with the group more comfortable. Even comforting. It reminded her of a few moments that she'd experienced with Chase and Aaron back in Trifecta, and when a pang hit her chest, she realized she missed that. Missed them.

It was all Nicu's fault, but in a way that wasn't necessarily bad. So when she made her way to the evening's bonfire, she wasn't quite as irritated as she could have been to see him already there, sitting on a folding chair with a tall cup in his hand, head tilted toward the dragon caretaker who was speaking to him.

Ember blinked slowly at this new version of Nicu. He appeared relaxed in a way she'd never seen him before, even with Branna or Edan. Would this be the version of Nicu that existed if he hadn't had to work as her guardian for all these years?

Guilt ate at the edges of Ember's long-held anger. She never considered there'd be a different side to Nicu than the domineering Fae who demanded control over her life. Yet, that erosive guilt pulled forward truths that illuminated how it hadn't been all bad between them. He'd saved her. Protected her. There were days he merely walked silently with her, knowing she had nothing to say, but recognizing she didn't want to be alone.

He'd sent Chase to her, which she'd originally been resentful about, but with her newfound nostalgia, she realized it might have actually been sweet. He'd given her someone safe. Someone supportive. A friend.

Nami appeared at her side, handing Ember a drink of something that popped and sparkled. She took a sip and hummed in pleasure at the fruity tang.

"So what is the real story of Nicu?" Nami demanded with a wink. As if they were waiting for that exact question, two other females joined them. Ember scrambled to remember their names, sure they'd been at yesterday's lunch. Laina and Evra.

"Yes!" Laina exclaimed, pulling Ember further from Nicu, likely so they could ask their questions without him overhearing.

"Oh, no." A male Fae came up behind the group of four, arms spread wide as he shoved them all toward the fire. "You ladies are not going to keep this story to yourselves. We all want to hear it."

"Karis," Laina complained, though her face split in a large smile as she maneuvered herself so she was close to the guy directing them. For Ember's part, she worked to walk ahead, finding an empty seat before she was forced into one. When she looked up, taking in a deep breath filled with pine and mist, her eyes connected with Nicu's where he sat five chairs down.

"Okay, first question," Evra claimed, sitting sideways in the chair next to Ember so she was facing her fully. "Is it true that you two are mates?"

"No!" Ember exclaimed, shaking her head. "Nicu's mate is Fae."

"That bond broke," Nicu inserted, and Ember's eyes flashed to his again. Evra squealed, and she twisted to meet him.

"It's because of the Fate marks, right? Something happened with Ember, and it broke your mate bond so you could come after the girl you really love?"

Ember choked on the fizzy drink and it rose up her nose, causing her to bend over in a thick cough. Love?

"How is that the rumor?" Ember demanded.

"He broke through the Veil for you." Nami's breathy voice came from her right, and Ember's mouth dropped open as if she might find words somewhere in the empty space of her brain.

"You are not at all like Terran Fae." Ember redirected her attention to Nicu. "What happened to Branna? Is she okay?"

Nicu hesitated, his gaze flickering over the crowd before he offered a small shrug. "Her temperament is much the same."

Which Ember interpreted to mean the necromancer was still incredibly angry at both of them.

"Ooh, what does that mean?" Laina asked, leaning next to Ember's ear, betraying that she'd been standing behind her the whole time. Ember's shoulders rose to her ears, and she glared at Nicu, who had pointedly looked away. Where was his convenient interference now?

"You do not get out of this," Ember declared. She opened the flow of power and shot a burst of energy in Nicu's direction. Still within the dragon field, the blue sparks were clearly visible as the fist-sized projectile aimed for Nicu's face.

Then his tattoos moved across his hands, a single line of Ink erupting from his skin to catch and wrap around the energy. The Ink glowed blue before Nicu released the power in a flash of light, changing her pure energy into cosmic glitter.

For a moment, the only sound in the night was the crackling of the large fire. Dozens of Fae eyes danced between Ember and Nicu, as if waiting for the second act of the show.

"I heard," someone murmured, "but I haven't been able to watch them practice—"

"What else can they do?"

"Is Shade going to make them an act?"

"Ember, can I use your power, too?"

Though the last question blended in with the rest, it gained her instant attention. Karis had been the one to ask, hunger brightening his eyes. His fingers flicked toward Ember, and she flinched. The crowd appeared ignorant of the tension growing between her and the man standing two feet away. Excited Fae filled the night with more questions, or turned to speak amongst themselves. Ember shifted in her chair, wondering if she dared to stand even as the Karis reached for her.

The party hushed when Nicu placed his body between that outreached hand and Ember, his own grip wrapped around the offending Fae's wrist.

"Do not touch her."

"So she can share with others?" Karis didn't retreat, his cheeks flushed with excitement. "She can give us a taste of magic again. An unlimited source—"

Nicu's free hand lashed out, tapping Karis in his throat hard enough to stop his words and knock him to the ground. Under the watchful eyes of the stunned Fae, Nicu faced Ember, his cold amber eyes locked on hers. No words needed, Ember rose from her chair and left her overly warm position next to the fire. In this moment she had no argument with him. Karis' simple question had turned the gathering from fun to dangerous.

"You're lucky it was Nicu," someone hissed in the background, likely berating Karis. "If Shade had seen that—"

Ember's stride increased as she walked as fast as she could

without breaking into a run. It wasn't fair. She'd just reached out. Just started making connections.

And once again, it was her power that ruined everything.

Ember eventually slowed to a stop, the landscape shifting into a more solid surface. Her leg caught against one of the rocks, and the sharp edges scraped her through the thin linen of her pants. She pulled away, backing up a step that left her pressed against Nicu's chest. Her gasp was barely in her lungs by the time he slipped to her side, looking down at what had stopped her.

"Ah. The rose garden."

Ember's brow wrinkled, her thoughts scrambled with his unexpected statement. "What?"

"The formations." He directed Ember to look down. What appeared to be a cluster of striped balls had risen from the ground, all stuck together. The lines angled around each other, almost in a sharp, geometric spiral. "This crystal is called a desert rose. These must have been here for a long time. It requires water to form."

Water that these Fae hadn't seen in ages. She looked back toward the gathering, wondering how many of them had lived during the days this land was lush. How many had been born later, and only knew this version of Gypsum? Would they ever get a chance to see green forests again?

A long, encouraging whistle floated through the air, and a thin arm waved against the fire-cast light, followed by a slightly vulgar gesture of encouragement. Ember blushed against the enthusiasm that poured off of Nami, and she shook her head.

"I guess that display isn't squashing any rumors."

"There was no stopping them, anyway." Nicu straightened and studied the group of Fae who took turns openly watching them. "May I ask a question?"

The request only added to the surreal atmosphere of the night. Why was he asking permission?

"What is it?" she responded cautiously. Was he going to bring up the idea of returning to Trifecta, or maybe dig deeper into why she was so determined to stick with Reyar and Shade?

"How do you know when I am approaching?"

"Pine and mist," she answered automatically. His brow lowered slightly as he silently requested more information. Since he already knew she could sense him, she didn't see any reason not to tell him the rest. "It's your essence, I think. I have always been able to perceive it. You. I thought you found me the same way."

"No," he replied quietly. "I studied you. I know your patterns. Preferences. And I never stop looking until I find you."

"Oh." Ember's word was short, her voice small. His answer was unexpected. Somehow intimate.

"We should talk about tonight," Nicu proposed.

"No."

"You saw. They know. It is no longer safe for you to stay here."

"I'm sorry to break it to you, Nicu, but I'm not safe anywhere."

"You are safe with me."

Ember's laugh was harsh. Dry.

"You nearly got me killed."

A heavy sigh escaped from Nicu. He did not deny the charges. He didn't defend them either.

"Look." Ember wrapped her arms around her torso. "We're kind of getting along tonight. Let's not ruin it."

Nicu answered with a slow blink, then a minute dip of his chin. He stepped back to give her more space. Then his body stiffened, and he jumped away from the spot he'd been standing.

"What?" Ember demanded, her power flaring to life, coating her skin, but Nicu wasn't acting as if he was ready for battle. He was cautious, slow, glancing at her out of the corner of his eye before he lifted a single hand, pressing his palm against the solid air he'd backed into.

Ember's own eyes widened, and she stepped forward, careful of the gypsum roses at her feet. Slightly in front of Nicu, she raised her own arm, knowing what she would find before she made contact with the invisible boundary.

"What does this mean?" Ember whispered.

Nicu shook his head, slipping his hands into his pockets as if he'd already come to accept this change in events, echoed in the flat tones of his easy answer.

"It does not mean anything," he assured her. "At least, it is nothing new."

23

NICU

In Trifecta, Nicu's days had often been monotonous, repetitive. Branna complained about it so often that he'd banned her from speaking of it. But his days had never dragged on like these last three in Gypsum had.

He thought that their display at the bonfire would push the circus Fae away. He'd been wrong. Every day after their practice, Ember had been claimed by Nami and her weapons performer group for lunch where, as far as he could tell, they talked about mock-battle strategies and offered Ember their own tips on her performance with the dragons. Nicu, on the other hand, had been adopted by the dragon caretakers, where he mostly ignored their probing questions.

It was community in a way he hadn't experienced, even for that single day with Altaya's hunters. It was comfortable.

It was dangerous.

He'd promised Devi to remember. He'd taken to carrying the Witch's bracelet token in his pocket as a reminder that they were not here to make friends. To create a home.

They had bought time by slipping into Gypsum's timestream, but that did not mean they were excused from what happened on Trifecta. Nicu needed to remind Ember of the same, but pinning her down was a challenge, and not just because of their newfound community.

Nicu did not want to disturb the peace strung between them like a web of fragile spun glass.

"By the way, you don't have to worry about Karis anymore."

Nicu looked up from his work on Torus to study Mize. The Fae's lips were thinned as if the news he wanted to share wasn't entirely pleasant, but he also didn't disagree.

"Karis?" Nicu asked.

"The Fae who talked about Ember's power," Mize explained. "Shade heard about it, and she told him to leave."

"Hmm," Nicu vocalized, returning to his task as if the situation was of no matter to him. But there was a change in Mize's tone that had ignited Nicu's need for answers. He replayed the short conversation, trying to pinpoint the exact shift that had caught his attention.

Shade had told Karis to leave. That's where it was. The slight catch in the middle suggesting distress was buried under general acceptance. From the fear of being fired?

With a flash, understanding settled into place. Nicu's fingers gripped the brush until his knuckles paled. Shade had a skill separate from her control of her Ink, one Nicu had no hope of replicating. One that instructed others what to do, and their bodies simply followed.

Karis had been told to leave.

Ember being ordered to stand. To follow Shade. Movements he'd disapproved of as proof of the Trimarked Child's lack of control.

But maybe it was by Siren command.

It took considerable restraint not to drop his brush in the bucket and rush away from Mize. He did not want to disrupt their routines, at least not with Devi still unaccounted for. Nicu thought of the bracelet in his pocket and wondered if he should use it soon. Or perhaps the Witch only needed a little more time.

He wasn't sure they had it.

Once he could disengage himself from Mize without drawing suspicion, Nicu withdrew to the small house he shared with Ember, Shade, and in theory, Reyar. Frustration settled at the base of his spine when he found it empty, having hoped Ember might come back for a short rest before her performance this afternoon. That perhaps fate and luck would be on his side and he could speak to her while Shade herself was performing. That she'd listen, and believe, and agree with him that it was time to leave. Then he could summon Devi whether or not she'd met with their Goddess and get them all out of Gypsum.

In a reckless move, Nicu drew forward the conundrum of his fate-mandated choice. Considering the weight of the Fae's needs against Ember's. Wondering if choosing to take her from here affected his agreement with the universal powers. Yet he felt no pressure from either Fate or Chaos. In fact, the Power retreated, clearly unwilling to be manipulated by such a simple, juvenile plan.

Then he would have to act on his own.

Nicu abandoned the small home, his strides cutting across the sand in a line so straight, he felt suddenly exposed, as if his every move was telegraphed. He'd never been able to accomplish such a direct path in Trifecta. Yet another reason to want to return home.

Once free of the ruins, he walked toward the arena's staff entrance, keeping his stride measured so it appeared as if he weren't in a hurry. There was little rush anyway, since he could not approach Ember before her performance. She could not miss it without raising suspicion. No matter how their conversation turned out, he didn't want the emotions of it affecting the clear head she would need for her battle with the dragons.

Mock or not, it was dangerous, and she needed to remain sharp.

Nicu listened from outside the big tent with his eyes closed. Since his arrival, he'd marked the general routine of the show. This side of the arena generally remained empty throughout the performance. The dragons rested in their field unless they were due to perform, and they always entered through the other end where the space was made specifically for the large creatures' entrance. Though Shade could, and did, interrupt the usual flow whenever she wanted, the rest of the acts followed the same pattern, including Ember's.

The bell toll gave away the start of her thirty-minute match. Nicu breathed through the seconds, counting down until there were only a few minutes left. Backstage, a different frenzy would have begun as they put finishing touches on the next act while preparing to accept Ember and the dragons from this one.

He slipped in, using the business of the Fae as his own cover. He was familiar to the crew now and did not draw unnecessary attention. Still, he did not search the area for curious eyes, not wanting to give off an air of suspicion. He timed his crossing well, stopping beside that space of in-between where acts had a moment to themselves after their performance. Nicu had learned it was one of the few times Ember was completely alone.

Raucous applause marked the completion of Ember's show, drowning out the sound of the timer going off. Nicu waited to ensure the ongoing act was in their respective space and not spilling into the outgoing chamber, and then he slipped in to wait.

Ember entered the dark room beyond the arena, her eyes already closed to take in what she assumed would be her solitude. Yet the way her head tilted and her eyelids weren't completely relaxed alerted Nicu that she was aware of his presence. Pine and mist, she'd said, assuming it was his essence.

Beside them, the next performers rustled and rushed out onto the stage floor, not wanting to leave it empty for long. Nicu retained his silence, grateful Ember kept hers. He studied her features, painted in shades of green and gold to mimic dragon scales. The paint was a work of art, highlighting Ember's inner strength in ways he hadn't noticed from a distance. The makeup artist had instilled Ember's spirit into those painted lines. Nicu's chest ached, and he couldn't decide if he liked it or not.

There was no surprise in Ember's eyes when they fluttered open after a few deep breaths, confirming she'd known he was there. Nicu wondered where his scent of pine and mist came from. Wondered why he couldn't sense her in the same way.

"I need to speak with you," Nicu murmured, flinching at the obvious nature of the statement.

"You want me to go back." Ember's tone was flat. Certain.

"I want us to go home."

The words came out with more force than Nicu expected. He raised his gaze above her head and took a deep breath.

"The barrier has cracked. Branna's powers have grown. The ghost of Edan—"

"Are you blaming me for that, too?"

The snap in Ember's words drew Nicu's attention back to her face. Her light gray eyes were narrowed, powerful even without the dragon scale makeup. The shift from calm post-performance was gone, replaced with the rise of a deep, hidden resentment. Her eyes were as hard as the first day he'd arrived here, the small threads of peace that connected them vibrating dangerously.

"If Branna's more powerful, you certainly don't need me."

"Edan disagrees."

"Again back to Edan." Ember took a step backward, her arms wrapped around her chest. "Is his death why you let that Fae shoot me?"

"I do not know why you are so upset."

"You don't know?" Ember's eyes narrowed. "That Branna attacked me even before your other Fae friend? That she tried to use her shadows against me before the humans' presence stopped her?"

"I did not." Nicu breathed through his nose. "Both of them acted without my permission."

"And that makes it okay?"

"No."

Ember's skin darkened, and her lips pinched as if holding back an explosion of words. An asynchronous note of pride filled his chest as she swallowed them down, showing her strength of control. Then Ember broke eye contact and looked around the small tent as if wondering about ears on the other side. Nicu didn't care who heard at this point, unless they tried to stop him.

"This is about more than you and me," Nicu countered, reaching deep to recall anything that would appeal to Ember and break through the emotions so she could begin to think rather than react. "There are enemies who want access to Trifecta."

"So you want me to defend the people who tried to kill me? Twice? At least twice. Have there been more, Nicu? Would you know?"

Ember's line of questioning forced Nicu to pause. A few weeks ago he would have answered that with what he believed to be a forthright denial of any unknown attacks. But after a week here, after seeing the dying world that Wist and the Council worked so hard to protect the Trifectan Fae from, he was no longer certain how far his people might go, or how deep their secrets delved. He could not give her an honest and true answer for the Fae, much less for the other races, so he turned to the facts he had.

"With this new threat, the Fae will close their borders, possibly the Coven as well. The Watchers will attack the humans. The Halfers. Chase and Aaron. Your mother."

Ember's eyes flashed with blue power. The coating on her skin wrapped over itself, creating a shell as thick as he'd ever seen her make for Shade.

She reacted as if attacked.

"The Watchers are worse than the Queen. Little hybrid—"

"You want me to go back to people who never helped me. Who used me and treated me like an amusement just so that I could bring home food to a mother who cares more for Halfer children than she ever did me."

Truth with exaggeration. Nicu did not have time for her temper tantrum.

"You have been protected your entire life by individuals you have regarded as nothing but jailers. People who have sacrificed their place in their own societies to make sure you were educated. Housed. Clothed. Who worked hard every time you made yourself known to ensure your actions did not raise suspicion. That an angry human, Fae, or Witch did not follow you to your home and set it on fire while you slept."

"As if anyone would care enough."

"You are correct only in the part that they would not care if you were harmed. That has always been the problem. You are insignificant to them. So easily erased in their minds. It would mean nothing to them to find you dead."

Ember's skin paled, and Nicu took a deep breath, hoping he'd finally gotten through to her.

"And those are the people you want me to help."

Nicu realized his mistake too late.

"No."

How could he have done this? Why choose those words? Why mention the danger to her?

What was happening? All he wanted was to regain control. To remind her why she'd listened to him for so long. To have her recognize his sacrifices, note all the actions he'd taken to ensure her safety.

Yet he'd lost control in trying to keep it. Expressed truths he never should have, shown emotions best left behind.

"Little hybrid."

Ember flinched at his quiet moniker and tried to brush past him.

Unbidden anger flushed through Nicu's body, and his hand wrapped around her upper arm before she got to his side. She stopped under his firm grip but refused to meet his eyes.

He didn't blame her, yet it was all her fault. He wanted to mark her, to remind her of who had always protected her. Who kept her on balance even when she dared to fall off. Falling all the way into Gypsum because she broke the rule to never cross the border. Agreeing to grow and train her power that should have never existed to begin with. To dare to break ties with him in favor of strangers who clearly meant to use her.

Nicu's tattoos swarmed, leaving his skin for hers, mummifying her forearm and tying her directly to his side. He wanted to wrap her entire body up then and there. To drag her to the place he'd arrived with Devi. Force her to open their way home and end this farce.

Like Brandt. Like Tristan.

Nicu ripped his focus from his tattoos and focused on Ember's face. Her features were flat, yet her eyes shone behind a thick layer of unshed tears. His heartbeat stuttered. He instantly retracted his Ink and released his hold.

"I am sorry."

He was the first of them to leave the tent.

24

EMBER

*E*mber stared at the point where the curtain closed on Nicu. Her chest rose and fell so fast, she might be taking flight if it weren't for the fact that her feet were firmly rooted to the ground.

How dare he.

How dare he!

Lecture her. Demand her what? Allegiance? Just because the Fae had ordered him to take care of her and he took his job a little too personally?

Applause from the arena shocked Ember into awareness. The act that followed her was finished and would be exiting through where she stood.

With full strides, she left the decompression room. By habit, she made her way to costumes but was so distracted, Vaelros kicked her out before she could offer any help. Assuming she would have. Ember was so lost in the storm within her head, she didn't recall changing, or having her makeup scrubbed off, or any of the things that were usually just hard enough to keep her attention on them.

Rather, she was sifting through the events of her life. Random memories floated up, all fighting for their time in the spotlight, screaming at her to remember when Nicu told her she could no longer go to school. That she wasn't allowed to visit human friends. Where Aaron struggled to understand why she chose to trust the humans over the Fae. Where her mother tapped out before Ember had turned ten, leaving her to figure out how to keep them alive even though she was just a child.

Each memory scraped against her heart, cut into her nerve endings. Each rendition became louder, every image so bright it blurred into a hurricane of pain and loneliness that blew away any shred of peace she'd managed to gather these months in Gypsum.

"Ember!"

The sensation of being shaken broke against the storm. Ember blinked, the features before her slowly morphing into a wide brow above deep, dark eyes. Shade.

"Yes?"

Shade's mouth opened and shut once, then she leaned back.

"Are you okay? You have been wandering amongst the dragons as if you want to get stomped by accident. You did not hear me call."

"Oh."

Ember looked around, noticing the dragon field for the first time. A few drakes glared toward her, and a large dragon pointedly shifted its head away. Apparently, she'd caused some trouble and wasn't aware of it. There were clear rules about wandering in the dragon fields as the adults could easily flick a tail and knock someone over. Had they been struggling to keep her safe?

"I'm sorry."

"Whatever. You are fine. They are fine." Shade paused. "Are you fine?"

"Just stuck in my thoughts. I'm sorry."

Shade let out a long breath and shook her head.

"Are you really sure? Because I have news and I do not want to overload you if there is something else going on."

"No, it's all past nonsense with nothing to do with the present. I'm sure whatever you have will be a good distraction."

Shade nodded, then strategically pulled Ember away from the dragon fields, keeping wide of the arena.

"I have news of Reyar." Shade's voice was low enough that it wouldn't travel across the desert landscape. "They have not been successful."

Ember's stomach dropped.

"Is Devi…"

Shade's hand slashed through the air. "They are not harmed. It is just not done. I was able to do the research I wanted. Our backup plan is risky. I do not want to lie to you about that. But there are precautions we can take."

"What is it?"

Shade hesitated long enough that Ember's frown grew deep. Was this a silence that hid something? Should Ember give Shade the benefit of the doubt and accept that some things were just hard to explain?

"It is a way to increase your power safely. To strengthen your body to accept it. To provide you with what is needed in order to rejuvenate the energies of Gypsum and offer us a chance to reset. To survive."

It sounded amazing.

"It sounds too good to be true."

"And it would have been when you first arrived," Shade agreed. "I would not have suggested it if I had not seen how you absorbed my lightning the other day at practice. If you had not shown how you could share energy with Nicu while maintaining your shield."

An uncomfortable weight settled between Ember's shoulder blades.

"Shade, Nicu and I are different."

"Because you are close."

"We are not that kind of close." Ember's words flew out of her mouth like a swarm of angry wasps. Shade's lips twitched up, down, then flattened, as if she couldn't decide on an emotion.

"You told me there was Promise Magic involved," Shade remembered. "That was broken? And it scarred Nicu."

Ember nodded. "There's more to our connection, though. I just don't know what it is."

"Whatever it was, it is gone."

Ember shrugged, but the weight didn't dislodge.

"You have been around dragons for the past week," Shade said. "If there were still strands of magic holding you together, we would have noticed them by now."

Ember understood Shade's logic, but she didn't believe it. They hadn't seen any magical ties connecting Reyar to Devi, either, yet there was no denying the powerful magnetism between the two.

"You said Nicu and I were god-touched," Ember recalled. "What if it's something like that? Something stronger than magic?"

"Then the question is: do you want to keep it?"

Ember noted the lack of denial. Maybe Shade noticed something, too, but without proof, they could only guess at the truth. And her question worked either way. Did she want to stay connected to Nicu? Her possessive, demanding, unfeeling Fae?

Ember flinched at her own thoughts. He was not hers. She was not his. Whatever connections that claimed them had no right to take her autonomy away.

"This procedure. Ceremony? What happens then? If there is a connection?"

Shade pulled them both to a stop and connected her gaze with Ember's.

"It will burn away. It will reach through space and time

and take apart anything that holds you to your old life and forge a new path forward."

Ember's lungs filled with air, her inhales and exhales keeping tight at the top. Her eyes widened as the edges of her vision faded.

A new start. One where she controlled her future.

"Do we go now?"

Shade turned back toward the distant line of the ruins. "No. I have a few things to gather. You clearly need some rest. Take a bath. Run through a few recovery poses. Sleep."

Ember shook her head. "Why not now? If Nicu finds out—"

"Do not tell him," Shade interrupted in her musical tones. "You cannot let him know."

"He has a way of learning things."

Shade pursed her lips, and her wrist twisted as if she might call forth her whip, but the Ink stayed put, wrapped around her arm.

"Straight to the tent. Bath, stretches, sleep. I'll take care of everything else, no matter what happens."

Ember nodded, and they walked the rest of the way in silence. Shade entered the tent with Ember to ensure it was empty, then with a glance heavy with warning, she went off to prepare.

Ember remained facing the door. She'd sensed what Shade hadn't. A whiff of pine and mist wrapped around the tent. Nicu had stayed out of sight, likely waiting for Shade to leave. Within moments, Ember's theory was proven correct as Nicu pressed his way inside. He stopped short, his jerky halt suggesting he was surprised to find she hadn't hidden in her room.

She showed no hesitation in meeting this gaze. She wouldn't back down. Despite what she'd said to Shade, Ember knew how to keep secrets from Nicu; she just didn't put it past him to find out in other ways.

Nicu's lips parted and Ember raised her hand.

"I am not in the mood to speak to you."

"I misspoke before. I should have chosen different words."

"You told me the truth as only a Fae can. Your tactics simply didn't work out like you expected."

Nicu's cheeks darkened, and he didn't add to the argument.

"I'm not saying something bad isn't happening in Trifecta," Ember validated. "Clearly, we have time on our side while we're in Gypsum. Let's wait for Devi before we make a decision."

"I would rather be ready to go when she arrives."

"I really don't care what you prefer right now, Nicu." His color rose, and he took a step closer to her, staring down at her with his heavy brow lowered to cast menacing shadows across his features. More of the same tactics she'd seen her whole life.

Here in true Gypsum, though, she was the one with an entire people behind her. He was the outcast just being allowed to hang around.

Ember stuck her hands in her pockets, finding the gem Devi had passed to her and taking it in her grip. She approached Nicu slowly, waiting for an opening to complete her next task.

"I'm curious," she murmured. "All that stuff you said. I know Fae always tell the truth. I also know that a Fae truth is relative."

Ember's empty hand reached out and gripped his forearm. Her fingers were too short to encircle his wrist as he could hers, but it didn't matter. She wanted to be skin to skin with his Ink trapped between them.

"Do you really mean that I don't matter?"

"Yes."

The answer stung. Ember snatched back her arm. Nicu growled as she turned away.

"That is not a simple question."

"Yet it was a simple answer," she threw over her shoulder,

refusing to face him. Refusing to show him the extra moisture added to her eyes. Never mind that she'd been the one to ask.

The question hadn't been important. It was only supposed to be a distraction.

That didn't stop the answer from breaking her heart.

"You will listen."

Ember ignored his shout on the way to her room. Her fingers trembled as she tied the interior knots, effectively locking the door. She sensed pine and mist from the other side and backed slowly away. Once in her private space, she breathed in, the air stuttering through the cracks in Ember's emotions, rattling her ribcage on each inhale. It didn't matter. It was done.

She'd used the distraction to drop Devi's stone into Nicu's pocket. Whatever the Witch had meant to do with it, the responsibility was no longer hers. One less loose end.

Two, actually. Nicu's answer had given her closure at least, and now she wouldn't have to see him until she wanted to.

After she was done with Shade, maybe never again.

25

DEVI

Devi groaned just a little less as she climbed the four flights of stairs to her room. After nearly two weeks of making the same trip, her body was used to the stress. Still, her thighs burned by the time she got to the suite, and all she wanted to do was collapse on the couch. But that would leave her exposed and vulnerable, so she headed toward her bedroom instead.

"There have been a lot of interesting rumors in the neighborhood."

Devi stopped in her tracks, raising her gaze to where Reyar stood in his room's doorway, arms crossed as he leaned against the frame. She hadn't spoken to him since the afternoon he'd interrupted her with Oren, and had only gone right back out the next day to find other ways to keep herself busy and away from him.

"Interesting," she replied, reaching for politeness. "I'm tired, though, so no need to chat."

She only made it two more steps.

"Apparently, someone is making the old fruit groves bloom." Reyar pushed from the doorway of his bedroom and walked into the living room, his glittering eyes and flat lips giving nothing away. "At first, they thought it must be one of the gods, of course. But then someone went to investigate and glimpsed cranberry curls and heard the sound of footsteps as the person escaped."

"Oh?" Devi asked, raising a brow. She hadn't been caught, so she wasn't entirely certain what his concern was.

"We discussed this. It is not wise to work Witch magic in a Fae city."

"We did not, in fact, have that conversation. And there are other Witches here working with the earth."

"Magic is only used for simple things."

"I would think growing food to be a simple thing. Especially since it can help save lives."

"It will all just die once you leave."

Devi stiffened, her chin raised in defiance.

"Not my spells."

Reyar's jaw clenched, and he stepped closer. The length of the couch stretched between them, a physical barrier that also held memories neither one of them wanted to dwell on.

"A few small groves will not save the realm."

"Isn't that what we're for?" Devi asked. Reyar's fingers curled into white-knuckled fists.

"I have done what I can. As has Shade."

"The goddess—"

"Azhirith demands too much! I am saving us from a sacrifice no one should be forced to make!"

Right, Devi remembered. Emotions. Desires. Connections.

"I would never force you to abandon what you love," Devi spoke quietly. The tension drained from Reyar and his torso leaned in her direction. The softening warned her that he was close to allowing his resolve to break. Then he would cross the apartment in a few long strides and take her in his arms.

She might be able to make it to her room first, but Devi's feet remained planted against the wood planks. Because it had been her talk of love that had stopped him, that had brought that light to his eyes, and she was losing the strength required to protect herself.

"Reyar," she whispered, and it was enough. He had her wrapped up against him, one hand buried in her hair as he pressed his nose against her neck.

"Devi." Her name was a vibration that originated in his chest and shook her entire body.

And between them, a scalding white flame that forced them apart.

"Wh-what?" Devi asked, eyes wide as her fingertips brushed her belly where she'd felt the burn. Reyar cursed, lifting his tunic to reveal his hip pack and pulled out the dragon bone fragment.

"Your timing is perfect as always, Azhirith," he grumbled. Reyar caught the bone in his palm and wrapped his fingers tightly, staring at her with the taut features of someone experiencing regret.

Because they were interrupted? Or because without it, they would have done so much more?

"I suppose we can't keep a goddess waiting," Devi said, aiming for a flippant tone while pretty sure it had fallen flat. She made her way to the door. As she opened it, Reyar appeared behind her, running his touch along the inside of her left arm until their fingers interlocked.

It was becoming a habit, she realized, the way that he took her hand. It might be what she ended up missing the most.

The walk to the temple was short but crowded as people jostled each other around food carts, then picked any empty spot to eat while those who couldn't afford to pay watched on with shaded, longing eyes. Devi frowned, knowing her work in the tiny orchards in the neighborhood was only a miniscule gesture, and hoped that no matter what came from this meeting with the goddess, there'd be a way to help out even more before she had to return to Trifecta.

As they had on that first day, Reyar navigated their way to

the steps of Azhirith's temple. The acolyte waited for them at the top. Reyar dropped the dragon bone into their open palms, and then the figure disappeared through the door. This time it remained open to the shadowed interior so they could follow.

Reyar's grip tightened on Devi's, stopping her from heading in immediately. He placed a hand on her hip, gently turning her so they faced each other, his lips parted as if a question balanced on the edge of his tongue.

Devi held her breath, wondering if he'd ask it. Wondering what her answer would be.

But it appeared neither of them liked to live in lies because Reyar tore his gaze from her and shoved their way in. Once inside, Reyar slipped his hand from hers, and he surged further into the surprisingly bright interior.

Devi's feet remained rooted in the entryway, using the excuse of taking in her surroundings. Despite the shadows she'd experienced from the outside, the interior was filled with white, reflective stone. A polished floor, like veinless marble. Small alcoves on either side of the entrance held statues about half her size. The one on the right was a long-handled torch with supple-looking curved flames. On the left, a deep black bone stood on a custom base, its length broken on either end. She approached it slowly, thumbing the ring on her right hand, wondering if the bones were from the same departed creature.

"Devi."

Reyar's breath brushed over Devi's curls, and she turned wide eyes to her companion. He'd adopted Nicu's stoic features again. Was it to hide things? To force himself to act as he wished to feel?

There was only one way to find out. Devi straightened her shoulders and nodded. It was time to meet a god.

Further into the interior, Reyar and Devi discovered a maze of squared-off pathways that all looked the same. The slate stone floors had soft depressions of elongated lines, echoes of the thousands of feet that walked them. The walls stood twice the height of Reyar, the ceilings flat, everything unadorned. Rectangular windows cut through the ceiling, showing off a sunset purple sky with only the brightest stars currently visible.

The most unnerving part was that there were no other people. Only Devi and Reyar's footsteps echoed in the halls. Only their bodies warmed the air.

"How do you know which way to go?" Devi asked.

"Practice."

One dismissive word and Devi's stomach bottomed out. She gave herself a mental shake, shedding the dark feelings trying to grip her heart. He was not worth it, not like this. She would not allow herself to care for someone who didn't care in return.

In another time. The whispered thought remained, clinging to a hope that refused to die. Devi narrowed her eyes against the false promise. She did not live in that other time. It wasn't promised to come. Devi believed in facts, made decisions based on what was. Exploring what might be only worked with magic, not people. Not unless they were exploring with you as well.

After Devi was truly and hopelessly lost, Reyar directed them toward what felt like the center of the maze as all hallways seemed to converge into one. A squared, enclosed structure stood separated and displayed the only set of double doors she'd seen. Reyar paused before them, whether for ceremony or due to hidden thoughts, Devi couldn't guess. She crossed her arms and waited, her toe tapping. The sound drew Reyar's attention to her for a second that dragged into a moment and then into minutes.

"There's no turning back." His voice spoke of a warning, but his eyes shimmered with loss. Devi was tired of guessing if he looked at her with truth or magic.

"I don't know my way back, anyway."

Devi strode forward and pressed her left hand against the

pale beech wood of the simple, paneled doors. They swung open at her touch and offered an invitation into the darkness. The sound of Reyar's footsteps betrayed his movement behind her, but Devi didn't wait and crossed the threshold without him.

The doors slammed shut, leaving her alone. A slow look around showed the room wasn't dark, only dressed in black, the exact opposite of the halls without. Though the exterior had presented as a large square block, the interior proved to be a round, cylindrical place. Black marble lined the floors and walls, which stretched on without the interruption of furniture. She'd expected an altar of some sort, maybe a statue, yet even those were lacking.

Reyar's fists pounded on the door, yet didn't echo, as if the space swallowed the unwelcome sound. If he shouted, Devi didn't hear it.

So he hadn't been meant to enter. Fine. Devi could do this on her own.

Not certain what was expected of her, Devi slowly paced along the outer edge of the room with mindful steps, remaining aware in case anything changed. A few spirals in, Reyar's pounding no longer reached her ears. He might have given up, or perhaps the space had eaten up all the sound energy at this point.

Devi let thoughts of Reyar fall away as she concentrated on her movements. Circling the room in smaller and smaller turns. The depth of the black marble intensified with her senses, invading more than her sight. Heavy bubbles filled her ears. Her fingertips danced over thickened air, and her nose cooled with the scent of earth and stone. She lost track of the spiral, unable to tell if she was getting closer to the center, or if she'd passed it and somehow continued inwards.

Turning one more arc, Devi saw the goddess's tail first. A sense of layered shadows lined with a red so dark, it was another shade of black. The long appendage shifted, exposing tapered talons at the end of four thick toes, which were instantly blocked from sight by the lowering of her massive head, an elegant bone frill tucked against her neck.

Bright purple eyes fixed on Devi, a curious angle to the slit pupils. Her chin lowered without resting on the ground, the gust of breath that eased from her towering nostrils surprisingly cool.

"You came alone."

"He wasn't worth it." As if Devi had thought it through. As if she'd slammed the door on Reyar herself.

"Is he the one who isn't worth it? Or is it the suffering you don't want?"

"No one wants to be hurt."

"Yet pain is necessary, and in many times worthwhile."

"And you'll guarantee my current heartbreak will result in a future reward?"

"There are no guarantees, little one. Only Truths."

Devi pursed her lips. She was here to be free of Reyar, not to talk about him.

"Reyar said you might accept a trade, one that would release us from each other."

"He really knows better."

The dragon turned her head so that one large purple eye focused on Devi. It looked like a challenge or a dare to see if Devi could piece together what the deity implied.

He knew asking was futile, but came anyway. He brought her along, claiming that their request would only be granted if they were together. He wasn't here, but that wasn't the reason Azhirith gave for why it wouldn't work.

Devi wished she'd gathered more information, but Reyar hadn't shared much. What did he think they could have accomplished? He clearly wanted their bond severed. He must have had a plan.

"I don't understand." The ill-tasting words dripped from Devi's mouth, and she pursed her lips against them.

"Not yet. But you will, which means it's knowledge that you can access, Goddess-born."

Goddess-born. Goddess-touched. Not Goddess-made. Yet?

The dragon's head retracted and cast a shadow over her body, the goddess's entire image fading into its depth.

Darkness filled Devi's vision again, but this time it was criss-crossed with millions of rainbow-glimmering woven threads. Devi gasped, spinning slowly within the transparent lights. She focused on one and her brain locked onto it, her eyes able to trace it from one end of the room to the other as it wove over and under, bent along the ceiling, then arched toward the floor. She didn't lose sight of it until she decided to let it go and try another thread, then another.

This was different from her sketches, different from capturing the pattern of a spell inside a crystal and expanding it. This was the makeup of the surrounding air, of the gaps between the walls. With long steps, Devi found the edge of the room. Her breath quickened with the discovery of more strings of power. Black, iridescent strands crossed each other with a surprising bright pink cutting through the center of the curved wall, and then a deep teal running from ceiling to floor. Her fingertips pressed against them, yet only felt the cool marble of the physical space even as her vision filled with the evidence of magic traveling through the stone and holding it all together.

She'd known the universe was composed of molecules, all interacting and linked, with nothing truly static. She'd noted the crystal-like patterns all things made, and used that discovery as the base of her experiments and her own use of magic.

Devi had never observed it in such a complete way before. Small sections were all she'd been able to grasp, and even then, complex systems had proven frustrating to trace and recreate.

In this moment, she saw it all.

The double doors appeared under her touch and sprung open. Reyar stood with his fist raised, ready for another knock, his eyes reddened, lips thinned, skin flushed. Bright white light concentrated within his body, yet pushed out further than the space of the hall. His aura and his soul.

She gasped as she felt her own spirit expand from the room of black marble. It didn't brush against the makeup of his, but filtered through it. Instinctively, Devi knew most auras brushed each other, passed by and through, yet remained separate at the same time. Her soul blended with Reyar's instead, as if their energies belonged tucked together.

The strands of the universe making up air parted for him. More spun up the height of his body, around its width. Thick, bright white ropes cut through it all, knotted in his center until it trailed to meet the knot within her. Devi instantly understood that these had been placed by Azhirith.

The Goddess of Unveiled Truth might not be willing to undo this spell, but Devi had no such reservations.

She stepped in closer, so focused on the energy she didn't realize she'd pressed against Reyar until his hand wrapped around the small of her back. The feeling filled her with warmth until it overflowed in a gasp, and she shifted her focus from the magic onto his own shifting rainbow gaze.

"Your eyes," he whispered. "They're pools of stars."

As if drawn into the galaxies dancing within her, Reyar leaned in. Their breaths mingled along with their spirits, molecules finally finding their way home. His lips settled on hers because they belonged there.

Devi allowed her lashes to drift shut, absorbed in the moment, not knowing how long it would last, not wanting to rush to the end. Yet this was what she'd come for. This was what she was meant to do.

The magic flared to life within Devi's mind, not needing her physical sight to exist or be seen. With tentacles of power, she reached deep into Reyar, finding the complicated knot at his center. With a gentle tug it released. The white light dissipated between them, taking apart the goddess-created connection with that one simple touch.

Reyar did not let her go.

He wrapped his second arm around her, pulling her in. His breath quickened, and hers rose in answer. Devi let go of the sight of magic, settled into the faded darkness behind her eyelids as she reveled in the feel of his mouth against hers, his body pressed into hers. The physical boundaries of their bodies intensified the connection of their souls, creating a delicious contradiction of sensations that drew goosebumps along every inch of Devi's skin.

Reyar broke the kiss, one hand on the back of her head, one low on her spine as he pulled her in as close as he could, his forehead bent to her shoulder and Devi's face pressed into his neck.

"This part is real, then," Devi breathed. A cooling relief bathed the heated pain she'd been carrying in her torso. Her flushed lips curled against his warm skin.

"The spell is gone." Her smile infected her voice, raising its energy and tone. "And we're still here. You're still here."

Devi suddenly found herself off balance, standing on her own. She reached behind her with blind desperation, finding the polished surface of the wall, leaning against it before she crashed to the floor. Reyar stared at her, features open and drawn as if the truth had pillaged him and left him raw.

Oh, fades. He hadn't known. He hadn't felt it.

His kiss might have been real, but he'd only given in because he thought it had been the magic. He still didn't want it, or her.

"I see." Her throat closed on the words, choking out the sound. She swallowed, but the muscles didn't loosen. "I'm sorry. I assumed you would know."

"Azhirith granted our request?" The height of his voice betrayed his doubt that their petition would be approved.

It was the lifeline she needed. The proof that, in some way, he'd lied to her. It lit a fire in her heart and provided the force necessary to stand on her own.

"It's done," she spoke without answering his question. "You can go back to Shade now."

He flinched, but this time Devi didn't pause to wonder why, didn't hope to think it might mean he hid a secret desire for her that would override a history of devotion.

Instead, she turned away, letting magic show her the way out, keeping her eyes forward and building up a thick wall of ice between her and the fires of loss that consumed her heart.

26

EMBER

Ember paced her room, her hair damp around her shoulders. Water droplets tickled, and she slapped them away, wincing at the accidental force.

How long would it take Shade to come get her? Not that Ember had a real idea of how much time had passed. She'd bathed and changed, but had been too wired to lie down for a nap. Had Shade meant she should sleep because it would take a while for her to be ready? How much could Ember pace before she wore a hole in the woven rug that stuck out from under her bed?

Are you sure you're doing the right thing?

How many questions without answers would she ask, continuing to drive herself crazy?

A noise sounded from the back of her room. Ember spun, facing away from what she thought was the only door to find Shade entering from a hidden fold in the canvas, a pack slung across her shoulders and sinking heavily along her spine. The Fae placed a long-nailed fingertip against her lips, then gestured for Ember to follow her out.

Twilight had fallen, painting the white sands peach and pink. The performers were gathered in pockets around the arena, small fires marking their gathering points as they ate, drank, and laughed. The guests would all be tucked away in their tents per the curfew, which kept them from wandering into the dragon fields or bothering the cast members after hours. No one paid attention to Shade and Ember as they skirted the ruins to pass beyond the rows of guest tents.

"You two are very alike, both pacing around like you might somehow break out of an imaginary cage," Shade noted.

"What are you talking about?"

"Nicu was stalking something across the main room," Shade answered. "It was why I had to create a back entrance."

So not only was he still in the tent, he was likely waiting for her to reemerge. As if she would after he confirmed that she didn't matter.

He was like the others, then. Like Tristan or the humans, just wanting to use her for whatever they thought was important. To drag her back to save his people at the expense of herself. The Trifectan Fae would never let her remain free if they saw how her power had grown. Ember placed a hand over the space between her shoulder and chest where the arrow had pierced her, pressed until the icy core she felt grew to encompass the remembered ache.

Nicu could go fall off. Ember wasn't stupid. She knew she was following another person who wanted to use her and her power. But this way Ember had a choice, and a chance to save not just a people, but a realm. This way, no one would be trying to kill her.

So Ember wouldn't feel. She wouldn't remember. She'd let the fires of her fury make ashes out of the phantom pain of the Fae arrow. Let it burn through the complicated knots lodged in her gut. Let it overtake the cold loneliness she'd lived with for so long, erasing all evidence of a life she didn't need.

Shade led Ember to the ravine that carved through the same physical location as the Pine River that flowed in the Terran realm. A small trail angled down the edge, and Shade's heavy boots knocked stones over the drop as she stomped along, uncaring of the hundred-foot plunge. Ember struggled to keep pace, catching her balance against the wall whenever she slipped.

"Careful now," Shade called. "We need to be at the bottom by moonrise, which gives you enough time to slow down and not fall and break every bone in your body."

Shade increased her pace after that warning. Ember paused, heart hammering over feeling left behind. She looked toward the sky, but without a horizon, she couldn't note how much further the sun had to set. Not that the sunset had anything to do with the moonrise, but it had a lot to do with how well she could see the path.

If Shade wasn't waiting for her, then there must be a reason, and the only way to find out was to finish the descent.

Ember made it to the bottom just as the last daylight faded from the canyon floor, shadows filling the deep crevice even as the upper edges still glowed pink under the vanishing sun. Shade had her pack open next to her, most of it having fallen over and collapsed. She knelt in front of a small fire that she'd surrounded with larger pieces of wood.

"Can I do something?"

Shade shook her head, pulling the bag closer as if she wanted to hide the contents. Ember shifted from foot to foot, a deep frown on her lips as she studied the path she'd just climbed down.

Was this a mistake? What was Shade hiding?

Ember had thought she'd been doing the right thing when she'd helped Tristan, too. Find a way to return the mages to their homes. She hadn't fully understood what that meant for the Fae, and wouldn't have cared if she'd known.

Then she'd met Reyar and Shade. The dragons, Nami, and the other Fae who ran and performed in this circus.

Did Ember want to help Gypsum? Yes.

Did she want to do it blind? Absolutely not.

"What's going on?" Ember rounded the fire so she could see Shade's face. The Fae glanced up, then back to the flames, checking to ensure they burned steadily before she reached into her bag.

"It has to be a natural fire, not a magical one," Shade surprised Ember by answering simply, not trying to evade. "The herbs have to be mixed in a very specific way. The altar needs to be laid out meticulously. I know you want to help, but this is really something I have to do on my own."

"And then what happens? Can you explain my part now?"

"It is complicated."

"So is saying yes to something you don't understand. Not knowing makes it easy to change your mind."

Shade paused her movements, her gaze locking onto Ember. She dropped the bag and carefully released a handful of dried herbs Ember couldn't recognize on top of an ancient tree-ring board.

"Have you ever heard of the god-made?"

Ember shook her head.

"It is an opportunity offered to all beings once they become powerful enough. For most, that can take centuries or more, unless they are god-born. That timeline is a bit more random, but usually shorter."

"And you need my help so you can be god-made?"

Shade snorted. "Hells no. This is all for you."

"I thought you said I was Goddess-touched, not born."

"I also said 'for most' it takes that long. You are well aware that you are different, Ember. Your conduit nature makes you exceptionally powerful, possibly dangerous. Which means you likely qualify."

"Likely?"

"If this spell does not work, then we will know that too."

"What does the spell do?"

"Opens a door to the universal plane. Sends you into the realm of Force and Magic. Presents you with the choice."

"To become a god?"

Shade nodded, and her fingers twitched toward the bag as she glanced at the sky. She was on a time limit, but Ember wasn't convinced.

"What does that mean? What happens if I do this?"

"It is like I said before." Shade returned to unpacking, the tension of her timeline overcoming her desire to meet Ember's gaze. "All your current allegiances are undone. You are reforged into a being of power."

"What's the cost?"

"Letting go of your old life."

Ember shook her head, not believing that was the cost. True, some might be driven toward the choice in order to cut all ties, but if it took centuries of cultivation, how many connections were left? And how many would have accepted that price, given that much time and that much work? No, letting go of an old life for a new one was a trade, not a payment. That was one concept Ember deeply understood.

"Your emotions," Shade elaborated, keeping her focus on shredding herbs into a large white mortar. "You have to give them up, become a neutral being. But you will still have your memories and goals. You will still remember this was all to save Gypsum."

Ember placed a hand on her chest and the other on her belly. As if called by Shade's words, her emotions surged forth, cutting into her nerves and weakening her muscles. With a shuddering breath, Ember recalled the raging flames that ate through everything she didn't want to hold on to.

She could remember Susan and forget feeling the pain of not being enough. She would remember Nicu's words, but not carry the wound he left.

No one could hurt her again.

The power to help Gypsum was fine, to give the Fae a safe place to return home and leave Terra. She was grateful for the chance to repair the damage to the Veil and ease the mistake she'd made with Tristan.

But never to be hurt again. To never brush Nicu's skin and listen to words she didn't want to hear. To be immune to Fae arrows, no matter how her power manifested.

"You have been quiet for a while." Shade picked up the pestle, but sat back on her heels, studying Ember's features as if to read her mind. "This is truly your choice, Ember. I cannot force you to do this even if I wanted to. Becoming god-made is not to be taken lightly. And you are right. There is a cost. I am hoping you will find saving an entire realm and its people worth it. To returning autonomy to Reyar and Devi, and anyone else caught up in this twisted situation."

"There really is no other answer," Ember murmured. "Do I wait here until you're ready?"

Shade's smile reflected the bright yellow light of the fire into the ever-darkening night.

27

NICU

Nicu passed the central tent pole for the seventy-third time, his eyes remaining on the ancient stone support even as his body took him by. He wondered if it would withstand a solid punch and if letting his energy out in a violent way would stop his feet from carving miles into the carpet of the tent's main room.

He could not redirect his movement. He missed the trees of Trifecta, yearned for the uneven ground that commanded his mindful attention to ensure his steps were quick, steady, and silent. Craved the physical release that came from crossing over the mountainside.

Anger rose, aimed at his lack of control. How could he not command his legs to settle when they were his own? How could he not hold his tongue from speaking words that ruined everything when he'd practiced silence for so long?

How could he not get Ember to see that all he meant to do was give her a space where she was safe?

Choose Ember.

How could he when she was showing signs of losing control? Not of her power this time, but of her logic and reasoning? How could he when he couldn't trust her choices?

Nicu shook the debate from his head, tension twisting around his heart with such strength, he rubbed the space with a knuckled fist. He needed to speak with her. But first, he needed to find a way to regain his personal control. He would start by simply standing still.

Yet once again, he spun on his heel and headed toward the midpoint support only to pass it and wonder if it would accept the force of his punch.

Power shimmered around him, raising the hairs along Nicu's arms. The sensation stopped him in his tracks when his own will could not. This was not Veil energy or organized magic, yet it filled the room with particles heavier than air. He threw out his senses, studiously examining the space, trying to find a spell when there was none.

Nicu looked toward Ember's bedroom, his heart pounding even as his stomach dropped. Would this be the moment she showed him she couldn't be trusted? That all the time he'd spent protecting and defending her had been for a girl who no longer existed?

One cautious step after another, Nicu slowed his breathing. His tattoos remained firmly on his skin, yet ready to move at his command. He pressed his hand against the canvas, expecting resistance of being locked. It parted with silken ease.

The bed was unmade, but as vacant as the rest of the space. Another deep breath, and Nicu stood before the bathroom entrance, certain she hadn't entered there but too concerned not to check. He hesitated for only a moment with a fleeting sense of wanting to respect her privacy, then he opened it while staring at the floor, looking for feet rather than the whole person. It was also unoccupied.

Nicu spun and searched the main room, his eyes wide open as if it might give him some secrets. His hands fisted unbidden at his sides. He didn't spare a thought for his body's subconscious motions, fully immersed in the realization that Ember was gone.

The organized energy of a spell broke into the space, but it didn't disperse the overall sense of power. Nicu gathered his tattoos, taking a moment to appreciate his advanced control over his Ink as it responded to his commands. The room before him blurred, a pillar of color appearing at its center that dissolved and solidified into Devi's shape and form.

When the magic dissipated, Nicu blinked, staring at the Witch with newfound respect. She had always been powerful, but that spell was impressive, especially on a world so drained. Her mint eyes sparkled like ice, her full lips were pale around the edges, and her hands trembled. Due to magic use or something else?

"What is that energy?" Devi demanded. The wild look in her eyes mirrored what Nicu felt inside, and a thread of control returned to him as if her reaction provided the anchor he missed.

"I do not know."

"Where is Ember?" Devi strode toward Ember's room, throwing up the flap just as he had.

"She's not here," Nicu answered.

"Verge it all. I gave her a tracking stone and it brought me here, to you."

Nicu's lashes fluttered closed as memory caught up with the moment. When Ember had gripped his wrist and he'd felt pressure against his hip, but assumed it was the result of her proximity. With the muscles in his jaw locking his teeth together, he reached into his pocket and pulled out a small black gem.

"Do you think she planned this?" He spoke the question aloud, only partially on purpose. He wanted to see Devi's reaction. Hoped she might help him understand.

"This is not Veil energy." Devi continued to search the tent, throwing each canvas door open as if one of them would prove Nicu wrong.

"It is not. But that does not mean she is not involved."

Devi stopped her search to face Nicu, arms crossed over her ribs, toe tapping silently on the rugged floor.

"What happened?"

"We argued."

"That is nothing out of the ordinary," Devi pointed out.

"It was this time." Nicu breathed deeply, hating the upcoming confession. "I misspoke."

Devi's mint-gem eyes widened, her lips parting on a small inhale. Then with a shake of her head, she reset, and for the first time in over a decade, Nicu found himself jealous of someone else's greater control.

"The world must be falling apart." Devi's words burst from her in a quiet hurricane, and she stared at the outer door, deep in thought.

"Maybe we can find her through you again. Like when we came from Trifecta."

Nicu remained rooted to the floor, uncertain if that was the path he wanted to take. Two weeks ago in Trifecta, he'd bent his loyalty to the Fae and joined forces with Tristan, all to get to the Trimarked Child as soon as possible. To reach through time and space to find her.

The Ember he met on arrival was not the girl who had disappeared. Once he'd been able to anticipate her every move, to foresee the path she would take and intercept her whenever it was needed. She'd argued against his guidance, but always complied in the moments that mattered.

Now he didn't even know if he could choose her.

Where Nicu hadn't been able to stop moving before, now his body remained still. Without his answer, Devi turned to face him, looking at him from toes to eyes as if his stature gave her answers. He desperately wished to learn what they were.

Nicu did not know what to do, and the realization was terrifying.

"You don't know if you can trust her."

Each of Devi's words added weight to Nicu's feet.

Choose the Fae.

Images swirled within his mind, tearing him apart between the forces of loyalty and decision.

Wist's angry eyes.

Mize's optimistic smile.

A deep pain for his people's plight.

A faint thread that tethered Nicu's essence to Ember and remained resolute against the storm of destruction.

An image from his time in limbo when given his fate-bound choice.

Mize's reminder that when dealing with dangerous creatures, it was best to give your full, complete focus.

The pressure of purpose settled onto Nicu's shoulders. Staring at Devi, Nicu knew he was not ready to make a choice that had no clear winner. No clear end.

"Reyar wouldn't tell me their whole plan." Devi turned her face away, swallowing with visible effort. "But I do know that they aimed to offer a substitute for the role Azhirith tagged us for. Given how much work they've put into Ember, I feel confident that they meant for that replacement to be our Trimarked Child."

Devi's eyes looked like frosted green gems when they met his.

"It isn't good, Nicu. They want her to become goddess-made. There will be no getting her back then."

Once again, Nicu spoke without vetting his thought.

"I can find her. I slipped a fragment of my Ink onto her."

It had been after her performance in a moment of weakness. He'd wanted to control her no matter how. Instead, he'd simply left a sliver of himself behind.

"You did what?" Devi demanded, the light in her eyes suggesting she wasn't showing disapproval, but excitement over this turn of events. Nicu did not have time to give in to her curiosity.

"She does not know," he continued. "So neither will Shade."

Devi took a deep breath, visibly pulling back her questions. With the new puzzle out of the way, a thin-lipped frown showed she redirected her thoughts to their current crisis.

"Fade it all. Does that mean we have to run?"

28

DEVI

Devi hated running, and yet she'd found herself engaged in the exercise more in the last few months than she'd hoped to do in her entire life. Ever since Tristan had cut his way back into Trifecta, she'd had to do more unpleasant things than jogging. She'd been pulled from her research. She'd had to cooperate with Fae and humans to save Halfers. She'd buried her mother.

The next time she saw the Wizard, she would imprison him in one of her crystals and carry him around on her neck, forcing him to watch the world she created in lieu of his own. It was better than he deserved.

Nicu led them past the arena, then they wove between the guest tents. His strides were sure, though not as long as normal. She wondered if he slowed his pace for her or if the resistance she'd observed was the reason for his current speed.

"Go faster," she ordered. Nicu's shoulders flexed at her command. Three steps, then four, and finally his stride length increased. Devi wrapped a magic tether around his waist. Nicu allowed it and she was able to share his speed despite her shorter legs and weaker stamina.

They rushed toward the edge of the ravine. For a moment,

Devi wondered if his urgency had returned and he'd launch himself into the air, hoping she'd catch them both. Instead, he took a sharp left, revealing a trail that angled down into the depths of the crevice in the direction of the flickering orange and gold of a small fire.

A bright, unexpected light on the horizon caught Devi's eye, and she dug in her heels. Nicu stopped with her due to their connection, and he raised his brow in question.

"Look," Devi ordered, pointing to the bright spot. "What are the odds that the Ternate has suddenly risen into the Fae sky?"

With stiff movements, Nicu returned to Devi and made his way back up the path, his eyes widening when they spotted the Ternate, which the Fae had ominously named the Chaos Star. Actually made up of three stars caught in each other's gravitational pull, it did not rise and fall with the usual celestial patterns. Instead, its appearance was a harbinger of change. Of power. Of chaos.

It had shown itself on Ember's birthday, then again just before Tristan cut his way into Trifecta. Its sudden presence here now was nothing short of a bad omen.

"We need to reach Ember." He turned back to the path, urgency in his jerky movements.

"Allow me to help." Devi stretched an arm out and twisted the space in front of Nicu. To his credit, he didn't slow his stride as the landscape blurred before him, launching him and her through the portal.

One step was on the angled path and the next they were on the flattened bottom, only a few feet from the fire. Another portal stood open before Shade, though this one spun dark and black, galaxies drifting within. This was how Charlah, the Witch Queen's eyes had looked. It was how people said Devi's eyes sometimes appeared.

Goddess-born. Goddess-made. Knowing before she learned.

This gateway wasn't for Ember. It was for her.

"You're too late." Shade threw the words over her shoulder, her eyes remaining on the cosmic entryway. "Ember passed through minutes ago. It will have been eons for her. Seconds until it's over."

"Is this all you?" Nicu demanded. Devi gasped when his tattoos eased off his wrists, wrapping around each other into braided ropes, one for each of his white-knuckled fists to grasp.

"It was her choice," Shade countered. "It had to be, or Force and Magic wouldn't have accepted her."

"But this is why you were training her," Devi argued as if her theory was fact. Shade confirmed her suspicions with a nod.

"It is a simple solution." Shade's voice was light, a wisp of hope wrapped around each word. "No one wants her. No one claims her. She is desperate for freedom and is willing to make sacrifices that are too great for the rest of us. It only makes sense that she is the one to go."

A twist of growl and pain drew Devi's attention to Nicu, shocked that the Fae had the capacity for such a noise. His ropes had retracted halfway, the very tips brushing against the ground as he stared at the portal, eyes wide and cheeks pale.

He looked as if his world had been taken away from him.

Devi checked the icy barrier she'd erected between her emotions and herself. If it broke, she knew she would look like him, feeling every bit as lost.

"Devi."

Devi flinched at the sound she hadn't expected to hear ever again. Reyar had somehow tracked her down, but then, was that so strange? The goddess spell had broken, but their soul connection survived, one that would demand they be each other's equal. His irises contained a shifting mirage of color that she'd thought was tied to his powers as the Dragon Lord. Suddenly, the pale colors meant something very different.

He too, was god-touched. He too, was god-born.

And he'd given nearly everything so he would not have to become god-made.

"Reyar!" Shade whirled, a grin brighter than the full moon lighting up her face. She ran to him, wrapping her arms around his neck. Reyar's hands fell against the Fae's waist, catching her mid-flight.

Devi turned away, eyes locked onto the portal. She felt the power reach out to her, whispering promises of untold knowledge. Of an eternity spent on learning. The ability to create something from nothing. An escape. She took a step closer, allowing its magnetism to draw in her own magic, her own energy. She only had to agree and her body would follow.

"It is almost over." Shade spoke with vibrant victory. "Ember is on her way. What did Azhirith tell you? Will the girl satisfy? Will Azhirith let you go?"

More confirmation. Reyar hadn't wanted to ask the goddess to release her spell, but to inquire if their project with Ember would work.

"Why did you even need me for that?" Devi asked without turning to face the couple. Through the portal of Time and Space, future knowledge drifted into her mind. She would learn it soon, so of course she knew it now.

"Ah." Her voice broke, but it was of no matter. The ice around her heart meant it didn't hurt. "Because you were afraid that I would stop Shade. That I held the power to keep Ember here. But you're both wrong. She isn't the perfect replacement."

Devi took a step.

"Devi." Reyar's speech felt distant, unimportant. The portal filled her vision as if she were already within, the rest of the world fading away.

"Reyar, let her go." Shade's sharp tone. The sound of a thunderclap suggested Shade had engaged her Fae Ink whip.

Nicu's voice drifted in through a fog, but Devi couldn't

make out the words. One more step and she lifted her hand before her, her fingers drifting through the energetic membrane that separated her from the place she belonged.

A crack in the ice surrounding her heart pulled her attention around. Reyar struggled toward her, the Ink and lightning whip spiraling up his torso, white sparks flickering between them as Shade worked to hold him back.

"Don't," Reyar commanded.

Like he could tell her what to do.

"Our choices are all that matter," she said, her tone full and hollow at once.

Devi pulled the matte black ring off the middle finger of her right hand. The power of the portal sucked on the spell surrounding it, tearing it apart into individual molecules that drifted into the universal realm of Force and Magic. She tossed the small piece of jewelry through the air, her aim perfectly marked for Shade.

Reyar's hand shot out, pulling the ring from its intended arc. His rainbow eyes brightened, and his own power surged forth, killing the lightning trying to shock him out of his focus, disintegrating the Ink so it burst apart and fled back to Shade, whose cry echoed through the canyon.

"This is for my fated lady."

Once upon a time, those words would have made Devi stop. Yet Reyar had already told her the only truth that mattered.

Devi turned away from the Dragon Lord and walked into the universe.

29

NICU

Nicu watched Devi slip through the portal with an odd sense of loss and acceptance. Hope snuck in through his breath, attention locked on the universe beyond, waiting for Devi's entrance to result in Ember's return.

Instead, the edges of the gateway shifted, twisting in, closing the space in a swirl of white light and blue-black shadow.

"Reyar, you will stop!" Shade shouted, her shrill growl slicing through the night.

The Dragon Lord appeared before Nicu, hands gripping both his shoulders. Copper strands had come loose from his thick auburn braid, and his hard, focused eyes were rimmed with red, heated emotions.

"You must act now or Ember will be lost!" Reyar's shout broke through Nicu's impassivity. Nicu stepped around Reyar, thrusting his arms forward with a wild force, his tattoos flying toward the diminishing portal. The rope unraveled and each length of tattoo reached for the edges of the magical passageway, yet never made contact.

Gravity collapsed against Nicu, forcing him to his knees. The blue scars across his body took on a deep, warning glow.

Choose.

Nicu grit his teeth and tried again, pressing his spine straight and lashing out with his arms. His aim was true, but his Ink slid away as if there was nothing to grab.

Choose Ember or have the choice made for you.

The portal jerked a few more inches closed. Nicu gasped for air, his eyes squeezed shut as he struggled to stand, striking at the portal again, trying to grip the magic, to break apart the spell and make it his. He leaned in, adding his physical body to the fight. His fingers were able to gain a slippery grasp as his Ink writhed around the magic, the tattoos appearing as faint shadows under the glow produced by the scars on his skin.

"What fool makes a deal with Chaos?" Reyar again, closer this time. Nicu turned to see the Dragon Lord had made it to his side. Shade was not with him.

"And Fate," Nicu threw in, wanting the Dragon Lord to truly appreciate the weight of his battle. "Help me."

Reyar stared into the landscape of black void and brilliant stars, his eyes wide and damp.

"I swore I would never enter the realm of Force and Magic."

Nicu grunted as his arms strained against another twist of the portal, another inch of opening lost. He would not be able to count on the Dragon Lord.

Choosing loyalty to his people had been easy at seven. The Fae had been prudent in their timing of the request, meticulous in Nicu's education up to that point and beyond. All Fae citizens needed to work together in the strange realm of Terra, to support each other against hatred, and to protect themselves against threats.

At seventeen, Nicu had seen much hate, shouldered considerable responsibility. Ember had been protected from most of the discrimination through the people's negligence and had been free to live her life without knowing the weight of the threat. She had not understood, and she had continued to fight and challenge. He'd been there every day to witness her fire, her determination to remain alive.

"Which side are you on?" Devi had once had the gall to ask.

For years he'd observed the Trimarked Child. Watched for signs of who she was, what she would become. He thought he had learned every facet of his little hybrid. Yet here, in true Gypsum, she'd shown him the person she presented as in Trifecta had only been a shadow kept small by rules. Always close, always linked, always bound. Kept weak by him.

In the end, he wasn't surprised she'd chosen a direction that looked like freedom. He just hadn't expected that her path might not include him.

Let go and choose the Fae.

Or choose Ember and have a chance.

Just a chance?

It was more than Nicu needed.

When all truths were fully examined, the fundamentals were decided. It had been Ember who had taught him that Chaos had its place. In that spirit, perhaps Fate was not always worth fighting.

The weight of the world lifted from Nicu's shoulders, unlocking the resistance placed on every fiber of his being. Power struck deep into his gut. He dropped one knee, then the next. Pain sliced through Nicu as his grip on the portal slipped. He lost his breath, pushed his Ink deeper in, gaining access to the interior that he hadn't held before.

Readjusting his fingers, his tattoos surged forward, wrapping around the gateway's edges, gripping at a dozen places along the diameter as he finally gained enough force to stop the magic from closing.

The Trifectan Fae would not approve. There would be no going back.

"Good." The relief that filled Reyar's voice echoed in Nicu's heartbeat.

"Reyar."

The break in Shade's voice reverberated in the cracks of Nicu's raw emotions. He glanced over to find her standing behind Reyar, though the Wizard's eyes were set longingly onto the space the Nicu struggled to hold open.

"You are too late." Shade gripped Reyar's arm with both hands, tugging him back with weak motions that suggested she knew she was too late as well.

"I know," Reyar answered simply. "And I am so sorry, Shade, that I cannot be what I promised for you. It wasn't the goddess spell after all. Devi really is a part of my soul."

"How do you even know that?" Shade demanded, placing her body between Reyar and the portal, her palms flat against his chest.

"She broke Azhirith's forced connection all on her own." Reyar's small smile weighed heavy with pride. "She's amazing, and I never stopped to see her."

"You swore you would never choose to be god-made!" Shade shouted, her words fast and her eyes wet with desperation.

"I know. The truth hasn't changed. I refuse to give up my emotions for something as mundane as power. But I cannot betray her any more than I have."

Shade gasped and released her grip on Reyar, her arms falling against her sides as dead weight. She nodded stiffly, then looked away and cleared her throat, shifting so she no longer blocked Reyar from his path.

Nicu grunted as the portal pressed against his resistance.

"I cannot hold this much longer."

"Thank you," Reyar said. "Make room, and I'll be through quickly."

Nicu shook his head, and Reyar's eyes locked onto his, lips pursed.

"Hold on to me," Nicu countered. "We will have to go together."

"And what do you think you can do in the universal realm?" Reyar demanded. "The choice will not be available to you."

The portal shifted again. Nicu's shoulders burned as he pressed deeper, past the edge of his resources.

"She will return," Nicu charged. "Or I will tear through the gateway despite your warnings. I will reclaim Ember."

30

EMBER

*E*mber floated among the stars for a million years. Head tilted back, hair fanned out behind her, her entire body relaxed in a state of weightlessness. She kept pace with an asteroid, matched her heartbeat to a pulsing star, and smiled each time a comet crossed the gorgeous clouds of the galaxies. She settled deep into the peace of having no place to go, nowhere to be.

Was that true? Surely she was in this space for a reason. Was she meant to arrive on one of the planets? Was she too late to watch a star become a nova?

Then again, what did it matter? There was no one to hold her accountable. Certainly, no one waited for her.

Right?

Questions didn't have a place here, she decided, and let them all fall away.

Ember refocused on the stars closest to her, wondering what section of the constellation she had visited today. Surely she'd been floating for at least two million years at this point, and the sights never failed to inspire and awe. Gratitude filled with the pleasure of being part of all this, grounded in the universe even as she flew with it.

A deep reverberation interrupted her thoughts. It shook her to the bones, and her heart rate increased as she looked around, eager to discover this something new. As if her desire called to it, her body sped through the empty space, celestial lights streaking beside her in a tunnel of brilliance.

Then all movement stopped, and Ember stood amidst a cavern of darkness. The billions of stars behind her were done lighting the way. This was the place she'd meant to visit, she recalled, though she didn't remember why. Digging through three million years of consciousness was a challenge, but eventually she followed the faint trail and found a distant memory.

She had made a choice to let her old world go. To have herself remade and to save a dying realm.

Ember smiled. In the air of the cavern, a whirlpool of black spun into existence, swirling before her. The ripples of shadows twisted and converged into an iridescent rosebud, the petals a deep, dark red that spoke of power beyond life and knowledge greater than passion.

Fingertips outstretched, Ember brushed the papery edges of the flower, curious to feel the velvet pull of energy that multiplied with each unfolding petal. The heart of the rose flared blue, a color so cold that even from a distance, it eased the burning core Ember had carried with her all these years. She'd built the blaze on a pyre of pain, and the arctic chill within the rose promised to quench the flames, to soothe the conflagration and silence her need for it.

A breath away from gripping the thorned stem, a deep sound echoed faint from the universe behind her. She glanced over her shoulder for only a brief moment; the starlight dazzled her vision after adjusting to the dark of the surrounding cavern.

Turning back, Ember frowned, stretching her arm to its full length. She was out of reach of the rose now. Her heart pounding, she leaned in, struggling to return to the icy strength she'd found in that flower.

She could stop burning. She needed to stop burning.

"Not you." It sounded like a whisper, but the shout was so far away. A distraction. A trick. She would not look this time, refusing to be fooled. The rose could be hers.

A shadow shifted beside her. As if she'd always been there, a figure in a flowing purple gown stood at her side. Bright cranberry curls framed ebony eyes that held the very image of the universe Ember had come to love. Over more years than Ember could count anymore, she dug out a memory that told her she knew this woman. Was this the person she was supposed to meet?

"Do you want it too?" Devi asked, drifting toward the infinite blooming of the flower. "It feels like if you touch it, everything will be optimal. Life will become strong and secure, and you'll never need to feel cold again."

Ember gripped Devi's arm, stopping her before she could get closer. There was only one rose. Only one of them could claim it.

"I came a long way for it. I was first," Ember claimed.

Devi's lips tangled as they fought between a smile and a frown.

Somehow, Devi was within reach of the expanding flower, but Ember was still too far. She struggled to use her hold on the Witch to close the distance, but could only watch as Devi brushed open the edge of the outermost petals.

"Hello, old friend," Devi whispered. As if she'd been here before. As if she knew the rose would shift from the darkest blue to the deepest red at her touch. A soft cry scratched through Ember's throat as she watched the flower burst with power, doubling in size with a multitude of layered petals.

Ember reached out, focused on the rose. With its larger size, maybe she could reach it. One brush of her hand and it could be her destiny again, not Devi's. She leaned closer, her fingers biting deep into Devi's arm in order to stay in place.

The Witch didn't seem to notice her presence at all, falling deeper into peace even as Ember gasped in desperate effort.

The rose did not change. She would lose it. One more thing gone, snatched from her before she had a chance to decide if it should be hers.

Another decision denied. Another path blocked.

"Do not make this choice." A voice from far away and further in time. One that came on a cloud of pine and mist, causing the fire within her to flare up, sending sparks across her awareness.

No, she didn't want this. She didn't want to reclaim the memories she'd used as fuel.

Ember shook the thoughts from her head. The rose had grown, and she'd held on. It had finally come close enough to reach. She thrust her free hand out, and the petal flickered blue, pushing into the red, swirling and mixing within. The resistance that kept her away vanished. Her power spilled out, matching and melding with the energy radiating from Devi.

Ice drifted off Devi, and fire burst from Ember, but they did not cross. Did not touch.

Devi sighed, her lips shifting in resigned acceptance. "Very well. One rose for two then."

"Yes." A voice full of sorrow and promise. "But a different two."

And there he was. Reyar, outlined by the stars, his copper-red hair twisted into a thick braid that rested over a pitch-black tunic.

Devi's power brightened, crystalline at the edges, pushing Ember's fire away. With another burst of growth from the rose, Ember was thrust aside. Denied in the presence of What Was Meant To Be. She let out a small cry that drowned in the distance between Reyar and Devi.

Reyar stepped before Devi, fingertips brushing from her elbows to her hands, interlocking their fingers at the end. They were beyond beautiful, standing tall and firm with the expanse of a universe between them despite how their skin touched.

He'd come to rescue her. Ember focused on the flower. She would claim it while they were lost in each other. The power could all be hers. Her fingers reached.

"You cannot stop me," Devi declared.

"I know," Reyar acknowledged.

Ember jerked, grasping at empty air as the rose drifted further away, centering between the other two. Devi never looked away from the promise of power. Reyar never removed his focus from Devi.

This is as it's meant to be, a voice as heavy as Fate filled Ember's thoughts. *Finished even as it begins*.

"I love you," Reyar murmured as the red rose bled into the surrounding blackness, bathing him and Devi in a crimson light.

Devi shifted from studying the rose, meeting his eyes with hers. There was no longer any sign of the Witch's gem-like irises, lost in the depths of the universe that had become part of her soul.

"I will not change my mind."

"I will not ask you to." Reyar lifted Devi's right hand and slipped a matte black ring on her middle finger. "I am your Dragon Lord. Forever beyond never, I am your servant."

Devi's smile lit up the universe. The brilliance of the rose flooded the void. The force of it thrust Ember away, stars streaking by even as she watched a new realm born in the place Reyar and Devi had stood.

"No." Ember gasped. Choked. The rose was gone. Her chance was extinguished. Airlessness closed in, stealing every breath. Tears floated gently before her face, caught in the endless fall of space just as she was. Lost without direction.

Fade it all. What was it all for? The thousands of years? The interminable days of floating. Why had she spent a lifetime looking for something not meant to be hers?

"Ember."

She forgot to breathe, hearing that word. But why? It was only her name.

She'd never thought he would say it, though.

The fire popped again. Memories older than the universe rose with the sparks. He'd never called her what others had. Never used her name as her mother did. Never called her the Trimarked Child as the rest of the world did.

Little hybrid, he'd named her a few decades ago. A reminder of the mixed blood that had marked her as cursed.

He always showed up when she needed him the most.

"Ember." More forceful this time, from out in the sky. She held on to the sound wave, using him as an anchor. Time rewound and Space condensed.

He was flying. Floating. Except his feet were firmly on the ground. Only the top half of his body had made it into the universe. Power circled him, closing in on his torso and threatening to cut him in half.

Nicu stretched out his hand. He would stay, she realized. If she decided to leave him, to float forever, Force and Magic would not forgive his trespass. He would not survive.

Or she could save him.

The choice was hers.

Ember locked her eyes on Nicu and reached for him. She'd lost her momentum from the birth of the new star, floating once again. But this time she knew she had a place to be. A person to meet.

Blue power flickered from deep inside her, though it belonged in a different world. The energy flowed around her, its edges undefined as it searched for its match.

Nicu grunted as the edge of the portal brushed against his shoulders. He ignored it, extending his reach. His tattoos burst from around his wrist, cutting through space.

There.

She directed her raw energy to his dark Ink, remembering

how he'd once collected her sparks, letting them free into the world in order to keep her secret safe.

"Ember!" he shouted, using her name again, soothing the flames that had driven her deep within herself.

The strength of command in his eyes had been a constant thorn in Ember's side for the last eighteen years. Now it was an anchor, a promise that he would rescue her. And she would protect him.

The portal closed in around Nicu's shoulders.

Ember's fingers gripped his, tattoos trapped between their skin.

You have always mattered to me.

ACKNOWLEDGMENTS

Writing *Tempered* felt like stepping into something waiting for me. That clarity came from the care and intention poured into every part of the series, and from the people who helped shape this book along the way.

Lauren, thank you for seeing both the story on the page and the writer behind it. Your insight and honesty helped flesh out a world ready for readers.

Kris, thank you for meeting this story with curiosity and care. Your feedback helped confirm that what I hoped would land, truly did.

Hannah of Dark Muse Words, thank you for your sharp eye and your respect for what this story is. You helped strengthen *Tempered* without losing its teeth.

To my kids, my cheering squad: thank you for your belief, your excitement, and for celebrating this world with me. Your joy reminds me why finishing matters.

To my ARC team, thank you for taking a chance on a new author and choosing to stay for the journey. Your trust, encouragement, and love for this series have meant everything.

And finally, to everyone who has ever had to be forged before they felt ready. This book is for you, too.

DRAFTING MY (5 STAR) REVIEW

MY FAN FICTION

MY CHARACTER ART

ABOUT THE AUTHOR

C.K. Sorens, a USA Today Bestselling author of Defiant Fantasy, writes dark fantasy and romantasy that explore fate, choice, and resilience. Known for her character-driven stories and compelling worlds, Sorens' works include the urban fantasy Trimarked series and the romantasy *Eighteen Wishes*. When not writing, she enjoys hiking, puzzles, and family adventures.

Discover more about C.K. Sorens' worlds of Defiant Fantasy and explore her latest releases at www.cksorens.com.

 instagram.com/ck_sorens
bookbub.com/profile/c-k-sorens

www.ingramcontent.com/pod-product-compliance
Lightning Source LLC
LaVergne TN
LVHW040138080526
838202LV00042B/2953